"YOU HAD BETTER
STOP FIGHTING ME.
I ALWAYS WIN."

The Duke of Vidal insisted on marrying Dominique—there was nothing she could do about it. She had the absurd feeling that she was being carried on a tide she could not halt.

He led her downstairs to the library, where the Vicar and the servants waited. Dominique moved as in a haze. During the ceremony, Vidal had to prompt her—the words swam around her, growing dim and far away. Dreamlike, she signed her name to the marriage document, turned, and fell in a heap at Vidal's feet...

Only later did Vidal realize Dominique had signed the marriage certificate with another name. ...Whom had he married?

"Deftly captures the manners of the period."
—*Publishers Weekly*

"Dawn Lindsey is headed towards a great writing career!"—*Chattanooga Times*

The Duchess of Vidal

Dawn Lindsey

PLAYBOY PRESS
PAPERBACKS

TO STEVE

All of the characters in this book are fictitious, and any resemblance to actual persons, living or dead, is purely coincidental.

Chapter One

The weather, though remaining cold and blustery, had not yet given way to the expected rain, and a few of the more optimistic of the stagecoach passengers had even begun to hope it might hold off until the evening's destination had been reached. England might boast of having the finest turnpike system in the world, with the new metaled roads making travel between such distant points as London and York the matter of a few days only, but inclement weather could still create unpleasant delays and render the journey, for the outside passengers at least, excessively miserable.

Those lucky enough to possess the price of an inside seat certainly fared better. But the public stagecoaches, unlike the more expensive mail coaches, were invariably poorly sprung and frequently draughty as well, so that the weather had remained the major topic of discussion throughout the long afternoon.

It was approaching dusk by the time Grantham was reached, but since most of the passengers were to spend the night some miles further, in Newark, the coachman did not linger. The steps were let down to permit a single female passenger to alight into the yard of the posting house. A small corded trunk and a portmanteau were hurriedly extricated from the boot, the door shut up again, and the coachman, with a last scowl at the rapidly gathering clouds, whistled up his team.

The passenger, left standing in the roadway, shivered slightly in the cold air and glanced up as well, as if calculating how many hours of daylight might remain. She was a little above average height, with slender build, and carried herself with an easy grace that belied the drab nature of her garments. These were seen to be serviceable only: her pelisse of some dark stuff was creased and travel-stained, and her bonnet was unadorned and some years past the current mode.

She was expecting to be met, but no one approached her. And although the yard of the inn seemed remarkably busy with any number of coaches, phaetons and curricles pulled up before the large brick building, beyond curious glances from one or two of the stable lads hurrying about their duties, no one paid the slightest attention to her. After a moment she shrugged and crossed to the entrance of the inn.

Inside the large hall an even greater bustle reigned. A great many fashionable gentlemen strolled about, engaged in conversation or warming their coattails before the fire, while the door to the coffee room stood open to permit a steady stream of waiters to hurry back and forth. Miss Forrester, hesitating on the threshold in some surprise, could only conclude that either Lady Thornton's notions of a quiet country town differed greatly from her own, or something untoward was taking place.

The landlord came forward to meet her at that moment and quickly confirmed her suspicions. He was sorry, but the inn was full to overflowing. She had best try elsewhere, though he doubted she'd have much luck. She must know every bedchamber in the town had been engaged for days past. The Quorn was meeting.

The information that she had come to Grantham during the meeting of one of the country's most famous fox hunts could not be without interest. But since she was unlikely to be given the opportunity of observing any part of it, she only said in her calm way, "Then it is fortunate I do not require a bedchamber, sir. My name is Forrester. I am expecting a carriage from Thornton Hall. I hope you can tell me if it has arrived yet?"

The landlord pulled on his lip, a slight frown in his eyes, and did not answer her directly. "Beg pardon, miss," he inquired obliquely, "but you said they was expecting you at Thornton Hall?"

Her own brows drew together slightly. "I had certainly believed so, sir," she said. "I am to be the new governess."

He nodded. "Aye, miss, I suspected as much," he said truthfully. "I'm sorry, but I've not seen old Timothy this past week. Nor do I lay much dependence upon seeing him tonight, neither, miss. Not with the weather what it is!" he added bluntly.

She regarded him in considerable dismay. "But do you mean you have had a message from Lady Thornton? She assured me I might depend upon her sending a carriage for me."

The landlord shrugged. "Nay, miss, I've had no message. But if you take my advice, you'll not expect to see her ladyship's carriage before morning."

It was apparent from his manner that he cherished no great regard for her future employer. She was not particularly surprised, for nothing she had learned from the agency that had employed her had led her to expect Lady Thornton would prove a kind employer, but nevertheless she was aware of a sinking feeling. She had not been looking forward to the coming interview, but to be left stranded in town until Lady Thornton condescended to send for her was hardly a welcome alternative.

She sighed, but after a moment said lightly, "Well, if it is as you say, I must be grateful to you for telling me, sir. At any rate, it does not matter a great deal. If Lady Thornton does not care to send her horses out in this weather, I was not looking forward to being obliged to go out again either, so it would seem we are both served."

The landlord's lips curled and he was betrayed into a most unprofessional utterance. "Begging your pardon, miss, but it's not *horses* her ladyship's concerned about!" he said contemptuously.

Miss Forrester was not easily daunted, but she had endured several exhausting days, and she knew she was not at her best. She was tired and more than a little dispirited, and she thought that if it had been at all possible she would have been tempted even yet to take the first coach back to London. It was, therefore, fortunate that the state of her present finances prevented her from taking such an undoubtedly foolish step. She had long ago made up her mind what she must do, and if it were not to be Lady Thornton, it must be some other, no doubt equally difficult employer. The options open to a female in her circumstances were very restricted indeed.

And since she was a sensible young woman, and there seemed no point in refining too much upon the landlord's pessimistic words, after a moment she only shook her head, a slightly weary smile on her lips, and said calmly, "Well, it seems I shall be requiring a bedchamber after all, sir."

"You cannot have been attending me, miss!" the landlord said in pardonable exasperation. "There's not a bed to be had this side of Stretton, and that's a good twelve miles away! I can only suggest you try to hire a vehicle to take you there."

She blinked, resigning herself to a fitting ending to a thoroughly miserable day, and meekly inquired of the landlord how much the hire of a vehicle was likely to cost her. If she were to be put to the expense of still another night's lodging, she very much feared she would have little left to pay for the hire of a vehicle.

He hesitated, then named a sum she knew to be beyond her slender resources. She had a good deal of pride, but she had little doubt the landlord must already be perfectly aware of her circumstances. She had long ago learned that innkeepers, of necessity, missed very little. After a moment she sighed and said frankly, "I am afraid that is out of the question."

He did not argue with her. "I'm sorry, miss," he said simply. "But it's probably just as well. I doubt you'd find anyone to take you in this weather anyway." He shook his head gloomily. "I can only suggest you try Mrs. Bailey just down the road. It's not what you'd like, but she might have something."

He spread his hands helplessly and shrugged. He had been kind, in his own way, but he clearly felt he had done all that could be expected of him. Nor could she blame him much. He had a house full of gentlemen with far more legitimate claims to his attention than an obviously penniless governess.

She inclined her head and thanked him civilly for his trouble. He looked a little guilty, but shrugged again and made no move to prevent her going.

She had just turned away when her eyes were caught by a tall gentleman standing a little way across the room from her. He appeared to be observing her closely, an unreadable expression on his face, but when she looked up he straightened himself and came leisurely forward.

He bowed and said easily, "Your servant, ma'am. I could not help overhearing part of your conversation. Perhaps I might be of some assistance?"

The words were conventional, but his voice was cool and she could detect no trace of friendliness in his eyes. She frowned and said frankly, "You are very kind, sir. But I doubt it is in your power to do so, nor can I conceive of any reason why you should trouble yourself on my account."

His black brows rose slightly, and he said in his colorless

voice, "That remains to be seen, ma'am. Might I be allowed to know what the difficulty is?"

She hesitated for a brief moment, then shrugged. "Very well, sir," she said evenly. "The difficulty is that I seem to have arrived at an unfortunate time. The landlord has been telling me that every bedchamber in town has been bespoken for days past. No doubt you are aware of the reasons."

His rather hard gray eyes continued to rest impassively on her face, but he said only, "I see. And yet that would not appear to be an insurmountable obstacle."

She looked up, a fleeting smile touching her lips, and said with a touch of humor, "Then I take back what I said before and can only beg your assistance, sir! I must confess neither the landlord nor myself has been able to come up with a solution."

The landlord had lingered, plainly feeling that some explanation of his conduct might be demanded of him. He reddened at that, and said defiantly that he was sure he was sorry, but the gentleman must understand that to find a room in a house filled to the rafters with sporting gentlemen was beyond his capabilities. Nor did he think the young lady would care to stay under such circumstances. He had suggested she hire a vehicle to take her to Stretton, where he did not doubt more suitable arrangements might be made.

The gentleman scarcely spared a glance at the landlord during this self-serving speech, merely continuing to regard Miss Forrester with a slight question in his eyes. She was beginning to find the expression in those gray eyes a little unnerving, and returned his look defiantly. She might admit to the landlord that to hire a vehicle was beyond her means, but she had no intention of being equally frank with this elegant stranger.

For some reason she was not obliged to. His eyes had narrowed a little, as if he were debating something within himself, but after a moment he said, "Then under the circumstances, ma'am, perhaps you would consent to accept a seat in my carriage. I happen to be going in the direction of Stretton, and would be most happy to convey you there."

Whatever she had expected, it was not that, but she could not deny the offer was tempting. A slight flush rose in her cheeks and she said with less than her usual composure, "I hardly know what to say, sir. I do not like to trouble you——"

"It is no trouble, I assure you, ma'am," he said indifferently.

She was not reassured, and stood regarding him frankly, a slight question in her eyes. She could not convince herself there was anything but a faint boredom in his face, and she had no idea why he had offered to help her. She would not have thought him one who concerned himself much with the plight of others. Indeed, she had been misled into thinking him as cold as the expression in those cynical gray eyes.

She might not move in the first circles of London society, but she recognized at a glance one who clearly did. Nor had she struggled for so many years to keep her father's wardrobe in good repair without recognizing the superior nature of that tailoring. He seemed to be on the point of going out, for he wore a many-caped greatcoat of white drab thrown open to reveal a blue coat and buckskin breeches beneath, and he carried a pair of driving gloves and a curly-brimmed beaver in one hand. His immaculate neckcloth was arranged in an intricate style, his waistcoat was elegant without being ostentatious, and his top boots were polished to a gloss that one who had never heard of the excellence of champagne as a blacking found a little difficult to credit. She might think his attire a little out of place in a mere country inn—in fact she *did* think it—but there was no other fault to be found with his appearance.

His expression was not warm, but his figure was excellent and he carried himself with the assurance of a man very much accustomed to being obeyed. His features were distinguished; his mouth firm and well-made and his nose finely chiseled. Only his eyes somewhat marred his countenance, for she thought them hard and without warmth, but he was without doubt a handsome creature.

At the moment a hint of amusement had softened his habitual expression, as if he were not accustomed to being stared at quite so openly and found the experience somewhat intriguing. His brows rose and he inquired lazily, "Well, ma'am? Do you mean to come with me or not?"

She thought dispassionately that the expression improved him, making him appear a great deal less haughty and unapproachable. But she had no intention of being charmed by the smile lurking in the hard gray eyes of a strange gentleman she was not in the least certain she liked, and she was very aware that her presence in a public inn under such circumstances might easily be misconstrued. She lifted her head and said bluntly, "Forgive me, sir, but I am a little curious why you have made me this very obliging offer?"

His expression did not change. "Indeed, ma'am?" he inquired smoothly.

Her color rose, but she repeated a little sharply, "Indeed, sir! I am perfectly aware that the circumstances might easily lead you to—draw certain conclusions—"

"On the contrary, ma'am," he interrupted drily. "I flatter myself I understand better than you think."

She frowned, by no means certain what he meant by that, and clamped her lips tightly together.

After a moment his face softened, the hint of amusement in his eyes no longer to be denied. "Forgive me, ma'am. I have not been deceived into thinking you an—er—*demimondaine* if that is what you fear," he said gently. He hesitated, then added mockingly, "In fact, you will forgive me, I know, if I tell you I have seldom seen anyone less like!"

A reluctant twinkle came into her own eyes at that. She was not vain, and had moreover an excellent reason for knowing exactly what she must look like. She laughed and said ruefully, "No, nor can I, sir! At least—I'm not certain what one looks like," she admitted cautiously, "but I very much suspect I look exactly what I am!"

His mouth quirked, but he said politely, "And what is that, ma'am?"

She hesitated, then lifted her eyes frankly. "I am to be governess to a Lady Thornton, sir. Unfortunately there has been some misunderstanding in the arrangements, and there is no carriage as I expected." Her color rose a little, but she added in her calm way, "In short, sir, although I feel certain I ought not to impose upon your kind offer—I am afraid I must do so, if—if you are certain it is no imposition?"

He shrugged. "You will find, when you know me better, ma'am, that I have rarely been known to trouble myself for anyone. If it is any comfort to you, my offer was quite genuine."

She frowned and regarded him searchingly for a moment, again uncertain of his meaning. Since there was not the least likelihood of her coming to know him better, she could only assume his words were a mere figure of speech. And since he chose to turn away at that moment to confer briefly with the landlord, there was nothing to be done but to stand quietly waiting for him to conclude his business.

He looked up once to inquire if her baggage was outside, and at her nod said something further to the landlord. In another moment the landlord had hurried away to do his bidding.

The gentleman turned back to her then, remarking calmly, "My phaeton will be brought around immediately, ma'am. I have instructed the landlord to fetch a rug for you, but I fear you may be cold. We must hope the rain holds off another hour at least."

She was not shy, but there was a certain awkwardness in her present position that she was very conscious of, and she only nodded again.

He stood looking down at her for a moment, an oddly speculative look in his eyes, then he said easily, "I am not perfectly certain what etiquette may prevail in such a situation as our own, ma'am. But I cannot help thinking it would be easier if we were to introduce ourselves. I am Vidal."

She suspected him of trying to put her at her ease, and was grateful for it. She accepted the hand he held out and said calmly, "Certainly, sir. My name is Forrester."

He retained her hand for a brief moment, his expression unreadable. "Indeed, ma'am," he said dispassionately.

Startled, she frowned and tried to withdraw her hand. The next instant the landlord had reappeared, and her hand was released, the moment gone. She could not even be certain she had not imagined the whole.

The landlord reported cheerfully that the phaeton was at the door, and he had himself superintended the bestowal of her luggage. She was not to worry, he would send word first thing in the morning to Thornton Hall of her whereabouts. If she would tell them at the Red Lion in Stretton that he had sent her, they would look after her right and tight. He bustled to hold the door open for them, plainly intending to escort them outside himself.

Miss Forrester, feeling absurdly as if she were abandoning her last friend, glanced once more at her rescuer, then thanked the landlord and walked through the door, her head high.

Unfortunately she was not attending closely enough to where she was going and collided almost immediately with a booted figure on the point of entering the inn. She might have fallen had not her arm been taken in a firm grasp and she been pulled back against her companion's tall figure.

The man she had collided with stepped back as well, saying hastily, "I beg your pardon, ma'am! Wretchedly clumsy of me! I hope you're not hurt?"

She had opened her mouth to reassure him when he looked past her to her companion. Immediately his expression changed. "Vidal!" he exclaimed in obvious delight. "Where did you spring from? Just the fellow I want, too! We've got Chalmondeley and Fitz and one or two others for a snug little game. You come too! Just the thing to take our minds off this weather!"

She looked up quickly and surprised a look of mild irritation in Vidal's eyes. Almost as quickly it was gone, and she had been set firmly on her feet, his hand retaining its grip on her arm. "Another time, George," he said easily. "Now if you'll excuse us?"

The man addressed as George looked quickly from Vidal's face to her own, and his mouth dropped open in almost comical disbelief. Then he had caught himself, and said automatically, "I—er—certainly, certainly! Beg pardon, ma'am! I didn't—er—that is—your servant, ma'am!" He bowed and stood back for them to pass, his face suddenly impassive.

Vidal, as if unaware of anything odd in his friend's behavior, nodded pleasantly and moved on. She was handed up into his phaeton, then he had picked up the reins and taken his place beside her. Without another glance at his friend he nodded for the lad to stand back from the horses' heads. He deftly tossed a coin as the lad sprang back, and in another moment they were moving out of the yard, threading an easy path through the crush of vehicles.

George, left standing in the doorway staring after them, shook his head at last and strode into the inn. He was hailed almost immediately. "There you are, George!" someone called out. "Been looking for you everywhere! Fitz has found a dozen bottles of a really remarkable claret. Landlord didn't even know he had them! The evening may not be a total loss after all."

George, always easily distracted, brightened and went off willingly enough to sample this unexpected treat. "I hope it's better than that stuff we drank last night!" he said feelingly. "Don't know when I've had such a head!"

His friend only laughed, and they moved up the stairs in companionable silence.

"Staveley," George said suddenly. "You didn't see that female Vidal's got with him, did you?"

Staveley looked interested. "No," he admitted. "You don't mean the Fair Caroline?"

"Of course I don't! Don't be such a saphead!" George said witheringly. "Is it likely she'd be seen openly with him here, where anyone of a dozen people could be counted upon to recognize her?" He grinned. "Not that I'd put it past her—or him either, for that matter! And wouldn't I like to see some of the old biddies' faces when *that* tale got around!"

Staveley considered it and at last admitted that it was not likely. But he added stubbornly, "Still, the odds are short-ening in her favor at White's, you know. Know for a fact Grenby's laid a monkey on the Fair Caroline."

"That don't signify!" George said contemptuously. "He said that about that Moreton chit, too, and you know how that turned out. Lost a bundle! I've lost count of the num-ber of females that have made a dead set at Vidal. Damned if I know how he does it, either! It ain't as if he encourages 'em, for you know he can be damned disagreeable!"

"You ain't worth £80,000 a year!" Staveley pointed out cynically.

Since this fact was all too true, a little silence fell, each pursuing his own thoughts for a moment. Staveley broke it first, saying reflectively, "That Moreton chit was a devilish fine-looking gal, too! Whatever happened to her?"

"Lord, I don't know," George said impatiently. "Married some country squire and settled down to raise a passel of brats, most like! Said she went into a decline, but that don't wash! Anyone could have told her the moment she began making such a cake of herself he'd be off. I'll say this for Vidal, he don't stand the nonsense!"

It occurred to him then that the conversation had wan-dered considerably from its original topic, and he added hastily, "But never mind! Point is, you ever see Vidal with any but an out-and-outer?"

Staveley did not require time to think it over. "No. What'd this female look like?" he asked with interest.

"Well, to tell the truth, I didn't get much of a look at

her," George admitted. "But I'll tell you what! Looked devilishly like somebody's country cousin to me."

"Poor relation, perhaps," Staveley suggested helpfully. "Lord knows we've all got 'em!"

"Yes, but *Vidal!*" George said incredulously. "If he's got any, *I* never heard of 'em! And even if he does, is he likely to be driving one of 'em out in his phaeton?"

Staveley, by now bored with the discussion, said soothingly, "Never mind, George. Ten to one it's all a fudge. You know what Vidal is! Anyway, there's still the claret."

George regretfully abandoned the attempt to second-guess the unpredictable Vidal. "So there is!" he said gratefully. "So there is!"

Chapter Two

It was perhaps fortunate for her peace of mind that Miss Forrester could know nothing of this conversation. But she would have had to be both blind and a great deal less intelligent than she was to have missed the significance of that exchange by the door. Her pride would not allow her to make a scene in the yard of a public inn, but there was an angry sparkle in her eyes and a decided tilt to her chin as she allowed herself to be assisted into Vidal's vehicle. She was aware that his eyes rested on her face for a moment, but she only thanked him in a cold voice when he tucked the rug across her knees. After a moment he took his place beside her and gave his horses the office.

Since his phaeton was a high-perch model built more for speed than safety, and his bays fresh, his attention was taken up for some minutes in threading a path through the congested yard, and controlling the initial fidgets of a difficult pair. Once the main road had been reached, however, he turned his head and inquired in a silky voice, "Yes, Miss Forrester? What is it?"

His tone should have warned her. But she was very angry indeed, and in no mood to guard her tongue. "Why, nothing, sir!" she said coolly. "Only I am a little surprised. If you are ashamed to be seen with me, why did you offer to take me up with you in the first place?"

"You must forgive me for not stopping to introduce you to all my acquaintances, Miss Forrester," Vidal said politely. "I had naturally assumed you had no wish to call attention to your presence in a public inn filled with men of that sort."

She flushed at that, but lifted her chin. "Well, I could hardly be expected to know it was *my* reputation you were protecting, could I?"

There was a moment of silence. "Miss Forrester," Vidal said grimly, "has it never occurred to you that that unruly tongue of yours is hardly an asset in your chosen profession?"

THE DUCHESS OF VIDAL 17

She glanced up quickly, a rueful expression coming into her eyes. "Frequently, I'm afraid, sir. I beg your pardon! I should not have ripped up at you when you have been so very obliging as to help me."

When he remained silent she could not resist asking, "Just why did you offer to help me, sir?"

For a moment she thought he did not mean to answer her. Then he shrugged. "Curiosity, Miss Forrester."

She laughed. "I might have known! But we have already agreed, have we not, that I look lamentably what I am? I cannot think the career of a governess will particularly interest you."

"But then I do not think you are just the usual governess, Miss Forrester. And you wrong me. *I* agreed to no such thing."

She had no intention of allowing him to provoke her again, and only said, "You may not agree, but I can assure you that your friend at the inn undoubtedly did. I think it more than likely that yours is the only reputation to suffer from our having been seen together."

"Yes, but I have always known George was a fool," he murmured enigmatically.

His bays claimed his attention then, his leader showing signs of discovering unsuspected danger in the shadows lengthening across the road, and she was spared the necessity of answering. She could not be sorry. She had no doubt that his words were idle, but it was not a topic she cared to continue.

So when he next looked up, remarking politely that he feared she must be cold for all her brave protestations, she answered him rather absently, in a manner that suggested her thoughts were elsewhere. After a moment he obligingly turned his attention back to his horses.

With a slight feeling of regret she, too, turned her attention to the road before them. As Vidal had said, it was very cold, the horses' breath steaming on the frosty air. The gray afternoon was fading rapidly and she did not think the rain would hold off much longer. But it was not unpleasant to be bowling along in such a fashion after the endless jolting of the stagecoach. She had long ago perceived that whatever else he might be, Vidal was an excellent whip, and it had been a long time since she had been behind such a team.

He drove his bays well up to their bits, effortlessly curbing every attempt of his leader to break into a gallop. The road was not a main one, and there was no other traffic, save for a farm cart soon overtaken. The road was narrow at that point, with deep ditches running on either side, and they were moreover approaching a sharp curve. The cart obligingly hugged the left side of the road, yet it did not occur to her that Vidal would attempt to pass it at such a point.

But Vidal, after a brief calculating glance, dropped his hands and urged his bays forward. In another moment they had swept past the cart with only inches to spare, Vidal feathering his turn nicely, skillfully looping up his rein and then letting it run free again. The bays did not even break their stride.

It was a beautiful piece of driving. She leaned forward, the wind whipping the color into her cheeks, and exclaimed impulsively, "Oh, well done! What beautiful goers they are! I do not know when I have seen their match."

Vidal's cynical smile appeared. "I am relieved you do not mean to cut me quite dead, Miss Forrester."

She was vexed with herself for having given him such an opportunity again, but only said ruefully, "No, no! I am determined you will not provoke me again! I find I am enjoying myself."

He glanced at her rather oddly. "Are you? It had no doubt escaped your attention that it is bitterly cold and like to rain at any moment?"

She did laugh at that. "No, of course not. But I hope I am not such a poor creature to fear a little damping."

"No, I am beginning to see you are not. Do you drive, Miss Forrester?"

"Why, I was used to," she said lightly. "But nothing like these beauties, I'm afraid. Do—do you live near Stretton, sir?"

"I have a house there," he admitted.

"Are you here for the hunt yourself, then, sir?" she asked curiously. "This is the Melton country, is it not?"

"Yes. Perhaps you might care to observe the run one day? You might find it interesting."

It occurred to her that she would indeed like to see Vidal mounted. But since the likelihood of that was almost as remote as her being given the opportunity of observing the hunt one day, she said prosaically, "I am unlikely to be at liberty to do so, sir. I imagine Lady Thornton has other duties in mind for me."

"Ah, yes," he said thoughtfully. "The mysterious Lady Thornton. I must confess I had forgotten her for the moment."

"She is hardly mysterious, sir. Nor can I conceive of any reason why you should be expected to remember her."

"No doubt you are quite right, Miss Forrester," he said immediately. "Have you been a governess long?"

"Not long, sir," she answered briefly.

If he was aware of any reluctance on her part, he gave no sign of it. "Who was your last employer?"

She turned her head and regarded him steadily. "Are you perhaps in need of a governess yourself, sir?"

"Since I have neither wife nor children that would be most unlikely, Miss Forrester."

"I see. You are merely exercising your—er—curiosity again?"

Vidal smiled languidly. "Oh, undoubtedly, ma'am!"

"Then perhaps you will not mind my saying I do not care to discuss my past history with you?" she said politely.

He was not attending. "What is your given name?" he inquired abruptly.

"It is Dominique. But pray give me leave to tell you that I find this discussion becoming—"

His brow cleared. "Ah, I thought I could not be mistaken in your accent. You must allow me to congratulate you upon your English, ma'am."

She bit her lip and said dangerously, "Sir!"

He met her eyes blandly. "Yes, Miss Forrester?"

She said a little stiffly, "I am perfectly aware you have chosen to find me amusing for the moment, but I—"

"But then you intrigue me, Miss Forrester," he murmured.

She pointedly ignored this interruption. "But I am afraid I do not care for your style of humor!"

He smiled. "Come, Miss Forrester! Admit you do not care a button what I think of you! You must know it is one of the things I find most intriguing about you."

Her lips curled. "No doubt I should find that flattering! It may amuse you for the moment to flirt with a mere governess, but *my* palate is hardly so jaded! I am beginning to find this conversation a dead bore!"

There was a glint deep in his eyes. "Ah, well done, Miss

Forrester!" he said quietly. "I might have known you would not disappoint me. But I assure you I have not yet flirted with you, you know. I do not mean I am above it, for I have already admitted you intrigue me, have I not? As it happens, you should be flattered. There are very few women who can make such a claim. My—er—jaded palate, no doubt," he added almost apologetically.

She met his eyes evenly, her color high. "I am well aware I should not have said that, sir," she said with dignity. "At any rate, you are quite wrong, you know. I learned long ago that the freedom to disregard what others think of you is reserved for those wealthy enough to afford such luxuries. It is amazing how conventional one becomes when faced with the necessity of earning one's own living."

For the first time she thought she had managed to surprise him. His eyes narrowed abruptly on her face, but he said only, "Very true, Miss Forrester. Accept my apologies. I begin to think I may have underestimated you after all. But you have not, I believe, answered my question."

"You must forgive me," she said with perfect truth. "You have asked so many I fear I have forgotten it!"

But if she hoped to embarrass him she might have spared her breath. He merely raised his brows and repeated patiently, "I asked who your last employer was?"

She sighed, then lowered her lashes and said meekly, "Why, of course! How stupid of me!" and immediately embarked upon an involved and extremely boring tale of her supposed previous charges and their more endearing traits, liberally interspersed with the doting comments of the more indulgent of their relatives. She knew little about children, but she had an inventive brain and managed to discourse for quite fifteen minutes in this vein, knowing full well that any gentleman would soon grow intolerably bored with such reminiscences as she chose to describe in minute detail.

She had reckoned without Vidal. He listened with a great show of interest, and when she at last wound down, said politely, "Delightful, Miss Forrester."

He waited until her indignant eyes flashed up to his before adding musingly, "But I must confess you hardly look old enough to be out of the schoolroom yourself, let along have undertaken what I feel must have been the years required to obtain such experience."

It had grown too dark to discern his expression clearly,

but there was no mistaking the mockery in his voice. She realized bitterly she should have paid closer attention to her own ramblings. Vidal was no fool.

After a moment he added conversationally, "You will find, Miss Forrester, that the most believable lie is always based closely upon the truth, you know. In this instance, you had only to inform me, at your most forbidding, that you were assuming your first position, and I would have been left at a standstill. Remember it next time!"

She was perfectly aware he was laughing at her, and could only regard him speechlessly, an angry sparkle in her eyes. She thought if it had been possible she would have demanded to be set down then and there. But since such conduct would only make her appear more ridiculous than she did already, she had perforce to remain beside him and could only hope Stretton could not be much farther.

It shortly began to drizzle, and she looked up sharply, before subsiding into her corner of the carriage in resignation.

Vidal glanced up as well. "I fear you will have to make good your boast you do not mind a little damping, Miss Forrester," he said mockingly. "I would advise you to wrap yourself up in that rug as best you can. Your coat looks far from waterproof."

"Never mind!" she said impatiently. "How far is it still to Stretton?"

He shrugged. "Not much more than four miles, I should think."

She sighed and accepted it without a word, merely attempting to halt the insistent trickle of icy water from the brim of her bonnet down her neck. The rain had quickly settled into a bone-chilling downpour that gave every indication of continuing for the rest of the night, at least. As he had predicted, her garments were far from waterproof, and she was quickly drenched through. She sat, cold and miserable, and thought longingly of the warm inn they had left behind.

Vidal, whose greatcoat and hat provided him with considerable more protection against the weather, turned his head briefly. "Regrets already, Miss Forrester?" he inquired unkindly. Then he laughed and said more tolerantly, "You look like a drowned rat. I suppose I had better spring 'em if you are not to catch pneumonia."

For answer she hunched an offended shoulder and turned away.

His laugh sounded again, and he did not wait for her permission before dropping his hands and allowing his bays to shoot forward.

She knew perfectly well that it was madness on such a road, but she thought she would see them overturned in the ditch before being betrayed into uttering one word of protest at the reckless pace. Vidal seemed almost to have forgotten her existence. He leaned slightly forward in his seat, his eyes intent on the road before them, and only his slight frown betrayed his concentration. He held his bays easily, almost carelessly, as if indifferent—or unaware of —the danger. The road had quickly become a quagmire under the horses' churning hooves, and the rain had created a peculiar half-light that made visibility extremely difficult, but Vidal seemed unaware of that as well.

Absurdly she was a little mollified. She might deplore the arrogance of the gesture, but she could not deny his undoubted skill. She thought she had never seen a better whip.

What happened next she hardly knew. One second she was huddled into her corner, watching with grudging admiration the performance of a man she had reason to dislike; the next she had been hurled across the seat, her bonnet pitched forward over her eyes and her face smothered against the wet fabric of Vidal's coat.

She struggled furiously to right herself on the pitching seat, aware that the phaeton was careening violently across the road. She could hear Vidal cursing softly and steadily under his breath beside her. Then she was thrust unceremoniously away, Vidal's whole attention concentrated upon calming his terrified bays.

She still had no idea what had happened to frighten them, but it was over then almost as quickly as it had begun. For a brief terrifying moment they had seemed to hang suspended over the ditch on the far side of the road, and she had watched in horrified fascination, convinced they must be overturned. Then even as the leader stumbled, the bays seemed to respond instinctively to Vidal's iron control. Reassured by the calming influence of his familiar hands, they regained their footing, the phaeton almost miraculously righting itself and the pace gradually slowing.

The first headlong flight was being checked, and she had just relaxed her convulsive grip on the side of the phaeton when fate intervened. There was a tremendous flash of lightning almost directly on the road before them, followed within seconds by a deafening clap of thunder. The bays, nervous and still badly frightened, shied violently, and plunged from the road down a narrow track running at an angle straight into the trees.

She ducked her head instinctively as low-hanging branches clutched at her, unable to believe for a moment that Vidal had lost control of his team. Then she had been pulled roughly against his shoulder once more, the smell of his wet coat strong in her nostrils.

His voice sounded close to her ear. "The traces have snapped," he announced briefly. "We're going to have to jump. Wait for a clear space and I'll tell you when."

Comprehension dawned then, but she could not help wondering a little hysterically what he meant to do if she refused. Throw her out? It was no easy thing to be obliged to jump from a rapidly moving vehicle fully five feet off the ground.

The trees still pressed in closely, and she was uncertain where he thought they were to find a space wide enough to jump, but she did not mean to let him see she was afraid. She gathered her skirts about her in a manner quite as cool as his own and lightly cast off the clinging rug.

"Good girl!" Vidal said approvingly. "I think there's an opening just ahead. Do you see—? Good! Get ready— Now!"

Even as she gathered her skirts for the jump she felt his hands close about her waist. In one swift movement he had lifted her and thrown her clear of the wheels. But the unexpected thrust of his hands and her confining skirts caused her to land badly, her weight coming down heavily on her left arm. Her wrist gave beneath her and her shoulder slammed into the earth with brutal force. Everything went black.

She could only have lain there for a minute or two before she came to herself and attempted to rise. But her left arm would not bear her weight and she nearly fell again. Then strong arms lifted her.

"Are you hurt?"

She looked up blankly. "Good God! You *did* throw me out!"

For answer he calmly set her on her feet and pulled her into the shelter of the trees. Memory returned then and she gathered her scattered wits about her. "No, no, I'm not hurt!" she said impatiently. "What happened?"

He shrugged. "As I told you, the traces snapped. Some animal—I rather imagine it was a deer—darted across the road in front of us, a circumstance my bays took pardonable exception to. But really, don't you think we might discuss this at a more convenient time?"

She had endured a trying half hour. She was shaken, in considerable pain and soaked to the skin, and she found his attitude at that moment inexcusable. She herself would have made light of the whole if he had shown himself at all properly concerned. He did not. She drew herself up and delivered a brief denunciation of his manners, his driving skill and his reckless disregard for the safety of others. If his bays were ruined it would be no more than he deserved, and she, for one, had no intention of standing in the rain a moment longer!

Vidal, completely unmoved, heard her out, then pulled off his greatcoat and fastened it about her despite her indignant protests. "Very true, ma'am," he said, bored. "Now if you are quite finished, I would suggest we attempt to find some shelter. I believe there is an old cottage not far from here."

She bit her lip, furiously aware that she was at fault, and uncertain which of them she was angrier with. "Oh, very well! I beg your pardon! But it was—*infamous* of you to behave so calmly!"

"No doubt, ma'am!" he said dampingly. "But it would hardly help if I were to give way to hysterics as well."

She gasped and said in mortified tones, "I have not given way to hysterics!"

"No, I beg your pardon! Merely a temper tantrum!"

It was a far more masterful set-down than her own had been. She was obliged to close her lips tightly together and endure the further ignominy of being pulled firmly against his shoulder as if she had been a recalcitrant child, and propelled forward.

But since the initial numbing pain in her shoulder and arm had subsided into a dull, mindless ache that was made worse by the pace he set, she had soon to be grateful for his support. The ground was wet and uneven, and she stumbled wearily against him several times, only saved from falling by the presence of his arm about her.

He seemed to be familiar with the country, for he hesitated only once or twice to look around him, and in a very short space of time had brought them out of the trees and into a tiny clearing. A small dark cottage stood within, slowly being reclaimed by the surrounding forest.

Vidal halted at sight of it. "Ah, good! I thought I remembered it being somewhere near here." Without hesitation he hurried her across the clearing, thrust open the door and bundled her inside out of the rain. "Much better! Now if you will remain where you are, ma'am, I will endeavor to see what light there may be."

She could only shake her head and lean breathlessly against the door, content to leave matters in his hands for the moment.

There was a thud and a muffled oath, as if he had stumbled into something in the dark, but then he exclaimed in satisfaction. In another moment a light shone forth.

He held up his candle and looked around the small room, an expression of distaste on his face, then shrugged ruefully. "I'm afraid it's not much, but it will do well enough. Do you mean to stand hovering by the door prepared for instant flight, Miss Forrester? You would be much better occupied in getting out of those wet things and helping me to find what other candles there may be. I can assure you you have nothing to fear from me."

She colored and came into the room, but said half in earnest, "On the contrary, sir! I think you are probably the most dangerous man I know!"

He stood looking down at her bedraggled figure for a long moment. Then unexpectedly his expression softened. "Poor Miss Forrester! I have not been very kind to you, have I? Never mind! I will make it up to you."

He smiled and added very softly, "Only I really think it is time you told me the truth, don't you?"

Chapter Three

The silence seemed to grate unbearably on her stretched nerves. She could only stand staring stupidly at him, her brain refusing to take in his last words.

After a moment he shrugged. "Come, Miss Forrester! I have been aware almost from the first that you are no more a governess than I am. You had better tell me the truth, you know, for I have every intention of discovering exactly what you are up to."

She stiffened abruptly and regained her wits. "I have not the slightest notion what you are talking about!" she snapped.

The slightly softened expression in his eyes died, to be replaced by his usual cynicism. "I would advise you not to continue to think me a fool, Miss Forrester. I do not think you will find it particularly wise."

"I will not be threatened, sir," she said evenly. "Nor do I care to be called a liar. I neither know nor care what absurd idea you have taken into your head, but I am growing weary of these constant innuendoes. I would appreciate it if you would tell me how far it is to Stretton."

He lifted his brows and regarded her indifferently. "There is not the slightest chance you will reach Stretton tonight, Miss Forrester. I would advise you to resign yourself to a night spent in my company."

Without a word she turned and crossed to the door.

Even before she had received the first icy drops in her face she had hesitated, furiously aware of how foolish it would be to set out in this weather when she knew neither the direction nor distance of the nearest habitation. The only thing she might depend upon was losing herself completely. To be wandering about all night in the storm would be as melodramatic as it was foolish, and was hardly calculated to improve her circumstances in the least. After a moment she closed the door again and turned back into the room, her face set.

"Very wise, Miss Forrester," Vidal drawled. "Now shall

we begin again?" Then his eyes narrowed abruptly on her face, and he said in a very different tone, "Oh, good God! Get out of those wet things while I light a fire, before you catch your death!"

She hesitated, then almost woodenly shrugged out of his heavy greatcoat and folded it across a chair before removing her wet pelisse and bonnet. Her skirts were stained and badly crushed, but she supposed they would soon dry. She ran her fingers automatically through her damp curls, then shook out her skirts as best she could, feeling sensibly that she was likely to require all the self-confidence she possessed to see her through the coming interview. Then, because she was by no means a coward, she turned to examine their temporary shelter with an assumption of indifference.

What she saw was hardly encouraging. There was a rickety table in the center of the room containing a great many objects tossed indiscriminately upon its scarred top. The only other furnishings in the room consisted of a narrow bed in one corner and a couple of wooden chairs, without any visible concession to comfort, pulled before the ancient hearth. This last had obviously been intended to do double duty as warmth and cook stove, for a roasting spit had collapsed partway into the ashes, and various pots were placed upon the mantel. A jumble of rusted traps and tools in one corner and an ancient fowling-piece hanging above the fireplace completed the whole.

From its location she judged it to be a gamekeeper's cottage, and it was evident it had not seen the presence of a woman for many years. Several faded blankets tumbled untidily upon the bed and a stack of firewood in a box gave some signs of recent habitation, but no one had seen fit to banish the cobwebs from the corners or sweep the floor in years. As if to add to the atmosphere, the wind whistled eerily through the chimney and the rain pounded heavily against the frail roof.

Miss Forrester, her housewifely spirit unstirred by all this disorder, nevertheless had no trouble in recognizing a setting worthy of one of the more lurid romances from the lending library. Her lips curled a little, but she only shrugged and went to warm her hands before the small blaze Vidal had succeeded in kindling in the grate.

He glanced up from his task of shaking the water out of his elegant blue coat. "I hope you are not afraid of rats,

Miss Forrester," he remarked calmly. "I have every reason to believe there is probably a large colony of them behind the woodbox."

She lifted her eyes and said contemptuously, "If you mean to frighten me, sir, you are very far off. I imagine I have had a greater acquaintance with rats than you could possibly have. At any rate, since it appears the whole place has been left to their devices, it seems clear we are the interlopers."

"I am delighted to see you are taking this so well, Miss Forrester," he said smoothly.

"Short of engaging in a show of hysterics which would hardly benefit either of us, there seems little at the moment I can do! I believe you have already expressed your opinion of temper tantrums, have you not?"

"So that rankled, did it?" he asked in amusement.

She ignored him, dragging a chair closer to the fire and calmly seating herself. "I think, under the circumstances," she said evenly, "it is time you explained what all this—" she hesitated briefly, "this—nonsense is about."

He pulled a snuff box from his pocket and withdrew a pinch, his eyes resting meditatively on her face. "You are really a most redoubtable female, you know, Miss Forrester," he remarked. "It seems clear I must discard my earliest theory."

She raised her brows. "And that was?"

"Oh, that you had run away from school," he said carelessly. "But I think you are perhaps a little older than I first thought you. Then too, I have yet to meet a schoolgirl with anything like your—er—*sang-froid.*"

When she only continued to stare at him with her clear gaze he added musingly, "It is, of course, possible that I have become the unwitting accomplice to an elopement instead. But if so, where, I must ask myself, is the elusive bridegroom?"

She could not help it. It was so ridiculous she burst out laughing.

He looked a little startled, then went to lean against the mantel, his hands stuffed into his breeches pockets and a dangerous smile upon his lips.

After a moment she gasped and tried to regain her composure. "I—I'm sorry, sir," she said frankly, "but it is f-funny!"

He did not move. "I have already warned you it is

never wise to underestimate me, Miss Forrester. I have known from the outset that you are very far from being what you would appear. Must I illustrate?"

She swallowed a little convulsively at that, but said defiantly, "Certainly! It should help to pass the time."

He shrugged and ran his eyes insolently over her figure. "Very well, Miss Forrester—or whatever your name is. Shall I tell you then that although your garments are well-worn they are not your own? You move in them as if they were unfamiliar to you and you were perhaps a little ashamed of them."

Her eyes widened in dismay, but she clamped her lips tightly together.

"You would do well to change your shoes, however, if you mean this little deception to be of any duration," he added almost carelessly. "They are obviously more expensive than the remainder of your wardrobe and draw comparisons I feel certain you wish to avoid."

It took a great deal of effort not to look down at her feet.

"With your permission I will pass over such anomalies as your hands and your voice—although I believe I have already complimented you upon your excellent English," he remarked.

"But you see, Miss Forrester, I do not think I am excessively cynical, and yet I cannot think of a single woman of my acquaintance who would consent to have in her home as governess a female with—may I say it?— your face and your figure."

As she stiffened he added coolly, "Your hair, by the way, clearly owes its color to art rather than nature." He idly lifted his quizzing glass to study her. "I think—yes I really think it must be Titian. Unusual for a Frenchwoman, but with those eyes almost obligatory."

"My mother was Scots!" she snapped, then promptly could have bitten out her tongue.

His lips quivered. "Ah, that no doubt explains it."

She rose abruptly and moved to stand before the fire, her back rigid. After a moment he spoke again, and the humor had quite left his voice. "I have, in charity, assumed that this little charade was not planned for my benefit, Miss Forrester, but I have every intention of discovering exactly what you are up to."

She jerked around at that, her eyes blazing. "Your benefit! *Your* benefit!" she gasped.

He shrugged indifferently. "Or, failing mine, some other gentleman's."

The furious color rushed to her face. "I see! Are women in the habit of seeking to compromise you?" she said derisively. "How very tiresome it must be! It is no wonder you are so very cynical!"

When he only shrugged again she added, "I can only wonder at your courage in risking so much by offering me a ride in your carriage! Surely one in your position must take every precaution to protect himself against such predatory females as myself?"

He seemed untouched by her contempt. "You will find I am not such an easy bird for the plucking, my dear," he drawled.

She knew an almost ungovernable impulse to smash something. She could not remember when she had been so angry. She would have given anything to have had a whip to slash across that arrogant face. She turned away, not trusting herself to look at him.

His voice came from behind her. "If it is neither an elusive bridegroom nor myself, Miss Forrester, that seems to leave only the unknown Lady Thornton. Now what business could you have with her, I wonder?"

She was aware he was goading her quite deliberately. She took a deep breath and turned. "Why, I mean to steal the family silver, of course," she said pleasantly.

Abruptly he inclined his head. "My compliments, Miss Forrester," he said quietly. "I do not believe I have ever met anyone quite like you."

"And I am quite certain I have never met anyone like you!" she said bitterly.

He smiled. "No, no! Do not get upon your high ropes again. Strangely enough, I meant it as a compliment. I admire your courage, Miss Forrester."

Her mouth tightened. "Indeed? I find I care no more for your compliments than your insults."

"No? But then perhaps you are quite accustomed to being stranded many miles from nowhere with a strange man, or being forced to jump from a rapidly moving carriage. I, on the other hand, cannot think of a single female of my acquaintance who would have acquitted herself so well."

She still could not believe him serious. "As I recall, you gave me very little choice in the matter! I seem to remember you threw me out whether I would or no!"

His lips quirked. "Yes, but I had not yet completely gotten your measure then," he remarked apologetically.

Her brows drew together haughtily. "And have you now?"

"Oh, I think so. You are headstrong, impetuous and possessed of considerable courage. You also have a ready tongue and a quick temper and are pretty much accustomed to doing exactly as you like. Is that not a fair assessment, Miss Forrester?"

"I had no idea you were a fortune teller, sir," she said coldly. "But I do not believe I have given you leave to use me as your subject."

He smiled sardonically. "You really do not like me very much, do you, Miss Forrester?"

"On the contrary, sir," she said immediately. "I make every allowance for the fact you are clearly mad, and must not be held responsible for your actions."

His smile grew. "So you think me mad, do you?" he said in amusement.

She closed her eyes for a brief moment, then sank into a chair, her hand to her brow. "Oh, good God!" she said wearily. "Let us have done with this!" Her anger had deserted her, leaving her only weary and unutterably dispirited. It no longer mattered what he thought of her, but if he had seen through her so easily, she could not hope to succeed. Maby had been right, and she had only made a fool of herself.

She started violently then as he said curtly, "Drink this!" Her eyes flew open and she stared at the silver flask he held out to her.

"Thank you! I do not care for anything!"

"No doubt such wounded dignity is extremely gratifying to your ego, Miss Forrester," he said witheringly. "But you will have some of my brandy if I have to pour it down your throat. I'll not have your pneumonia laid at my door."

She glared up at him, but since she had no trouble in believing him capable of carrying out his threat, gave in with ill-grace and accepted his flask. She sniffed suspiciously at its contents, her nose wrinkled in distaste, but under his mocking gaze forced herself to swallow a

small amount of brandy. She choked, the unaccustomed
spirits burning down her throat, and coughed miserably,
tears flooding her eyes.

Vidal's harsh laugh sounded then and the brandy flask
was taken from her hand. "My God! What a situation!"
he said in exasperation. "I suppose you're going to be sick
on me now? It wanted only that!"

She lifted her head with great dignity. "Certainly not!"
But since the room seemed to have developed an uncomfortable tendency to tilt around her, she then carefully
leaned her head back against the chair and closed her
eyes.

When next she opened them Vidal was standing over
her, a steaming mug in his hands. She only stared blankly
at him, and after a moment he took her hand and curled
her fingers around the cup. "Contrary to your obvious
expectations, Miss Forrester," he said drily, "it is neither
poisoned nor drugged. Some thoughtful occupant before
us very kindly left us a packet of tea."

She flushed and repeated stupidly, "Tea—? But who—?"
Her eyes widened. "Surely *you* did not make it?"

"If I had any doubts, you have now told me exactly
what you think of me," he remarked silkily. "I cannot
help feeling that you, of all people, should learn not to
trust to appearances, Miss Forrester. I am quite capable of boiling a pot of tea when the occasion demands."

She sighed and sipped gratefully at her tea. After a moment Vidal added easily, "I thought you would find that
a little more to your liking than my brandy. There is a
packet of biscuits as well, but I hesitate to recommend
them to you. I can only guess how long they may have
lain here."

"I fear I lack your discriminating taste, sir," she said
truthfully. "I find I am hungry enough to eat nearly anything."

He shrugged and produced the biscuits. They were indeed quite stale, but once she had drunk her tea and
eaten one or two of them she felt a great deal better. She
set her teacup aside, saying a little stiffly, "Thank you,
sir. That was—was very kind of you."

"Not at all, Miss Forrester," he said politely. "I must
admit you look a little better. Dare I hope your temper
has improved accordingly?"

She shook her head in disbelief. "I collect it would be

quite useless to point out that I am in no way responsible for this—this remarkable situation?"

His brows rose mockingly.

After a moment she laughed reluctantly. "Good God! Are you never at a loss?"

"Very seldom, child," he remarked indifferently.

Her color rose, but she said musingly, "That seems to be the first thing you have said that I can find myself in complete agreement with! In our brief acquaintance you have subjected me to a cross-examination on my past, thrown me out of your carriage in the mud, insulted me, accused me of I know not what—and all with the air of the merest commonplace. I dare not speculate on what would manage to strike you as out of the ordinary."

"Yes, but I did not accuse you of being mad," he pointed out in amusement.

"No, indeed you did not!" she said, much struck. "Must I thank you for this unlooked-for forbearance?"

"You may do so in the morning. Now I think it is time and past that you were in your bed."

She raised her eyes quickly. "I would be happy to be so, if you will tell me where you desire me to sleep."

"You will naturally sleep in the bed, Miss Forrester."

"And you?"

"Pray content yourself, ma'am. I shall manage well enough in a chair before the fire. I assure you it will not be the first time I have done so. You have nothing to fear from me, as I seem to have been called upon to repeat with unflattering frequency."

She shook her head. "No, I am smaller than you and will be able to pull two chairs together. I can assure you that I, too, have spent my share of nights thus."

His eyes lit. "Come, this is intriguing," he said immediately. "I must confess I had put you down as a product of an extremely proper background."

"I am perfectly aware that you have done nothing of the sort!" she said bitterly. "Or that I have given you any cause to think me other than a—a—" She broke off, and after a moment continued stiffly, "In actual fact, I have spent much of my life traveling with my father. There have been many times in Portugal and Spain when I have known far worse accommodations than this."

Then she drew herself up, a little angry to have said so much, and conscious as well of a strange expression in

Vidal's eyes. "But that was many years ago. And I was forgetting. You still persist in thinking me a runaway heiress or some such!"

She smiled derisively and stood up. For a moment the room swam unpleasantly, the product no doubt of brandy and fatigue. Then she moved determinedly to tug two chairs together.

Before she quite knew what had happened Vidal had gathered her into his arms and dumped her unceremoniously back into her chair before the fire.

"Good God, you little fool! What the devil do you think I am——?" His black brows were drawn together in an ominous line and the humor had completely disappeared from his face. She could only stare at him in bewilderment, uncertain what she had done to bring about this sudden anger.

After a moment the anger died from his eyes and he laughed harshly. "Ah, perhaps I deserved that! You have a chastening effect upon me, Miss Forrester, and I find it damnably uncomfortable."

Then the mocking light returned to his eyes, and she could not be certain which of them he mocked more. "Quit glaring at me with those enormous green eyes of yours, you ridiculous child. Come, you had best have some more of my brandy. I think we are both likely to need it before the night is out."

Remembering his former threat she drew back hastily. But when she would have turned her head away he gripped the back of her neck and tilted the flask ruthlessly. The brandy she gulped made her choke and cough and set her head to spinning.

His voice sounded curiously far away. "Forgive me, my child. I am a brute to have kept at you so. I think you must be pretty much all in. No, don't fight me!" as she again tried to push his flask away.

She was forced to swallow more of the fiery liquid, then weakly closed her eyes and leaned her head back as the warmth of the fire and the brandy seemed to fuse within her.

Sometime later she roused slightly, to discover Vidal had removed her shoes and stockings and was chafing her cold feet. "No, no!" she murmured, greatly shocked.

He looked up for a moment, then calmly continued with his task. She attempted to stop him, but somehow the heavenly warmth enfolding her made her eyelids too heavy to lift.

When Vidal looked up next she was asleep, her long lashes dark against her cheeks like an exhausted child's. But when he lifted her to carry her to the bed her eyes opened sleepily. Her face was very close to his own, her brows drawn together into a puzzled frown. "You—?" She shook her head fretfully. "I don't understand you . . ."

"Don't let it disturb you, my dear," he said drily. "At the moment I'm not certain I do myself."

She sighed then and her lashes drooped.

He laid her on the bed and tucked the blankets closely around her, then stood looking down at her, a wry expression in his eyes. Suddenly he shrugged, picked up the brandy flask and settled himself before the fire. It was going to be a long night.

Chapter Four

As it happened, the landlord had done Lady Thornton an injustice. Timothy Smallwood, coachman to my Lady Thornton, had in fact been sent to fetch the new governess. But since his road led him past the village inn and he knew the stagecoaches to be habitually late in these parts, he had seen nothing wrong in stopping for a brief tot to warm him up for the long drive.

It was not until considerably later, when it had begun to rain, that Timothy's by now somewhat fuddled brain was recalled to his original errand. But by the time he had paid his shot and struggled back into his heavy coat, and then had the horses set-to again, the rain was falling heavily, and he was of the strong opinion that Lady Thornton would not wish him to risk the horses in such weather, governess or no governess. Lady Thornton was not what you might call an open-fisted lady, as Timothy Smallwood would be the first to tell you.

And since it was rare indeed for his employer's penury to match so exactly with his own inclinations, he gratefully turned his team toward home.

Since Lady Thornton spent the afternoon visiting her dear friend Mrs. Winthorpe, she did not learn of the matter until much later that evening. It was then brought forceably and unpleasantly to her attention by Nanny, who stood, arms akimbo, in the doorway of the drawing room just as dinner was announced, and with dark satisfaction demanded to be told what was to become of her promised half-day, since the new governess had failed to arrive.

In truth, Nanny had not been looking forward to the arrival of still another governess, for she thought them flighty, namby-pamby creatures more interested in their own comfort than the well-being of their charges. But she endured an exhausting week. The weather had for days made it impossible for her five exuberant nurslings to reduce their energies in outside exercises, with the result that they spent their time in devising pranks designed to set the whole house about its ears. Nanny was therefore understandably pointed in her remarks about governesses who failed to arrive when they were expected, and households where a nanny was expected to take charge of children who should by all rights be in the schoolroom.

Her words were produced more for effect, however, than the vague likelihood of producing results. Lady Thornton considered herself a fond mama as long as nothing more strenuous was expected of her than a brief visit from her beloved children before dinner, but in any crisis where prompt action or an immediate decision was required of her, she was more than likely to retire to her bedchamber with one of her spasms, too unwell to be disturbed.

But for once Nanny, too, had underestimated Lady Thornton. Since the high spirits of her darling William had led him to introduce a frog into the scullery yesterday morning, causing cook to faint and the kitchen maid to fall into strong hysterics, she was nearly as concerned as Nanny might have wished at the unwelcome news.

A rapid succession of governesses had somewhat dimmed Lady Thornton's hopes of finding exactly what she wanted, since the last five governesses had complained incessantly of the climate and had even gone so far as to lay wicked and wholly false accusations against her innocent lambs.

But Miss Forrester had been highly recommended, and was French as well, which was seen in this context to be a decided advantage. Not only could she instruct the elder daughters in the French tongue, but she might reasonably be expected to fill out her time in doing odd sewing. Lady Thornton was not, as a rule, fond of foreigners, particularly the encroaching French, whose impecunious nobility had flocked to England during the revolution in their own country some years before. But one could not deny that they were unusually handy with the needle. And there was, now that the dreadful Napoleon had been defeated at last, a decided cachet in having French servants.

With these thoughts in mind, Lady Thornton was stirred to unaccustomed vigor and was in turn extremely heated in her remarks to Timothy Coachman on the folly of returning without the new governess. If he valued his position he would see that she was found promptly.

For all the world, Timothy grumbled to himself, as if she were a parcel to be retrieved from the side of the road. He wisely interpreted her ladyship's demand for promptness to mean tomorrow, however, and passed a comfortable night untroubled by any twinges of conscience.

He was up earlier than usual the next morning, however, and spent a disagreeable few hours in making useless inquiries between Grantham and Stretton. The landlord in Grantham informed him with a great deal of contempt that the young lady had been obliged to accept a seat in a gentleman's carriage to convey her to Stretton, since there was not a room to be had in Grantham—a fact certain parties might have foreseen if they had troubled themselves to give the matter any thought.

As if that were not bad enough, his inquiries in Stretton met with equal failure and were greeted moreover with what he could only consider quite unnecessary ribaldry. There was a great deal of laughter, and not a few remarks about the mislaying of young females. Had he checked with the local magistrate? Perhaps he should call in the Bow Street runners.

His temper considerably frayed, Smallwood turned his horses back on the road to Grantham, his immediate future bleak. Lady Thornton was not one to take such news calmly, nor was it likely to weigh in the least with her that he could in no way be held responsible for the lapses of the new governess. He sighed and shook his head over such patent injustice.

Since he was by no means eager to return, his pace had slackened considerably, but even so, he was nearly halfway back to Grantham before he remembered the old gamekeeper's cottage in the woods. It was possible the storm might have driven the governess to take shelter there. He turned his horses immediately and made for the cottage, grateful for any reprieve.

In truth he did not actually place much faith in his own theory, so that when he reached the cottage some fifteen minutes later he blinked in considerable surprise at the sight of smoke drifting leisurely from the chimney. He scratched his head, spit expertly between the shafts, and muttered to himself in disbelief, "Wull, I'll be damned!"

A slow grin spread across his face.

Vidal had spent a most uncomfortable night, roused alternately by the cold when the fire died down and by the torturous confines of a chair he could only assume had been placed there as punishment for his sins. It was thus not in the most amiable of moods he was wakened the next morning by the unmistakable sound of steps outside.

He swore softly and gained his feet. He was leaning negligently against the mantel, his hands in his pockets and a dangerous smile upon his lips, when the door was banged open.

Smallwood, expecting to be met by a tearfully grateful female, was checked on the threshold at sight of that smile.

He swallowed, shifted his feet nervously, then muttered, "I beg your pardon, sor! I didn't know anyone was here. I be looking for a young lady, sor. You hadn't seen her, has you, sor?" He gulped and ground to a stop, jerking his cap off under Vidal's gaze.

Vidal lazily lifted his quizzing glass to survey the man from head to toe. Far more valiant men had quaked under that withering glance, and Timothy paled perceptibly.

His inspection complete, Vidal allowed his quizzing glass to fall. "I see. And exactly where did you . . . er . . . lose this young lady of yours?"

Smallwood, wishing himself anywhere else, muttered thickly, "Sor, she's to be the new governess up to Thornton Hall. She—I—" he broke off, his eyes looking wildly around for inspiration, and edged slightly toward the door.

It was at that inopportune moment that the slight figure in the bed sat up, the blankets clutched about her. "Oh! *Qui est là?*" she cried, her eyes still fogged with sleep.

Smallwood's eyes nearly started out of his head at this apparition. Vidal's lips thinned, but he moved slowly to the bed and pulled her against him.

"Tais-toi, m'amie," he murmured, his fingers pressing

her shoulder in warning. His eyes did not leave the figure at the door.

After a moment he spoke again, and his voice was no longer lazy. "You have disturbed my wife! I would suggest you remove yourself with all possible haste and seek your . . . young lady elsewhere."

The man quailed before that look and backed thankfully through the door. After a moment Vidal followed him from the room for a low-voiced conversation, then stepped back inside, calmly closing the door behind him.

"How are you feeling this morning, Miss Forrester?" he inquired politely.

Her eyes were abnormally large and she still clutched the blankets convulsively about her, but some of the shadow left her face at his prosaic question.

"Very well, thank you," she answertd impatiently. "Who was that man?"

He shrugged and said indifferently, "Merely a case of mistaken identity, ma'am. It need not concern you."

She did not look to be wholly convinced, but after a second allowed the subject to drop. Vidal, never at his best in the morning, looked her over coldly, a distinct curl on his lips.

He had told her the truth when he said it had been curiosity that had prompted his unusual offer. He had known within a very few minutes of setting eyes upon her drab figure that she was far from being what she appeared. His curiosity had naturally been piqued, and since he was feeling decidedly bored at the moment, he had given in to the impulse to find out a little more about her.

It had required little intelligence to surmise what her difficulty must be, but he had meant to do no more than exert his influence in her behalf to obtain her a room. He hardly knew why he had offered her a seat in his phaeton instead, except perhaps that on closer inspection she proved to be even prettier than he had thought.

But Miss Forrester, far from being grateful for this unexpected offer, had regarded him skeptically out of a remarkably beautiful pair of eyes, and coolly demanded to know the reason for his offer of assistance. Vidal was unaccustomed to being summed up and so obviously found lacking, and certainly never by a dab of a female in the worst bonnet it had been his misfortune to lay eyes on in months. His interest, before only mildly engaged, had been thoroughly aroused.

Intrigued and even amused he might be, but no doubt he would have set her down in the village in the end and thought no more about her had fate not intervened in the guise of the storm and the subsequent mishap to his carriage. Resigning himself to a thoroughly miserable night, and with the slightly malicious intention of repaying her a little for his missed dinner and the mistreatment of his bays, he had set himself to discover exactly what she was up to.

But far from displaying the horror natural to a young lady finding herself in such a compromising position, Miss Forrester had parried all his questions, refused point-blank to be bullied and had even laughed at him. Vidal, whose cynical humor was directed at himself quite as often as at others, was obliged to admit that for the moment, at least, the honors were decidedly with the lady.

Then she had succeeded in flicking his conscience on the raw, a thing that did not happen very often, and he found that for the moment he did not like himself very much. It had been an uncomfortable feeling, and one that he had quickly rejected. He had few illusions, and he doubted whether his Miss Forrester was a great deal different than any other female of his acquaintance.

Nor had he the least intention of allowing himself to become embroiled in her ridiculous masquerade, whatever its reason, and he now saw clearly that he was in great danger of doing exactly that. In the sane light of morning he had lost all interest in the reasons for that masquerade. What had amused him before, now took on overtones of exactly the sort of ill-bred behavior he most despised. As for himself, he desired nothing so much as his valet and his breakfast. He would be rid of the tiresome creature as soon as he decently might, and let that be a lesson to him in future!

In a thoroughly bad temper, he raised his quizzing glass for the second time that morning and directed it at her face, an unpleasant smile upon his lips. In the clear light she was even younger than he had supposed. Her preposterous hair hung in muddy locks about her face, but her eyes were the clear, startling green that had first drawn his attention to her. They were framed by enor-

mous dark lashes and were the color of rain-washed seas.
Her nose was short and straight, her mouth had a lovely
curve, and her complexion, though at the moment too
pale and marred by dark smudges under her eyes, was
oddly translucent. Only her chin was a trifle too firm for
real beauty, and her eyes were at present glittering angrily.

Vidal, an acknowledged arbiter of beauty, was impressed. He bowed mocking. "Decidedly *not* a governess, Miss Forrester," he murmured maliciously.

She had flushed becomingly under his scrutiny, but
now she became very pale. "I see," she said quietly. "Perhaps you would be so kind as to hand me my shoes and
stockings."

His brows rose. She had spirit, the little governess. He
obediently gathered her shoes and stockings and turned
back in time to surprise her eyes resting on his chair before the fire. She glanced up, then lifted her chin and
said politely, "I trust you had a comfortable night, sir?"

He met her eyes and smiled grimly. "On the contrary,
Miss Forrester. You hope I spent an excessively uncomfortable night, since it's clearly no more than I deserve!"

She actually had the temerity to laugh at that. His eyes
narrowed and he regarded her in silence for a moment
before handing her her shoes and stockings and walking
out.

When he returned some ten minutes later she was once
again wearing her stained pelisse, and there was a
slightly rueful expression in her eyes as she gazed at her
ruined bonnet. At the sound of the door, however, she
turned swiftly, her face suddenly impassive.

Vidal's lips quirked involuntarily, and he said sympa-
thetically, "Perhaps it will be salvageable with new ribbons, ma'am."

She sighed and said truthfully, "I fear more than ribbons are necessary to restore this to its former beauty,
sir." Then she glanced up, and at his expression added
sharply, "Well, it *must* have been attractive once!"

"Probably before your time," he remarked drily. "Shall
I consign it to the flames?"

Miss Forrester smoothed the ribbons and said calmly,
"By no means, sir. I can assure you bonnets are not so
easily come by on a governess' salary."

Vidal's lips curled. "At any rate I can believe that

particular bonnet was not readily come by, ma'am," he said. "I imagine you must have turned through the attics for some time before hitting upon just what you required."

She flushed and defiantly placed the much-maligned bonnet upon her head, tying the ribbons firmly under her chin. But since the brim showed a marked tendency to collapse over her eyes and her bow was lamentably lopsided, the effect of this gesture was somewhat diminished.

Vidal, unable to resist, straightened it for her and solemnly retied the bow under her left ear. She stood rigidly under his hands and thanked him in a frigid voice.

Fast recovering his sense of humor, he bowed mockingly and moved to don his own still-elegant blue coat and straighten his cravat. His buckskins bore little trace of the storm and his fine cambric shirt was not too badly creased. He might be sadly in need of a shave, and have a very good notion what his extremely fastidious valet would have to say about his appearance, but he knew himself to be little the worse for wear.

Miss Forrester observed these actions with growing resentment and was at last moved to remark sarcastically that she hoped he had not ruined his beautiful coat.

He met her eyes and said gravely, "No, I think I have been lucky, ma'am." He transferred his gaze to his boots and sighed. "But I fear it may be otherwise with my no-less beautiful boots. I dread to think what Clay will have to say."

She frowned, torn between disgust and sudden suspicion. "Who is Clay?" she demanded.

"My valet." He shook his head gloomily.

She stiffened, glaring at him, but then her lips betrayed her. She attempted to firm them, failed miserably, and at last laughed reluctantly. "Oh, very well! I can only say I would give a great deal to see your valet give you a thundering scold! If there is anyone who can get the better of you—which I don't for a moment believe—I would very much like to make his acquaintance!"

He smiled guilelessly. "Why, how can you doubt it, Miss Forrester? I seem to recall that you bested me several times yourself last night."

"I would be very glad to think so," she said frankly. "But I seem to recall exactly the opposite!"

She hesitated then, her color a little high, and added

with obvious reluctance, "But in truth, sir, I believe I must thank you—"

"You were not so grateful last night as I recall, Miss Forrester," he interrupted mockingly.

She sighed. "No, I know I was not. You made me very angry, but indeed, sir, I am not ungrateful—"

He swore softly under his breath as he discovered he was unlikely to hear what this abominable girl might be grateful for, because at that moment she raised her head, and his own ears caught the sound of a carriage arriving. After a moment he shrugged and strode to the door to meet his groom.

As he went to the horses' heads Hollings grinned and was heard to reflect upon the conduct of some cawkers who sent their highbred horses home in the rain without them. But since Hollings had put him on his first horse, Vidal merely laughed and asked after the bays.

"Well, sir, one of them has strained a fetlock, but I've put a poultice on it and I've no doubt it'll be right as rain in a few days." He dropped his voice. "That fool of a coachman from Thornton Hall you sent was putting it about that you was here with a lady you said was your wife, but Lymings was able to shut his mouth and we figured I'd better come myself to get you."

Vidal's eyes darkened, but he turned politely as Miss Forrester emerged from the cottage. Hollings quickly relieved him of the horses and he handed her into the carriage and spread a light rug over her knees. He then returned to the cottage to retrieve his hat and greatcoat, took his place beside her, and signaled to his groom to climb up behind.

After a moment Miss Forrester said quietly, "I hope your bays sustained no hurt, sir?"

He shrugged. "No. Hollings assures me nothing more serious than a strained fetlock."

"I—I am glad, sir."

After that they rode in silence. The road was rutted and pitted after the rains, making the journey rough-going even in his well-sprung curricle. After several minutes he glanced down at his companion. She was staring straight ahead in a fixed manner, her face drawn and her lips tightly set.

"It is not much farther now, ma'am."

She glanced up with a start. "What? Oh! Thank you,

sir. Will there be some vehicle in the village to convey me to Thornton Hall?"

Twenty minutes ago he had wanted nothing so much as to be rid of her, and even ten minutes ago he had vowed to rebuff any appeal she might make. She made none. She only looked up at him, her eyes growing a little puzzled at his delay in answering her question.

Vidal, looking down at her, realized ruefully that he had no particular desire to see this chit thrown to the mercy of the local gossips. He had no illusions that their early morning visitor would hold his tongue. For perhaps the first time in his life he had cause to regret his own lamentable reputation.

He knew himself to be on the brink of disaster. A great many years' experience had taught him that it would be the rankest folly to encourage the claims of one who had shown herself, however engaging, to be totally impervious to the conduct expected of a well brought-up young lady. He still had no idea what her motives might be, but her escapade was inexcusable, and her conduct from first to last had been outrageous. He had, furthermore, a constitutional dislike of laying himself open to being bled, and he was perfectly aware he had already done exactly that.

Against this remained only a nagging intuition that this ridiculous child was much more likely to curse him for interfering in her plans than to demand large sums of money from him. Then, too, he had not yet discovered the reason for the dyed hair. He thought that was what intrigued him most. A beauty such as he had every reason to believe Miss Forrester to be was capable of many things, but they usually did not include dyeing her hair and attempting to pass herself off as an unattractive governess. He grinned at the thought of some of the more celebrated beauties he had known even contemplating such an action.

Whether it was that last that decided him, he hardly knew. He only knew he was not yet ready to see the last of Miss Forrester. He therefore looked away and said indifferently, "I believe there may be, ma'am. I am not, however, taking you to the village, but to my own house first. When you have freshened up you may have one of my carriages take you wherever you wish to go."

She frowned. "Does your—your family reside there with you, sir?"

"I have already informed you, I believe, that I have no family, Miss Forrester. I keep a house in this country for the hunting."

"I see." For a moment he thought she would say something more, but then she inclined her head and thanked him in a colorless voice. He was conscious of an irrational feeling of disappointment.

The remainder of the short journey was accomplished in silence. He pulled up before a small, beautifully situated Georgian manor and helped her down, then stood back for her to precede him through the door. After the briefest of hesitations she did so.

"If you will step in here, ma'am," he said easily, holding the door to a small sitting room open for her, "my housekeeper will attend you shortly. Lymings, ask Mrs. Hedges to see me immediately." He bowed, and closed the door upon her.

His servants were too well trained to betray the least trace of emotion, but he was perfectly aware that his butler had stationed himself in the hall to forestall any of the footmen from opening the door before him. He had no doubt that news of the morning's happenings was already spreading throughout the house.

But not even mild curiosity showed in the butler's face as he took Vidal's hat and coat and announced that he had taken the liberty of having breakfast laid out in the morning room.

An hour later, refreshed by a change of clothes and breakfast, his grace, the fifth Duke of Vidal, sat unseeingly at his writing desk. His expression was not pleasant.

Vidal was well aware of his worth. A dukedom, a large fortune and vast estates would have made him an extremely eligible *parti,* had he been ugly or even squint-eyed. But since he was blessed with a harsh, but not displeasing countenance, an elegant figure that showed to distinction the somewhat plain but beautifully tailored clothes he wore, and the possession as well of a singular charm when he chose to exert it, he was perfectly aware that he was considered to be the most eligible bachelor on the Marriage Mart.

Having ascended to the title at the age of nineteen, when his father had been killed in a hunting accident, he had also inherited the vast responsibilities that went with the maintenance of an extremely large fortune, no less than six houses and any number of servants.

He had quickly become aware that his title and possessions would mask a multitude of faults as far as the polite world was concerned, and it was to his credit that he had not become a great deal more autocratic than he was. If his manner was cold, and many a foolish person had been withered by his cynical stare, he did not single out young girls for his attention, only to forget their names at the next meeting, or refuse to answer invitations, or deal rudely with his servants. Such conduct was beneath him. He possessed a keen intelligence, and it could not be said that he neglected a single one of his responsiblilities.

In fact, many a fond mama, despairing of her daughter ever gaining his attention, could almost have wished that he would squander his money away. But although he often played deep, and was forever laying large sums down upon ridiculous wagers, his luck was prodigious and he almost invariably emerged more wealthy than before.

He was generally acknowledged to be a nonpareil in all matters of sport and turf, a devil to hounds, and kept a stable that was the envy of his friends. And if he sometimes drank to excess, and was famed for the beauty of the high-flyers known successively to be in his keeping, it was only to be expected of a man in his position.

For the rest, he was an acknowledged leader of the *ton,* one whose whim could make or break the career of anyone aspiring to figure among fashionable circles. Any young lady lucky enough to gain his favor was assured success, while one frown from his cynical gray eyes could depress the brightest hopes forever. Those he numbered among his friends found him amiable and not the least high in the instep, but outsiders were apt to consider him cold and disagreeably rude.

The fact that he had reached his thirty-fourth year without succumbing to any of the various matrimonial lures thrown out to him was due as much to his cynicism as to his keen intelligence. For although he was well-practiced in the art of love-making, and had conducted any number of well-publicized affairs, he had never yet met a woman who did not heartily bore him within a very short space of time. He had begun to believe he would not do so, and although he was well aware that he must eventually marry, knew of no one upon whom he wished to bestow his title and fortune.

He frowned now. He had grown inured to young ladies wrenching their ankles when his arm was near to be leaned upon, or having their carriages break down just outside his gates, but he was damned if he knew what game the little Forrester was playing at.

His brain told him that despite all appearances he might trust her, and he prided himself upon being an excellent judge of character. But he was aware that anyone else would be justified in thinking he had taken leave of his senses. She was obviously lying to him. Despite their early morning visitor he could not believe she was the governess she claimed. And not only had she made no demur about being obliged to spend a night in his company, but she had willingly accepted shelter in his own home as well.

His eyes narrowed. He did not know who the devil she was, but he certainly meant to find out. She had taken him for a fool, and that rankled above all else. He smiled grimly in a manner that boded no good for the mysterious Miss Forrester.

Chapter Five

When Dominique woke, the hands of the clock on the mantelpiece told her it was late afternoon. She stared at it stupidly for a moment, then looked around the strange room in puzzlement. For a brief second she was unable to think where she might be.

Then as her memory returned she rose quickly and wrapped a dark blue dressing gown around herself. It, like the nightgown she wore, was borrowed and much too large for her. There was no sign of her own clothes.

She was conscious of a nagging pain behind her eyes and she did not seem able to concentrate properly. She should not be here, of course. She did not know how she had come to consent to it, she who prided herself on her good sense and her ability to look after herself. But under Vidal's cold eyes and the inhibiting influence of his groom she had not known how to avoid it.

The ways of the world were strict indeed. She knew very well that last night had been bad enough, were it to become known. But she could not imagine what Vidal was thinking of to bring her to his own house and thereby compound the matter a thousandfold. She smiled grimly. Well, no doubt it amused him to defy the wagging tongues of gossip. She, unfortunately, could not afford such a gesture. The morals of a governess must be above reproach.

She was not fanciful, and if for a brief moment this morning she had feared Vidal's intentions, she was sensible enough to know that if he had had seduction on his mind he would scarcely bring her to his own home and place her in the care of his kindly old housekeeper. Nor had he behaved toward her with anything but polite, if mocking, disinterest during the night they had been forced to spend together.

But his behavior this morning had shown exactly what he thought of her, and she was conscious of a sinking fear that he meant to insult her. She knew she had only herself to blame if he did, and knew herself capable

of handling any importunate advances he might make,
although the thought of him doing so was somehow ridiculous. But she desperately hoped he did not mean to offer
her his protection. Despite everything last night she had
found herself somehow liking the arrogant Vidal. She had
a sudden strong aversion to discovering he was no different from the fashionable unfaithfuls she had more
than once encountered in the last few months in London.

She sighed and looked around her. The room was
lovely in apricot silk hangings and soft carpets. Everything she had seen in Vidal's house spoke of money and
elegant taste. A hunting box! Good God! She knew gentlemen often kept houses in the country that they used
only a few weeks of the year during the hunting season,
but she had never imagined they would be like this. Vidal
must be very wealthy indeed.

She frowned distractedly. The sooner she left his
house the better. Last night had been a strange interlude
that was best forgotten. She could not even explain her
own behavior, let alone Vidal's. And if he had been surprisingly kind after his suspicions about her, it was clear
that he was already regretting it. She had rather thought
he despised her this morning.

Yes, the sooner she had taken up her new life the better. She pulled the bell resolutely.

She was at least refreshed by a bath and a nap, and
therefore better prepared to meet her future employer.
That Lady Thornton was very likely going to be extremely
angry could not be helped.

Maby, her own old governess, had not understood why
Dominique could not continue to live with her in the
little house on the outskirts of London. But Dominique's
fierce pride would not allow her to become a burden upon
her old friend. She had let too many months slip by as it
was since her father's death before she had at last roused
herself to think of her future.

But since she was possessed of a shrewd intellect and
what she knew to be an excellent education, she had foreseen no difficulties in obtaining a position as a governess.
The knowledge that she was temperamentally unsuited
to the post and had been too long her own mistress to
readily accept being little more than an upper servant in
someone else's house she had ruthlessly suppressed.

There was, after all, little else a well-born young lady in straitened circumstances could do.

But it had been swiftly borne in upon her that her prospective employers were less interested in her qualifications than they were in her youth and appearance. A succession of fashionable London matrons had taken one look at her and politely but firmly informed her that she would not do at all.

The weeks had slipped by and the agency had become more and more reluctant to refer her at all. Then a Lady Thornton, in Leicestershire, had sent an urgent request for a governess. Since she had had five governesses in the last eighteen months, Lady Thornton had not been in a position to be too particular, and the agency had thought she might find Miss Forrester suitable.

Miss Forrester privately thought it was the agency's way of washing its hands of two of its more trying clients, but she was certainly in no position to be too particular either. She had therefore taken her own somewhat desperate steps to see that she would not be dismissed for her appearance, and had resolutely closed her ears to every plea from Maby.

There had been many. Maby had said roundly that she had known Dominique to take a great many idiotic notions into her head, but she had never thought to see the day when her former pupil would dye her hair and dress herself up like a scarecrow.

"And what your father would say to my letting you do it I don't like to think!"

But at that Dominique had had to laugh. They both knew perfectly well that as likely as not Gerard would squint up his eyes in that absent-minded way of his and advise that of course she must do as she saw fit. His concern, though genuine, had been erratic at best, and he had rarely exerted himself to exercise his parental authority.

But she missed him more than she had expected. He had been gay and irresponsible, and had never allowed the presence of a daughter to hamper his activities, but they had enjoyed a camaraderie based on a perfect and mutual understanding.

Her thoughts far away, when the tap on the door came she did not even look up, expecting Mrs. Hedges, or perhaps the maid Rose who had helped her with her bath.

But it was Vidal's voice that said mockingly, "Ah, much better! But then your hair is almost copper, isn't it?"

She jerked her head up furiously, bitterly aware that she seemed destined to appear a complete fool in front of this man whenever they met.

One of his black brows rose lazily and he drawled, "Quite charming, Miss Forrester!"

She flushed under his scrutiny, then shrugged. It was clear he was firmly embarked upon his chosen course. She was to be the poseur and the interloper, and those few minutes last night were to be denied. Well, she could not blame him. He was, in his way, perfectly correct.

But now he was frowning slightly. "My housekeeper tells me you sustained some injury in your jump from the carriage. Why did you not tell me?"

Despite herself her lips quirked a little at his choice of words for the manner in which she had left his carriage, but she let it pass and said only, "It is a very minor injury I assure you."

His eyes still rested on her face, but there was a soft tap at the door then. He hesitated, then shrugged and went to admit his groom and housekeeper. "With your permission, ma'am," he said smoothly, "I have asked Hollings to have a look at your shoulder. He will be able to determine if anything is broken." He bowed and moved toward the door.

Hollings smiled kindly at her, but his face was plainly embarrassed. "If you would permit me, miss?" he asked diffidently.

She forced herself to dismiss Vidal from her mind and smile warmly at his groom. "Indeed, I think my injury is but slight," she said frankly, "but I would be grateful for your opinion, Hollings. I know my father always trusted the advice of his groom over any doctor he knew."

Hollings' answering grin was relieved. "Well, miss, we do have a deal of experience with broken bones and such."

He then stepped discreetly to the window while Mrs. Hedges adjusted the dressing gown over Dominique's injured shoulder. That stout lady then took up a protective stance beside her as Hollings came to probe her shoulder gently with his rough hands.

Dominique glanced from one to the other and wondered maliciously what Vidal had told them to explain her presence in his house. Neither of those kind faces betrayed the least awareness of any impropriety attending the situation. She, very much aware of it, could only smile ruefully.

"Well, miss, you do have a nasty bruise," Hollings was saying gently. "I'll do my best not to hurt you."

She nodded reassuringly, but was soon forced to clench her lips tightly together against the pain. Hollings was very gentle, but her shoulder was tender and the slightest movement jarred it painfully. By the time the groom had completed his examination and stepped back with obvious relief to allow Mrs. Hedges to replace the robe, his face was almost as pale as her own.

"There, miss, I'm sorry! I know that hurt!" he said gruffly. "I don't think anything's broken, luckily, but you have a bad strain I'm afraid."

She smiled up at him and said teasingly, "Why in that case, if only I were one of your horses, you could prescribe a bran poultice for me!"

Hollings' eyes lit in an engaging twinkle. "Aye, that I would, miss!"

She extended her hand. "Thank you, Hollings. You've eased my mind. And thank you, Mrs. Hedges."

"Well, miss, as I said, I don't think you've broken anything. But I don't like the looks of it all the same," he said bluntly. "I'd feel better if you was to have a proper doctor to look at it."

She merely smiled again and shook her head. Hollings hesitated, then sighed and followed Mrs. Hedges' round figure from the room. When the door had closed behind them, she sank tiredly into a chair and closed her eyes.

"Here, drink this!"

He eyes flew open. "I thought you'd gone!" she said irritably. Then as he held the glass of brandy to her lips, "No, no, thank you! I have had enough of your brandy! I dislike it excessively!"

His brows rose in the gesture she was coming to know. "My dear girl, this brandy is a great deal older than you are, and entered the country without benefit of any tax, two properties my father considered indispensible in a good brandy. He also placed unshakable faith in its medicinal properties. Surely you do not mean to question his wisdom?"

She had to smile and in the end drank a few drops.

"No, that's quite enough, thank you. Is your father still alive?"

"No, he died when I was nineteen." His eyes surveyed her. "I will have a doctor in if you'd prefer it."

She sat up, a martial light in her eyes. "I have not spent this much time in your company without knowing that you have absolutely no interest in anyone's wishes but your own! You have no intention of sending for a doctor!"

His mouth quirked. "Well, I own I'd prefer not," he admitted. "But if you are worried . . ."

Her color rose. "No, of course not!" she said quickly. "I shouldn't have said that. I assure you I have complete faith in Hollings." Her eyes softened a little. "He's very nice."

"Yes, he is, isn't he? He's been with me since before I was breeched."

She stared up at him for a moment, then said somewhat stiffly, "D-do you make a long stay here, sir?"

"A few weeks, Miss Forrester. I hardly know."

"I see. It is a very large house," she remarked.

His mocking smile appeared. "Yes, I do keep a full staff here year round, and no, I have no idea how they occupy themselves while I'm away. Probably drink my brandy!"

"I was not going to say either one of those things!" she said indignantly. Then her lips curved. "Although it is a shocking waste!"

"No doubt, ma'am." He suddenly reached out a finger to smooth the line between her brows. "Does your head ache?"

She drew back, startled. He was much too observant. "A—a little."

There was a little silence. "Miss Forrester," Vidal said rather stiffly, "I believe I owe you an apology. I promise you that had I known of your injury I would certainly not have confronted you as I did last night."

She fixed him with a fascinated eye. "Why, this is a handsome apology indeed! I think I am to assume from it that you regret none of the abominable things you said to me, only the fact that I was somewhat incapacitated at the time!"

His expression softened. "As you wish, ma'am. But you

may rest content in the knowledge you have been offered something few before you have."

She found she could readily believe that he seldom apologized for his actions. "In that case, sir," she said lightly, "I must naturally accept your kind apology." She hesitated. "In any event, I think we were perhaps both of us guilty of certain—remarks—that can only be attributed to the peculiar circumstances. I hope you will accept my apologies as well?"

He pulled a chair close to her own and calmly seated himself. "Certainly, ma'am. And perhaps now that we have both of us apologized so dutifully, you will allow me to attend to your wrist?"

"My wrist—?"

"I wish to see your left wrist, Miss Forrester," he repeated patiently. "I think you also sprained it in the fall. You have been favoring it for some time."

She clasped her hands firmly in her lap. "I assure you there is not the least need for that, sir. If it needs attention perhaps Hollings might see to it later."

"Surely you would not have me ignore one of *my* father's old maxims?" he asked gently.

She bit her lip. "And what is that, pray?"

"Why, only that a man should be able to do anything he asks his groom to do."

"A very good maxim, sir," she said primly. Then she laughed and held out her wrist. "Come, sir! This is ridiculous! Why is it I can never seem to get the better of you?"

He had rolled up the sleeve of her dressing-gown and was examining her swollen wrist with cold fingers, but now he looked up from his work. "I hope you will keep that in mind, ma'am!"

He held her eyes for an instant before returning his attention to her wrist. She frowned and remained silent, a little embarrassed by his touch and the close proximity of his sleek dark head to hers.

He completed his examination and remarked without malice, "You *are* a little fool. This is a bad sprain. Why didn't you say something?"

She had glanced up sharply at his first words, but then colored and made no answer.

He was studying her again. "I must confess that you puzzle me, Miss Forrester," he said frankly.

"You puzzle me as well, sir, as I have said, so we are equal. But since we are unlikely to meet after today it hardly matters," she said lightly and changed the subject.

"Were my bags safe?"

"Yes, although they were a little the worse for wear. My staff is cleaning and pressing their contents." He unhurriedly tied off the cloth he had wrapped tightly around her wrist. "There. Does that feel better?"

She nodded but would not be diverted. "I would appreciate having my clothes returned as quickly as possible, sir. And then perhaps you would be so kind as to lend me a carriage to convey me to the village?"

"Certainly, if you wish," he replied calmly. "But there are several matters we must discuss first."

She stood up and took several steps away before turning back to him. "Sir, I do not believe there can be anything for us to discuss. It only remains for me to thank you for your kindness, which I do most sincerely."

He took the hand she extended and stood lightly holding it, a question in his eyes she could not read. "In good time, Miss Forrester. What do you intend to do then?"

She smiled wearily. "I intend to take up my post at Thornton Hall, sir." She tried to withdraw her hand.

His black brows rose in cynical disbelief. She flushed and said defiantly, "That was unnecessary, sir! You have already made your opinion of me perfectly clear."

"I was not aware that I had yet reached an opinion about you, Miss Forrester," he murmured.

She met his eyes evenly. "I do not think there is anything to be gained from continuing this discussion, sir. It is plain we are unlikely to agree. You have been very kind—"

"I am never kind, Miss Forrester."

She ignored his dry interruption. "You have been very kind, sir," she repeated firmly, "but nevertheless, none of this concerns you. I would much prefer not to discuss it."

"No doubt, ma'am," he remarked calmly, "but I'm afraid it does concern me. Perhaps I should tell you that our early morning visitor was the coachman from Thornton Hall."

She recovered herself quickly and turned away, but not before Vidal had seen the stricken look in her eyes.

His eyes narrowed abruptly and he said blankly, "Good God! You don't mean you are—" He broke off, his eyes grim. "I see. It would appear we are in the devil of a coil, Miss Forrester."

She turned on him then, her voice shaking with repressed anger. "No, *I* am in the devil of a coil, thanks to your—your *curiosity!*" she said bitterly. "I have no doubt *you* have found the whole vastly entertaining! You meant to from the first, did you not?"

There was an odd expression in his eyes. "I fear you are right, Miss Forrester. Under the circumstances, I will say nothing of your own part in this affair. But I must confess I still fail to see why you felt it necessary to engage in this masquerade in order to take up a position as governess—"

He checked suddenly, a look of chagrin in his eyes, then said in a very different voice, "I beg your pardon, ma'am. I seem to have been uncommonly dense last night. For the very reasons I have said, of course. There can be little demand for a beautiful governess."

When she refused to meet his eyes he added matter-of-factly, "I assume Lady Thornton hired you sight unseen. But I am a little curious how you managed to prevail upon an agency to be a party to such a scheme?"

She reddened and answered reluctantly. "I don't think they much cared, one way or another, but of course they had no idea what I meant to do. They had not found either one of us a particularly profitable client."

He looked amused, but there was a good deal of comprehension in his eyes as well. "It would not have worked, you know," he said almost gently. "A sharp-eyed matron was bound to see through you even sooner than I did. You really are a most beautiful girl."

Her lips curled bitterly and she went to stare out the window with unseeing eyes.

"Forgive me," Vidal said quietly, "but have you no family, Miss Forrester?"

"Why certainly!" she said flippantly. "A wealthy father and—what was it?—ah yes! an elusive bridegroom as well! Surely you have not forgotten?"

He frowned and said bluntly, "You had better give up the notion of becoming a governess, Miss Forrester! It will not work."

Her eyes were suddenly bleak. "Shall I be a chambermaid then? Or do you mean that I must resign myself to the only occupation my face and background qualify me for?"

"I have suggested neither of those, ma'am! Nor can I believe that such straits are at all necessary."

"I have no intention of being dependent upon my relations or my friends," she said evenly.

His brows rose. "You are very proud, ma'am."

After a moment she shook her head and said wearily, "Perhaps, sir. But that is my affair. If it is as you say, then I can only return to my own old governess until I can obtain a new position."

"Does she live in London?"

She only nodded, too tired to combat him any longer.

After a moment he spoke lightly, but his voice held a note she had never heard before. "I have not often known remorse, Miss Forrester, but you are fast teaching me. I said you had a chastening effect upon me, did I not?"

She looked up quickly, her eyes shadowed, and said with difficulty, "I find I am a little tired, sir, and not in the best of spirits. If I have said anything to make you believe I hold you responsible for this—this mischance, I beg your pardon. Please believe that I do not. I—" She broke off and smiled a little crookedly. "Never mind! I said nothing good could come of this discussion, did I not? It is more than time I took my leave of you. Will you be so kind as to have my bags restored to me?"

He stood looking down at her, a frown deep in his eyes. "You are right, my dear," he said quietly at last. "We will not discuss it now. But you will certainly not leave here tonight. It is nearly dark and it would be impossible to find accommodations for you at this hour. After you have rested we will discuss what is best to be done."

"Sir!" she said sharply, "I cannot stay here! You know that as well as I!"

"Nonsense! If I must remind you, ma'am, you have already spent a night in my company under far more suspicious circumstances."

"I—!"

He laid a finger lightly on her cheek. "Get some rest. You will feel much better after you have slept."

She stared at the door he closed behind him and could have wept. Then she shook herself. What was the matter with her? She never cried! Vidal was right, she was just tired.

But she would not have been reassured by the bitter smile on Vidal's lips as he moved to the library. He poured himself a brandy and went to stand before the fire.

He did not think he was a fool, but either the unknown Miss Forrester was a consummate actress, or she was indeed telling the truth. It hardly mattered. In either case, he was caught like the merest whipster.

After a moment he shrugged and tossed off his brandy. Well, no doubt this chit of a girl would do as well as the next. Perhaps better than most. She should at least be sensible of her position. She appeared to have a modicum of intelligence and a certain spirit. Given the proper gowns and jewels he didn't doubt she would show to advantage.

And as long as she refrained from enacting for him any Cheltenham tragedies, or carried on too outrageously, he did not doubt that they would manage to rub along tolerably well together.

Chapter Six

When Dominique woke again the maid Rose was standing over her. It was dark and the candles were lit.

"I'm sorry to wake you, miss, but his grace has ordered supper for nine o'clock. It's half-past eight now. I let you sleep as long as possible, but I knew you'd wish to tidy up a bit." She had a lovely robe of spidery green silk over her arm. "He sent this for you to wear since your things are still drying, miss. Isn't it lovely?" She chattered on as she helped Dominique into the robe and brushed her hair.

Dominique scarcely heard her. Her mind, still fuzzy with sleep, was grappling bewilderedly with Rose's first words. After a moment she said hesitantly, "Rose . . . his grace—?"

"Why, yes, miss. He asked if you could be ready at nine o'clock, and Mrs. Hedges felt that would be satisfactory. Is something wrong, miss?"

"But—but—who are you talking about?" she asked desperately.

Rose giggled. "Why, miss! His grace, the Duke of Vidal, of course!" Her eyes widened suddenly. "Miss! Are you ill?"

She shook her head wearily. "No, no, of course not, Rose. I can manage for myself, now. Thank you." She did not even see the puzzled little maid leave the room.

Good God. What a fool she was. She had not long been in England, but even she had heard of the Duke of Vidal. He was reputedly one of the richest men in England. All of London talked of his mistresses, his stables, the vast sums he won and lost nightly. Her mouth twisted bitterly. That she had unwittingly become involved with one of the most talked-of rakes in England was almost laughable. She had no illusions as to what would become of her reputation if the day's activities should become known. She had lost one position because of him, and the fact that she was blameless of any wrongdoing would not make a particle of difference to her chances of obtaining another.

Her mind refused to take in the consequences of this last enormous jest. She turned almost blindly as a light tap sounded on the door. Then her mouth tightened into an uncompromising line as Vidal entered.

He looked her over slowly and his eyes held the cynical glint she most disliked. "I knew that robe would suit you, ma'am."

She inclined her head regally. "You are very kind, your-r gr-race." To her chagrin her accent, usually barely discernible, had deepened and her tongue stumbled over the difficult r's. His eyes narrowed mockingly.

She was very angry indeed, and her temper was not improved by being forced to hold her tongue while a small table was laid for supper. Until the servants withdrew Vidal kept up a steady flow of aimless chatter that tried her patience to its limit.

As the door at last closed behind the footman, Vidal politely held a chair for her. She only glared at him.

"No doubt, ma'am!" he said coldly. "But I prefer not to air my disputes in public! Now what the devil are you so incensed about?"

Her eyes glittered fiercely. "Why, indeed, your-r gr-race, I should no doubt be flattered that the most notorious Duke of Vidal chooses to dine tête-à-tête with a— gouvernesse in her bedchamber."

"I did not suppose you would enjoy dining downstairs in a dressing gown, ma'am!"

She smiled derisively. "Why, I cannot suppose your servants would find it out of the ordinary! No doubt they are very used to finding strange females in your company!"

"Indeed, ma'am?" he inquired icily.

She had a fiery temper, but she was also scrupulously just. After a moment the anger died in her eyes and she took a deep breath. "Forgive me, your grace. I should not have said that. I believe you were acting kindly, but I can only think it was very wrong of you to bring me here. I must leave immediately."

"Madam, you have been in my house for nearly twelve hours. To what do I owe this sudden attack of maidenly modesty?"

His words were biting and she flushed, but lifted her head. "It was only within the last hour that I learned your identity, your grace."

His eyebrows rose in disbelief.

"I am well aware you will not believe me!" she said stiffly.

"Particularly since I myself told you, ma'am!"

"I—I know. But I have not long been in England and I did not connect— It is my fault, sir. I should not have accepted your offer of assistance." Her voice was very low.

Vidal regarded her for a long moment, then some of the harshness left his face. "Miss Forrester—Dominique —I am afraid we are both of us caught in a tangle not of our making. Forgive me for losing my temper. You are exactly right. I should not have brought you here. As for the rest, well . . ." He shrugged lightly. "Under the circumstances, ma'am, there can be only one solution. Will you do me the honor of becoming my wife?"

She gasped, not believing he could be serious, and searched his face incredulously. What she saw there caused all the color to drain from her face, leaving her deathly pale.

His brows rose again. "You are surprised, Miss Forrester," he remarked flatly. "Now what—ah! I see. You thought I meant to offer you a carte blanche."

When she turned her head away and twisted her hands together tightly in her lap he smiled sardonically. "What a very pretty opinion you must have of me, my dear."

She raised her eyes. "I am sensible of the great honor you do me, your grace, but I must naturally decline your kind offer." Her voice was as colorless as her face.

"Why 'naturally,' Miss Forrester?" he inquired politely.

At that some of her color returned. "You are being intentionally obtuse, sir! You must know the reasons as well as I! We hardly know each other. We—we certainly have no regard for each other! And our stations are very different."

"Those are not insuperable difficulties, Miss Forrester. Ours would not be the first marriage made on such terms."

"No doubt you consider that an eligible match!" she said tartly. "I can assure you the world will not!"

"I care nothing for the world's opinion, Miss Forrester."

"No doubt! I, on the other hand, am not of your exalted station, and must care."

After a moment he said quietly, "May I inquire what you intend to do, then?"

"I have told you, I shall return to my own governess until I can obtain a suitable post." She spoke evenly. "If you really wish to help me, perhaps you could put me in the way of someone in need of a governess."

"My recommendation would hardly help you. Dominique . . ."

"I have not given you leave to use my name!"

"Then give me leave now," he said calmly. "I think it is time we were frank with one another."

She drew a ragged breath. "Why is it that when people desire to speak frankly it is almost invariably something you do not wish to hear? I would much prefer you do not, sir."

He ignored her interruption. "You and I both know, my dear, that you will not obtain another post as governess." He held up a hand as she stiffened. "Oh, not only because of this. It is possible I could keep that fool of a coachman quiet. But you are not stupid, my dear, and I might add, neither am I. You did not appreciate my advice earlier, but I am right, you know. It is too much to expect a woman to have a governess that looks as you do."

She held her head proudly. "Nevertheless, you have not told me how any of this concerns you, sir!"

"Madam, acquit me of ruining innocent females!" he said acidly.

"And acquit me of seeking a—a—*mariage de convenance!*"

The anger died suddenly from his eyes, to be replaced by a glint of rueful humor. "Do you always lose your English when you are enraged, Miss Forrester?"

"I am not enraged!"

He returned her look blandly, and after a moment a reluctant twinkle came into her eyes. "Well, perhaps just a little," she admitted. "But you should not have provoked me so!"

"Really, my child, how long did you think you'd be able to control that abominable temper of yours and maintain the modest demeanor of a governess?" he asked in amusement.

"Oh, oh! The devil!" she uttered wrathfully.

He politely raised his eyebrows. She bit her lip and

after a moment said accusingly, "You did that on purpose to make me lose my temper! Admit it!"

He smiled and slipped easily under her guard. "Oh, readily, my dear." When her lips curved involuntarily he added gently, "You had much better marry me, Dominique. I at least am not shocked by language I can only assume you to have learned in the stables!"

This time she refused to be drawn. "I swear I do not understand you, sir," she said frankly. "I think you despise me, and yet anyone would almost believe that you *wished* to marry me."

His expression was unreadable. "I do not despise you, my dear. And I assure you I am becoming more reconciled to our marriage by the moment."

She colored a little, but replied shrewdly, "I think the truth is that you cannot bear not to have your own way."

"That too, dear ma'am."

When she smiled he said instantly, "Ah, that's better! I really think we should have some of this excellent supper. I have already survived a magnificent rage from my valet. You really cannot expect me to face the ire of my chef as well."

After a slight hesitation she allowed herself to be seated at the small table. Vidal poured her a glass of wine and began lifting covers from the dishes. "Ah, good! I do not think the sole is completely ruined. Pray allow me to give you some. My chef has a way with fish that I particularly like."

When he had filled her plate he added matter-of-factly, "Now, ma'am, allow me to tell you of the arrangements I have made. I have obtained a special license that will enable us to be married immediately. The Vicar will attend us here in an hour. I presume you are of legal age?"

Her fork clattered and she eyed him in amazement. "I have never met anyone like you before, sir! Have you not heard a single word I've said?"

His eyes held hers. "You had much better stop fighting me, my child. As you observed yourself, I always win."

She pressed her fingers distractedly to her temples, trying to clear her head. Her headache had returned again, nagging behind her eyes and making it difficult to concentrate.

He did not miss the gesture or the too-bright color in her cheeks. "Come, child," he said gently. "You obviously have no relations or you would not be forced to earn your own living. Since I am responsible for any damage to your reputation that has caused you to lose one position and will likely preclude you from obtaining another, you can see I must make what restitution I can."

"I can see only that you have turned everything around to suit your own ends as usual!" she said bitterly. Then as the meaning of her own words struck her she blushed furiously. "Oh! Now you have even got me talking as if it were the dearest wish of your heart to marry me."

"Why, since we scarcely know each other, that is naturally not true," he said frankly. "But I am a practical man, my dear, and I see no reason to exhaust myself in railing against what cannot be helped, as you are doing."

Her eyes were suddenly bleak. "I see. And do you always do your duty, no matter how distasteful to you?"

He reached across the table suddenly to clasp her hand lightly. "I do not expect you to believe that I particularly desire this marriage. But I hope you will believe me when I say that I see no reason why we should not deal extremely well together. I shall gain a chatelaine for my estates, and the not-inconsiderable relief of protection from matchmaking mamas." Though she smiled, it did not reach her eyes and after a slight pause he continued smoothly, "While you will be spared the necessity of a lifetime of being a drudge in other people's houses.

"By the way," he added suddenly, "how many children does the estimable Lady Thornton possess?"

"Five," she said briefly.

"Five! Good God! And you prefer her offer to mine?" he was clearly shaken.

She did laugh at that. "Come, sir, you are being nonsensical! It has nothing to do with preference." She hesitated and added a little defiantly, "What I do prefer is to be beholden to no one!"

"That is scarcely possible, my dear," he said quietly. "We are always beholden to someone, if only to our friends. Life would be very poor without that."

At her frown of surprise he added mockingly, "Come, Miss Forrester! Did you think I had no friends? I assure you my reputation is not as bad as that!"

"No, of course not!" She toyed with her wine glass for a moment, then sighed. "You are right, of course, sir," she admitted. "B-but having friends is one thing, and taking advantage of their kindness is quite another." She lifted her eyes and said simply, "I doubt you have ever been in that position, sir. But I think you can perhaps understand it very well."

"Yes, I do, my child. Are both your parents dead?"

"Yes, my mother died when I was quite small. My father died six months ago." She spoke steadily.

"And you have no other relatives?"

"I—No."

His eyes narrowed slightly, but he said only, "Who was your father?"

"I doubt you would know him, sir. He was only another of the many thousands displaced by the French Revolution. After my mother died we moved around Europe, living here and there, never staying long in any place. By the time the war was over he no longer had any desire to return to France."

"And your mother?"

"Why, I know little of her. She was Scots, as I told you, but I don't know what happened to her family." Her mouth softened. "So you see, sir, no skeletons in the closet, no irate papas. Mine is a very common and quite unromantic tale."

Then she started suddenly at the tap on the door. A young footman entered at Vidal's invitation. "The Vicar is here, your grace."

She jerked violently, but Vidal took her hand firmly, his eyes strangely compelling. "Come, Dominique. The Vicar is waiting."

She parted her lips but no sound came out. She had the absurd feeling that she was being carried on a tide she could not halt, caught up in a strength she could no longer resist.

Somehow she allowed herself to be led down the stairs to a library, warm and dimly lit. Her hand was taken in a warm clasp and words swam around her, growing increasingly dim and far away. Once Vidal prompted her and she responded automatically, then he placed a heavy ring on her finger and she felt his lips cool on her brow.

As in a dream she signed her name to a document the

Vicar, a small and slightly flustered man, held for her. Vidal's hand checked slightly before adding his name beside hers.

She turned then to find the kind faces of the butler and Mrs. Hedges swimming before her. She accepted the glass handed to her, only to have it drop from suddenly nerveless fingers. For a long moment she stared down, appalled, at the shattered glass on the rug. Then she too was falling . . .

"Your grace!" Mrs. Hedges fluttered around as he lifted Dominique easily and carried her up the stairs. He moved to a different room on the first floor and laid her on the bed.

"Have Lymings send for the doctor, Mrs. Hedges, and bring cool water and cloths. Her fever is pretty high."

He stood looking down at the still figure until Mrs. Hedges returned with the cloths. He took one and laid it across her burning forehead.

"I will tend to her, your grace."

He looked around absently. "Oh. Thank you, Mrs. Hedges. I will wish to speak with the doctor when he has seen her."

"Certainly, your grace."

Nearly an hour later Vidal looked up from his contemplation of the fire as the doctor was ushered into the library.

The doctor, a rather stout gentleman of indeterminate years, crossed the room and shook hands firmly. "Ah, your grace, I'm Dr. Willton."

He accepted the glass of claret Vidal handed him and sank into a chair. "Thank you, your grace. This is very welcome." He took several appreciative sips before recalling himself briskly to his duties.

"Well, sir, I don't wish to alarm you," he said frankly, "but I don't deny your wife's condition is quite serious. She has pneumonia, complicated by what seems to be a generally run-down condition. She is also much too thin."

His rather intelligent blue eyes rested on Vidal's face for a moment, but after a slight pause he continued. "With careful attention I have no doubt she'll recover. Someone should stay with her. I've given your housekeeper some drops for her and any instructions I think she'll need. I'll drop by again in the morning."

His eyes were puzzled as Lymings showed him out. Something havey-cavey going on there, unless he missed his guess. Well, you never knew what a man like Vidal would take it into his head to do. Wife indeed! He had no wife that anyone around here had ever heard of. He felt a sudden pang of regret for that young girl, whoever she might be.

Vidal watched the doctor leave, a cynical light in his eyes. Then he shrugged and moved once again to stare down at the document on his desk. There, beside his own name on the marriage certificate, was her signature in a clear, well-formed hand: Dominique Estelle Marie de St. Forêt.

His eyes were thoughtful as he folded the document and put it carefully away.

Chapter Seven

For nearly a week Dominique's condition remained unchanged. The doctor reported daily to Vidal that her fever had not yet abated.

"She is slightly delirious some of the time, and her fever is likely to climb still higher, I'm afraid." He hesitated, then added frankly, "I don't scruple to tell you that most doctors would bleed her under these circumstances, your grace. But I don't hold with such practices. I have every confidence the fever will soon break."

But as Dr. Willton climbed into his gig his kindly face bore an expression that was at odds with his optimistic report. His usually gentle eyes were hard, and his mouth was set in a firm line. He frowned and reminded himself sharply, as he did every day, that it was none of his business. If that poor young creature had chosen to become involved with such a man, there was nothing he could do.

But even so, he muttered a few well-chosen epithets he was not often guilty of using and shouted at his placid mare with such unwonted violence she was surprised into a sharp trot before she remembered herself and subsided into her usual rolling walk.

Mrs. Hedges and the housemaid Rose took turns in sitting by Dominique's bedside. After that first night Vidal made no attempt to enter the sickroom. He did, however, remain close to the house; even foregoing the hunt, and riding out only briefly each morning for exercise.

The upper servants maintained a discreet silence, but of course everyone from the lowest scullery maid knew of the happenings of the past week. Clay, the superior manservant, knew his place too well to engage in idle gossip with the servants, but Mrs. Hedges confided anxiously to Lymings that she thought the young lady soft-spoken and well bred, no matter what was said about how she came into the house.

Lymings, who had been with Vidal for a number of years, replied pacifically that his grace always knew what he was about. But it was to be seen that the butler's manner was somewhat graver than usual.

One of the young stable hands made the mistake of winking broadly at the undergroom and saying cockily, "Aye, properly dicked, 'e is!" in Hollings' hearing and was soundly cuffed. But it was Hollings, who had been with his grace since he was in short coats, who secretly nursed the deepest concern. He did not need Lymings' warning to know that Vidal was sitting up night after night in the library with a bottle of brandy for company.

He had even dared to broach the subject on one of the rare occasions Vidal had gone out driving, and had been roundly cursed for his pains.

' Vidal had then given his lazy smile and said, "You think I'm badly dipped this time, don't you?" He laughed mockingly. "What is the saying about old sins coming home to roost?"

But at the genuine concern in his old friend's eyes, he added softly, "Never fear, Jeremy, we shall come about again as we always do!"

Hollings had grinned slowly, the memory of some of those old times fondly in his head.

It was shortly after midnight a few days later that a hesitant Mrs. Hedges tapped lightly on Vidal's bedchamber door. He had not yet retired and was seated before the fire with a book, resplendent in a brilliant brocade dressing gown.

At his lazy invitation to enter she stepped just inside the door. "I'm sorry to disturb you, sir, but it's young miss—er—her grace," she amended hastily. "She has been much worse these past few days, sir. Now she's out of her head and keeps crying out in a foreign tongue. I—I think we should send for the doctor to come back."

Vidal's eyes were instantly alert. "You were right to come to me, Mrs. Hedges. Send James to fetch the doctor. I will see to her grace."

"Oh, yes, sir!" she said in relief. "That will be just the thing!"

A daunting scene met Vidal's eyes when he stepped quietly into Dominique's bedchamber. A very frightened Rose was trying to keep Dominique from climbing out of bed. The tangled covers and tossed pillows gave mute testimony to the struggle.

"Oh, miss! You must lie still! You will only make yourself worse. Doctor says you are on no account to upset yourself!" She started at the hand on her shoulder, then exclaimed in heartfelt relief, "Oh, your grace!" and promptly burst into tears.

"It's all right, Rose. I will see to her grace. You have done an excellent job and I'm very grateful to you. Now go to bed."

"Oh, your grace!" she wailed again, and fled.

He smiled a little grimly at their simple faith that he would know just what to do. He did not suppose he had ever been in a sickroom before, and he himself was never ill. But that Dominique was very ill he could not doubt. Her face was flushed with fever and her movements were agitated.

After a slight hesitation he sat down on the edge of the bed and took her hands firmly in his "Dominique, listen to me!"

His voice seemed to penetrate into her consciousness for she turned enormous eyes on him. Encouraged, he went on firmly, "You are behaving in an extremely ridiculous manner, my dear! I certainly thought you had more sense."

"Papa?" she cried wildly. *"C'est toi?"* She tried desperately to sit up.

He pressed her back on her pillows, but she had subsided now and was shaking her head sadly. "Ah, *non! Papa est mort . . . !"*

"Dominique!"

"C'est tout fini . . . tout fini et Papa est mort! Tout fini . . ." It was a litany.

After a moment though, she closed her eyes and he drew a breath of relief, thinking she had perhaps fallen asleep. But then her eyes flew open again and she tossed wildly and murmured disjointed phrases that made no sense to him. He did not make the mistake of relaxing again. For nearly an hour he could do little more than attempt to keep her still while she babbled incessantly.

Then suddenly she grew very still. The hands he held clung feverishly to his fingers and she whispered clearly, "Papa is dead. They killed him, you know, and I didn't even know. Isn't that funny?" She shook her head. *"Mon pauvre Papa . . .* It was the only thing he cared about, and I never even knew . . ."

He looked around a little desperately and spied a glass

on the bedside table. He sniffed at its contents, then ruthlessly tilted it down her throat. She gagged and tears stood weakly in her eyes, but after a moment it seemed to calm her.

She lay silently for a time, then her eyes opened again, and he thought there was recognition in their depths. "It's you . . ." she said. "I must go. You see that I must go, or Lady Thornton . . . no, no!" she corrected herself. "*Not* Lady Thornton any more! Must go back to Maby, and then it's all to be done over . . ."

He smoothed back the hair from her burning forehead, and after a brief hesitation lifted her and smoothed the bedclothes and pillows before laying her back, straightening her nightgown, and tucking the covers around her once more.

"Thank you," she said calmly, quite as if he had handed her a book or her gloves. Then she turned her head on the pillow and murmured pettishly, "I'm so thirsty!"

He poured her a glass of water and lifted her head while she drank thirstily. Then she lay back and closed her eyes exhaustedly.

For a while she seemed to doze, then she grew restless again and tossed and murmured agitatedly. He sighed and spoke sharply to her. "Dominique! You must be quiet!"

Her eyes met his and she struggled wildly against him. "No, no Let me go! I will not!" she cried.

He held her firmly, speaking slowly and soothingly, as to a child or a frightened animal, and at length she relaxed against him. But when he sought to lay her down again she clung desperately to him.

When the doctor was at last ushered into her bedchamber, he found Vidal in a deep wing chair before the fire, Dominique asleep in his arms.

Vidal's glance met his, full of self-mockery. "An affecting sight, is it not? I regret bringing you out, doctor! The fever has broken."

A flustered housemaid opened the door of the modest cottage on the outskirts of London two days later and promptly dropped her duster at sight of the elegant gentleman leaning against the post.

Two seconds later she whisked into the parlor, where two ladies sat before the fire, holding a visiting card as firmly by one corner as if she expected it to leap out of her hands at any moment. The stouter of the two ladies looked up with a frown.

"Well, Elsie, what is it?" she grumbled.

The girl Elsie gulped and then whispered thrillingly, "Oh, mum! There's a gentleman come to see Miss Mabington. Says he's a Duke!"

Her breathless announcement produced as startling an effect on her two listeners as she could have wished. Mrs. Biddlecombe dropped her knitting and the ball of yarn promptly rolled under the couch. Her hands flew to her cap. "Mercy me!"

The other occupant of the room certainly looked surprised, but she merely closed her book and calmly retrieved her sister's yarn. Then she took the visiting card firmly from Elsie, who appeared to be permanently transfixed in the middle of the room, and read its elegant lettering.

"Well, well." She looked up absently. "Well, don't just stand there, girl! Show his grace in."

Vidal's firm step sounded at the door.

The trim woman who calmly held out her hand to him was well past her youth and had never been handsome, but he found himself favorably impressed by her dignified bearing and frank eyes. She was a little below medium height, with soft brown hair and a pleasant, easy manner.

"I am Miss Mabington." She shook his hand firmly and presented her sister. Since that lady only managed to gape in slackjawed amazement, Miss Mabington adjured her calmly to close her mouth and invited his grace to take a set.

"You wish to speak with me, sir?"

"In truth, Miss Mabington, I am the bearer of a message for you. Miss Forrester had fallen ill—no, no!" as she started up, "I assure you she is in no danger and much recovered. But she charged me to bring you to her, if you will accept my escort."

Miss Mabington frowned, but after a swift glance at her sister bit back her questions. "Certainly, your grace," she said calmly. "Allow me ten minutes to pack a few things, and I will be ready to accompany you."

Fortunately she was as good as her word, since Mrs. Biddlecombe had at last found her voice, and spent the time regaling him with what she had known all along would be the outcome of such a mad-cap scheme.

"For I tell you to your face, Duke, I knew nothing good could come of dyeing her hair in that heathenish way—as if that would have fooled anyone over sixteen anyway, and so I told her! But then there was never any stopping dear Dominique when she took a notion into her head, as Sophie could tell you if she would, which she won't. Never a word will she utter against the child! Or that father of hers! Dragging them all over the world and sometimes not enough food in the house—!"

"That's enough, Mary! I'm sure his grace is not interested in our private affairs." Miss Mabington stood at the door, a large basket and a portmanteau in her hands.

She allowed Vidal to take her bags and quickly bid good-bye to her sister with an admonition not to worry, that she would write immediately when she knew anything more. Then with admirable aplomb she opened the door for Vidal and whisked him outside before Mrs. Biddlecombe could voice even one of the protests trembling so clearly on her lips.

Tht postilion sprang to take the bags and corded them on behind while Vidal handed her into his traveling chaise. In a matter of seconds they were driving away. But the rapturous voice of Elsie could be heard quite plainly.

"Oh, mum! He *must* be a *duke!* He's got a crest on the door!"

Miss Mabington met his twinkling eyes and gave a bark of laughter. "You have provided them with a nine-days' wonder, your grace! I don't think Elsie has been that excited since the circus came to town."

Vidal's lips twitched. "Are my attractions rated above or below the circus?" he inquired with deep interest.

"Oh, below, I should think," she replied promptly. She stared at his shaking shoulders for a moment, then explained helpfully, "You are not unusual in yourself, you know—simply out of your accustomed surroundings, your grace."

"Miss Mabington," Vidal said appreciatively, "I am at last beginning to see where your former pupil learned her outspoken manners."

She laughed, but disclaimed immediately. "Oh, no, sir. I fear the shoe's on the other foot. I picked up my habits from her." She colored then and added reluctantly, "I hope you will disregard anything my sister may have said this morning, sir. She is sometimes a little—foolish.

"Now, your grace," she continued briskly. "I didn't like to say anything before, but Miss . . . Forrester," her hesitation over the name was infinitesimal, "was to take up a position as governess in the house of a Lady Thornton. How do you come to be involved?" she asked bluntly.

She listened in silence as he succinctly outlined the events of the past week. The glance she bestowed upon him at the conclusion put him forceably in mind of his own old governess when he had been caught out in some misdeed, and he smiled ruefully.

At his smile she appeared to come to some sort of conclusion. "Well, your grace, I don't pretend to understand all you've told me. And I don't doubt there's a great deal you haven't told me as well," she added shrewdly. "But I won't deny that to see Dominique married to a respectable gentleman is what I've prayed for."

She eyed him steadily for a moment. "I hope I may speak plainly, sir?"

He frowned a little, but at her questioning look laughed harshly. "Oh, by all means, ma'am. Miss Forrester pointed out to me recently that whenever anyone desires to speak plainly they are bound to say something unpleasant! I beg you not to spare my feelings!"

She did not flinch. "Yes, sir. I will not scruple then to tell you that I am—aware of your reputation, your grace. I love Dominque more than anything else on earth. I'll not stand by and see her mistreated."

Anger flared in his eyes for one dreadful moment. Then it slowly died out. "I give you my word, Miss Mabington, that I shall not mistreat her." He held out his hand. "Friends?"

She searched his face carefully. What she saw there must have reassured her, for after a moment she slowly laid her hand in his.

A few days later Vidal strolled into White's. Although fame of that club had somewhat dimmed since the unfortunate departure of Mr. Brummell for the continent a year or so before, it was still wildly renowned for its famous bay window and the dandies who habitually sat there.

He looked around idly for a few minutes, politely refusing several hearty invitations to join various of his friends, and made his way slowly to an elderly gentleman seated in a comfortable chair, his foot swathed in bandages and propped up before him.

The man looked up from his papers and waved his hand affably. "Ah, Vidal! Been weeks since I've seen you, m'boy! Just talking about you at Watiers t'other night and wondering if you'd deserted us for good!"

Vidal laughed. "No, no, Sir Reginald. The truth is I've been on a repairing lease. But I'm sorry to see you're still in queer stirrups. May I offer you some claret, or are you forbidden to drink it?"

"Oh, aye, I'm forbidden to drink the stuff, but those damned sawbones take delight in making long faces! Never could abide the fellows! Never believe a word they say!"

"Perhaps that's why your gout gets no better, sir." Vidal grinned wickedly.

Sir Reginald imperturbably waved the servant to fill his glass. He then rolled the claret on his tongue with evident enjoyment and pronounced it a very good year.

"Eighty-nine I think! I have a pipe of it laid down at home, y'know. An excellent year!" He took another mouthful, then said shrewdly, "But you didn't seek me out to discuss my cellars! What can I do for you, m'boy?"

"Why, sir, I was hoping you could give me some information. I know you spent a great many years in France before the war, and no one knows more than you about the noble houses. I'm seeking information about a family by the name of de St. Forêt."

"The Marquis de St. Forêt," Sir Reginald replied promptly. "Oh, aye, I've known him any time these last forty years." He thoughtfully fingered a button of his coat for a moment. "But you won't be interested in him. Wouldn't surprise me at all to learn he's dead. Now what do I know about the sons . . . ?"

Vidal made no comment and after a minute Sir Reginald sat up energetically. "Ah, now I've got it! Middle one disinherited or some such rot for marrying to suit himself. Always had his eye to the main chance, did the old Marquis, and expected his sons to marry to improve the estate. Pity. Always liked Gerard the best of the lot of them. Took after his mother. Pretty little thing when I first knew her. Years of living with de St. Forêt soon cured that!"

He became lost in his recollections for a moment,

then said briskly, "But that's all a long time ago. I always thought the other two sons may have had something to do with the whole sad affair. There was never any love lost between any of the family that I could tell.

"I saw Gerard in Lisbon in '08. He was doing some work for our troops. Had a pretty little red-headed gal with him—must've been his daughter, though what he meant by dragging her into that mess I don't know. I don't need to tell you things were pretty hot just then." He shrugged, then shook his head. "Sorry. Afraid I can't tell you much more, m'boy."

They talked of other matters for a few minutes before Vidal excused himself and walked thoughtfuly back to his house in Berkeley Square.

The next afternoon he walked into his sister's drawing room unannounced to find her engrossed in a romance from the lending library. She glanced up idly then hastily threw aside her book and jumped to her feet.

"Vidal! You wretch! You promised faithfully to attend my drum last week!"

At his thunder-struck expression she merely laughed. "Oh, never mind! Charles was kind enough to notify me you were held up on urgent business." Her eyes twinkled merrily. "I hope she was very pretty!" she said cordially.

"Oh, very!" He moved to pinch her chin and said solemnly, "Sally, I stand before you a reformed man. I have at long last taken your advice."

She did not appear to be impressed. "Why that would indeed be a surprise! But I have given you so much good advice over the years, I assure you I cannot recall the half of it!"

He sighed pensively. "And I thought only to please you, my love."

She laughed. "What a whisker! You have never sought to please anyone but yourself in your whole life!"

"Why, my dear, I assure you, you would not know me! I wonder, has it ever occurred to you the sad existence our governesses are forced to lead?"

Lady Sarah, inured to her brother's odd humors, merely sighed resignedly.

"Ah, you see! You, like the rest of the world, do not care! But I have become intimately acquainted with their problems, since I have two of them in residence at my hunting box."

At last a light dawned in Lady Sarah's eyes. "Well, I can readily believe that you have two women ensconced in that wretched hoouse in Leicestershire, but that they are governesses I will never be brought to credit!" she said roundly. "And why you have come to me with this faradiddle of nonsense I do not know!"

"Why, Sally, I hoped you would help me," he said gently. "You see, I have married one of them."

"Justin!" She shrieked. Then she searched his face accusingly. "Why, it is another of your Banbury stories—!" After a moment she sat down quietly. "Good God! You had better tell me the whole."

When he had finished she sat stunned for a moment. Then she sat up briskly and said, "Well, is she presentable?"

"Oh, yes," he said, idly drawing out his snuff box and taking a pinch. "I've no doubt you will think her quite beautiful."

She stared at him in perplexity, apparently . caught by something in his tone. "But—but Justin, do you *like* her?"

He smiled rather grimly. "Well, as to that, Sally, I don't really know. She says whatever pops into her head, is apt to lose her English when her temper is aroused," his lips quirked, "which seems to happen entirely too often for comfort! She is damnably stiff and proud when she thinks her ability to look after herself is being questioned, and has a deplorable sense of humor that has prompted her on several occasions to laugh in my face."

She stared at him, a frown between her eyes. "Why, Justin, it sounds as if you—" She firmly closed her lips on whatever she had been about to say. "Well, I shall look forward to meeting this—this hoyden of yours. I— you know it goes without saying that I will help you in any way that I can."

He did not stay much longer, saying that there was naturally a great many details to be attended to under the circumstances. He would be going to WainCourt in a few days and hoped to wrap all the settlements up there. He left, unaware of exactly how much he had left Lady Sarah to think about.

Lady Sarah was generally thought to be a flighty woman, but in fact she possessed a great deal of her brother's shrewd intelligence, if not his cynicism. As little Sally Waincourt she had taken the town by storm and could have had her pick of any of the town's most eligible bachelors. It had, therefore, been a considerable surprise when, at the end of her first Season, she had chosen Richard Ambersley.

Lord Ambersley was of excellent family and fortune, but it was a respectable marriage only, and not the brilliant alliance Lady Sarah might have made. That had been eight years ago, and after having duly presented her lord with two infants she had promptly taken her place as a leader of society and given every appearance of being perfectly content.

She was not blind to her brother's faults and excesses, but she knew, as no one else did, exactly how much a strict and rather cheerless childhood coupled with too-early an ascension to a great title and possessions had contributed to Vidal's naturally reserved nature. She was, in truth, very fond of him.

She knew exactly how much he despised being toad-eaten and pursued, and had nearly give up hope of his ever marrying. She reviewed the afternoon's disclosure, a frown between her eyes. She was puzzled. She thought Vidal had revealed a great deal more than he had intended, but she could not quite credit the natural interpretation his words had invoked. He had spoken lightly, but even so, she had never known him to speak in exactly that way about any woman.

At last a smile curved her lips, and she went in search of her husband.

Chapter Eight

It was nearly a month later that Vidal rode briskly down the road from London. He had driven most of the way in his phaeton, but when they had left the inn that morning he had felt the need to stretch his legs and had left Hollings to tool the phaeton while he mounted a showy chestnut he had recently purchased and was bringing up with him.

It had been early when they set out and he had reveled in the cool morning air, soon leaving the vehicle far behind. At mid-morning he had pulled his chestnut up for a breather. His eyes idly scanned the landscape, noting the first signs of an early spring in the fields and trees. Then his attention was caught by a slight figure in a mad gallop across the fields. His eyes narrowed.

There could be no mistake. He certainly knew that black. She was a spirited filly, not quite up to his own weight, that had taken his fancy recently and he had bought her with the idea of racing her. She was only half-broken and Hollings reported her wild to a fault. But whoever the devil the lad was on his back, he seemed to have her well in hand.

He watched grimly for a moment and then spurred his horse sharply forward. By God, if her mouth was ruined! He cut swiftly across the field to intercept horse and rider.

Hearing the approach of another horse, the lad turned his head for a long moment, then dug his heels in and veered sharply away. Vidal's mouth thinned and his eyes were cold slate as he settled into the chase.

The youth had the advantage of his light weight on a faster horse, but the black showed signs of skittishness at the sound of another horse thundering behind her. The lad leaned low over her back and obviously soothed her as he fought her head.

Vidal's gain was slow but implacable, until he drew up beside and just behind the black. The filly reared with

fright and the lad held her with difficulty. Good God!
The boy could ride!

Vidal urged his horse slowly forward, and reaching out
an arm, grabbed the black's bridle just above the bit. She
veered in panic, but he held her steadily and slowly
brought both horses to a standstill. He was out of the
saddle in a flash and savagely pulled the slender figure
from the blown horse.

He stared in utter amazement at the copper braid that
fell from her cap.

Dominique jerked away, her eyes blazing. "What the
devil do you think you're doing?" she cried furiously.

"I might ask you the same question, my dear wife!"
Vidal's face was a cold mask as he slowly surveyed the
short jacket and buckskin breeches she wore. He put up
his quizzing glass. "Is this your normal mode of . . . er
. . . attire?" he drawled.

She suddenly lifted her crop to slash at him, but he held
her wrist in a steely grip and pulled her against him. "I
think not, my dear."

His face was very near to hers and he studied her for a
long moment before slowly releasing her arm and straightening himself. "I assume you are completely recovered
from your recent indisposition," he said smoothly. "I
must apologize for any rough treatment." He dusted his
jacket idly and straightened his cravat. "Perhaps you will
be good enough to tell me what you mean by taking my
horses without my permission?"

She rubbed the wrist he had released and replied
stiffly, "I had Keatings' assurance that this horse was not
up to your weight."

"You are not seriously telling me he approved your
riding Serena?" His brows met in an ominous frown.

"He satisfied himself thoroughly that she would come
to no harm with me!"

"Keatings knows full well that this is no fit mount for a
lady. She is headstrong, skittish and half-wild—a description I might apply to you as well!" he said succinctly. "If
she is not lamed or her mouth ruined I shall be extremely
thankful."

She looked up at him a moment, then laughed. "Pooh!"
she said airily. "I am fully capable of handling Serena,
as you well know. And if she is as skittish as you say, you

had no business crowding her. She is not yet used to being followed closely," she added kindly.

He reached out suddenly and took her slender neck between his fingers. "If I do not end by murdering you someday, I shall be very surprised, you abominable girl," he murmured ruefully.

She stood quietly under his hands, her color a little high. "Why, not in the least, your grace," she replied politely. "I mean to make you a very complaisant wife."

Enlightenment dawned his eyes. "Was this . . . er . . . exhibition designed to convince me of your unsuitability to be my wife?"

"Certainly not, your grace." She frowned suddenly and seemed to recall another grievance. "As a matter of fact, since I have heard nothing from you in over a month, I could hardly know you were expected today!" She ignored his sardonic grin. "But if you find my conduct not to your liking, pray do not hesitate to tell me so. It must naturally be an object with me to please you, your grace."

"Ah, so you do have claws, do you? Well, if you mean to rake me over the coals, I suggest we return to the house instead of standing in the middle of a damned draughty field." He cupped his hands in preparation to throw her into the saddle.

Her eyes widened. "Why, certainly you are not going to trust me to ride Serena back, your grace?"

"I believe it will be safe since I am here to see she comes to no harm," he assured her judiciously. As she bridled he laughed and tossed her into the saddle.

He stood surveying her with his lazy glance and after a moment said idly, "I believe I will have to make you a present of Serena. But I think—yes, I really think we shall have to acquire a more . . . er . . . suitable wardrobe for you."

In reply she tossed her head and spurred sharply forward. They had traveled for some minutes in silence when she seemed to recollect a debt she owed him. "I understand I must thank you for bringing Maby to me," she said stiffly.

His eyes gleamed at her obvious reluctance, but he said lightly, "Always at your service, ma'am. How is Miss Mabington?"

"Very well. She, at any rate, has fallen prey to your charm," Dominique replied bitterly.

They drew up to the house in silence and she allowed him to help her down. She entered the house quickly before him and had just reached the stairs when his voice overtook her.

"When you have changed, will you kindly join me in the library, my dear?" His voice became contemplative as his eyes moved over her slender figure. "Strange . . . that garb somehow suits you . . ."

She stiffened and hurried up the stairs.

When she entered the library some fifteen minutes later she was demure in outmoded gray merino, relieved only by white collar and cuffs. Her bright hair was confined severely at her nape. But if she expected to draw a rise from him she was doomed to disappointment. His face was impassive as he handed her to a chair and offered her a glass of sherry.

"Now then, your grace," she began purposively.

"Don't you think that under the circumstances you might call me Justin?" he interjected smoothly.

"Your grace," she repeated firmly. "I think this charade has gone on long enough."

"I assure you it is no charade, ma'am."

She bit her lip in vexation. "You know perfectly well what I mean! This—this—"

"Marriage?" he supplied helpfully.

At her look of loathing his lips quivered, but he maintained his gravity. "You were saying, ma'am?"

She took an agitated turn around the room. "I might have known I could expect this sort of behavior from you," she said bitterly. "I am asking you to release me from our—agreement."

"No!" he said bluntly.

That brought her around. Her eyes were very bright and she controlled her voice with an obvious effort. "Your grace! I will say nothing more of the fact that you forced me into this—this—marriage—against my will! I must believe your motives were kind . . ."

"I never have kind motives, my dear. Remember it!" he advised sardonically.

She ignored his interruption. "But my objections must still stand. Nor will I be bullied as before. I demand that you release me!"

"Come, child, surely nothing is to be gained by these histrionics," he said drily.

She flushed under his amused gaze and slowly sank into a chair.

"That is much better," he approved. "Now, if you like, I will freely admit that I took advantage of your illness to . . . er . . . coerce you a trifle. But I am a great deal older than you, my dear. Allow that I know a little more of the ways of the world."

He looked at her smouldering countenance and could not resist. "In point of fact, ma'am, you should be grateful to me. I don't believe I have ever seen anyone less suited to the position of governess. It is clear you would not have lasted the week!"

"I am surprised you are so knowledgeable, your grace," she murmured sweetly. "I have never heard it rumored that your taste ran to governesses. I understood actresses were more in your line. But no doubt I was mistaken."

"Do not fence with me, my girl! You are not up to my weight!"

"I think you would find yourself mistaken, sir," she challenged softly.

His attention was caught. "Do you fence?"

"Why it is but one of my many talents. You see, your grace, despite your opinion, I am possessed of excellent qualifications. I speak five languages fluently and three more with enough skill to get by. I read Greek and Latin, and am equally well versed in mathematics, history, geography and the use of the globes."

"Accomplishments, indeed." One eyebrow rose.

"No," she said truthfully. "I have no accomplishments. I cannot paint, or play upon the pianoforte or the harp, and I have no patience for needlework or any of the other genteel occupations expected of a lady of quality." She lifted her head defiantly. "But no doubt those faults will not weigh too heavily against me in my new life.

"For the rest," she continued indifferently, "I have lived in every country in Europe as well as several in the Near East and Africa. I am a devil to hounds—is that not the expression?—I can drive a team to an inch and can shoot the heart out of a card at fifty paces. I have lived in a castle one day and a hovel the next, depending upon the luck of the cards. I can instantly tell a Captain Sharp from a Johnny Raw, and I number amongst my acquaintance soldiers, gamblers, drifters and poets. In short, sir, your first opinion of me was exactly right. I have been an adventuress all my life. Shall I now have a try at being a *Duchesse?*" She met his eyes cynically.

"A strange life for a child," he remarked softly.

"Spare me your sympathy, sir!"

"I never waste my energies on useless emotions, my dear," he drawled and lazily flicked open his snuff box. As he withdrew a pinch, he added idly, "Did you think to shock me, my dear?" His cool gray eyes compelled her green ones.

"I believe I forgot to mention that a notice of our marriage appeared in the *Morning Post* three weeks ago. Cards have already gone out for a ball I shall give to introduce my wife to the *ton.*" He delicately flicked a grain of snuff from his blue sleeve. "So you see, my dear, this conversation, however enlightening, is quite useless."

Her face had grown very pale. "I see. If you will excuse me, your grace?" She turned and moved swiftly toward the door.

But there she stopped. "Why are you doing this?" she asked quietly.

"I have told you. I do not ruin innocent young females."

She turned then. "That is no answer. I had no claim upon you. At most you could have given me money to go away."

"Would you have accepted it?" he asked with interest.

She flushed. "N-no. But even so, there might have been some gossip, but you must be used to that." She looked up into his face. "I do not understand you, your grace. You know nothing of me. You do not even like me. Please let me go."

"No, my child, I cannot."

She stiffened and said defiantly, "Ah, there's the rub! Cannot or will not?"

After a moment his face softened and he said truthfully, "Both, child. Come, my dear, no good can come of this discussion. I can assure you we are irrevocably married. Can you not trust me?"

For answer she lifted her chin and turned abruptly away.

Her hand was on the door when his quiet voice stopped her. "One other thing, my dear."

For a moment he thought she meant to ignore him. Her hand tightened, but then she turned jerkily to face him, her expression set.

He stood regarding her intently, his eyes unusually alert behind his lids, but his expression was unreadable and he said quite casually, "I will need your father's name and family, as well as his place of birth, for the marriage certificates."

She stared at him, her eyes very dark. Then her lips twisted and she said deliberately, "Certainly. His name was Gerard Forrester. He was born in Paris. He had no family." She turned and walked out without looking back.

Vidal watched her go, wondering cynically why he should be disappointed that she quite evidently had no intention of telling him the truth.

Dominique, moving blindly, had not yet reached the sanctuary of her room when Maby's voice assailed her. "My dear! I have just been investigating the herb garden with Mrs. Hedges. Did you know they have hyssop? I remember my mother was always used to keep hyssop for rheumatism. Why, my dear? What ever is the matter?"

Dominique returned some vague answer, but Maby was not to be put off, and drew her into a small sitting room on the first floor. "Now, you'd better tell me what it is." Her eyes narrowed. "He's back, isn't he?"

"Oh, yes, he's back!" Dominique replied bitterly. Maby's apparent failure to understand the difficulties of Dominique's position had come as close as anything could to putting her out of sympathy with her old friend. "He discovered me in my breeches and riding one of his horses without his permission!"

Then at Maby's horrified expression she suddenly laughed harshly. "Well, it served him right! He was furious, of course, and I was glad to get a little of my own back! No doubt if he thought of me at all during the last month it was to picture me demurely twiddling my thumbs, content to wait until he condescended to remember my existence! For all he knew I might have been dead."

"Now, my dear," Maby protested. "That is not quite fair. He did not leave here until your fever broke, and then only to fetch me to you. If he had business to attend to in London, I'm sure it's not to be wondered at, and he has received daily reports since."

At Dominique's incredulous stare she continued calmly, "Yes, my dear, and now that I come to think about, Mrs. Hedges told me that he himself nursed you through the worst part of your fever."

Dominique did not appear to be gratified by this information. "Oh! That makes it worse!" She paced the room as if it were too small for her. "Now he calmly announces that invitations have gone out for a ball in my honor! It of course did not occur to him to consult me before making his plans. *I* have nothing to say about it! It is obvious that I am simply an obstacle to be overcome like a—a lamed horse or an impertinent servant!"

Her eyes narrowed dangerously. "Well, his grace will find he has mistaken his man this time. He'll rue the day he ever dared to cross swords with me!"

"Now, Dominique!" Maby said sternly. "You'd better be careful how you tangle with Vidal. I don't think he's the man to put up with your starts. Do not cross him too lightly!"

Dominique turned, a strange light in her eyes. "No, Maby," she said softly. "I do not mean to cross him lightly."

Maby watched her go, a frown on her face. At last she shrugged. There was never any reasoning with Dominique when she was in this mood.

A week later they returned to London. Dominique and Maby made the journey in Vidal's well-sprung traveling chaise, but he had spurned riding in the closed carriage, choosing instead to gallop ahead. Dominique, too, would have preferred her dear Serena to rocking endlessly in the stuffy vehicle, but she was well aware that such freedom was not allowed women.

She had seen very little of Vidal in the past week. They seemed to meet only at dinner, and then the sight of her in her drab gown made him tighten his lips and turn away. She was perfectly aware he thought she wore it to anger him, but in point of fact it was her most presentable gown. The last few years of her father's life the luck had seemed to run consistently against him.

Those dinners had not been happy affairs. Dominique had steadfastly refused to do more than reply shortly to any question put directly to her by Vidal, and Maby had sat between them in unhappy silence.

They had been installed for two days in Vidal's house in Berkeley Square when there was a tap at the sitting room door that she and Maby had adopted as their own. When Vidal entered Maby instantly rose.

"Good afternoon, your grace. I was just about to return to my room for a rest. Such an appalling habit, but quite necessary at my age, I find. If you'll excuse me?" She curtsied briefly, ignoring the message in Dominique's eyes, and left the room.

"Well, my dear, your *cicisbeo* had deserted you," he observed in amusement.

"You wished to speak with me, your grace?" Her voice was politely indifferent.

His face hardened, but he propped his wide shoulders negligently against the mantel and observed her through narrowed eyes. She defiantly lifted her chin.

"You are treading on dangerous ground, my dear," he remarked softly.

"Indeed, sir?"

He took a quick step toward her, then controlled himself and resumed his lazy posture. "Make sure you don't try my patience too far." His voice was silky. "My sister will dine with us this evening. I have asked her to advise you on modistes and mantuamakers and the like.

She raised limpid green eyes and then lowered them indifferently. He lifted his shoulders and strolled to the door.

"I would advise you to be civil to her." His tone was curt.

She glared at the door he softly closed behind him.

A moment later Maby stuck her head back in the door. "Has he gone so soon, love?"

Dominique looked up from a somber contemplation of her hands. "A nap indeed! What a whisker!" she said indignantly.

Maby merely laughed and came on into the room. "Well, my love, you can't go on avoiding him. It's bound to make life excessively uncomfortable, you know."

Despite herself Dominique's lips curved at the calm good sense of this remark. "Oh, Maby!" she said ruefully. "What would I do without you?" Impulsively she hugged her old friend's slight figure.

"Hmph!" Maby said gruffly. "I imagine you would do very well, since you never take my advice anyway! Nor have since I've known you."

Dominique grinned. "At least not in this case when I know what your advice is." Then she sighed and her mouth twisted. "His sister will dine with us this evening. I didn't even know he had a sister. What must she think of me?"

Then she purposely shook off her mood as Maby's kind face grew worried, and laughed lightly. "Yes, yes, I know! You think me more than a match for him! Perhaps I should have held out for more than a mere duke! They say Prinny always has his eyes out for a pretty young girl!"

But for once Maby did not laugh at her nonsense. "When are you going to tell him who your father was?" she asked quietly. Then as Dominique stiffened she added calmly, "He has a right to know, Dominique."

Dominique, her eyes suddenly unnaturally bright, said harshly, "And what shall I tell him, Maby? That it was all a misunderstanding, and I am not the penniless governess he thinks me? That therefore I am worthy to marry into his exalted family, no matter how much he may despise me?" Suddenly she closed her eyes and said wearily, "I'm afraid that only happens between the covers of a romantic novel, Maby. The truth is I am exactly what he thinks me—the penniless daughter of a ne'er-do-well father—no matter what my name is. And God knows I have little enough to be proud of in that name."

"Dominique . . ."

"No, Maby!" Dominique said stubbornly. "I won't have him find out now. It doesn't change anything."

"You are too proud, my dear," Maby said unhappily.

She shrugged. "Perhaps. He said that too. But you are not to tell him either, Maby."

There was a little silence as each of them pursued her own thoughts. Then Maby sighed and said slowly, "And your uncle?"

Dominique shrugged again. "As far as I am concerned I have no uncle." Then she relented. "Come, Maby! You have been indulging in too many novels. I have nothing to fear from my uncle. Nor is it the least likely I will ever hear from him again."

Maby only shook her head and looked unconvinced.

After a moment Dominique stood up. "Well, if we are to have guests for dinner, I must take extra care over my toilette." She grinned impudently. "Somehow I think Vidal is growing tired of my gray silk!"

As it turned out she was first downstairs when Lady Sarah was shown into the drawing room. Lady Sarah was some few years younger than Vidal, but despite a pair of disturbingly familiar gray eyes, bore little resemblance to him. She was very lovely. Her dark hair was dressed in the height of style and her high-waisted crepe gown was without a doubt both extremely expensive and chic. Dominique was more conscious than ever of her dowdy gray silk.

Lady Sarah observed her with interest for a brief moment, then exclaimed impulsively, "Oh, my dear! Justin said you were beautiful, but he much understated the case!"

Since Dominique found it difficult to believe Vidal had said anything of the sort, she merely smiled and politely invited Lady Sarah to sit down.

Lady Sarah smiled frankly. "Excuse me if I offended you, my dear. My tongue is forever running away with me. Ambersley says it's my besetting sin! Pray let us have a comfortable coze before the others come down.

"I hope you will forgive me," she continued lightly, "but Vidal has told me the whole." She smiled gently as Dominique stiffened. "He had to, you know, my dear, for you will need my help. Please don't be angry with him. I vow I have not been so diverted in years. I had nearly given up hope that someone would manage to throw a rub in his way at last."

She eyed Dominique's heightened color and said shrewdly, "Do you dislike him, my dear? If half of what he told me is true, you have good cause. But he is not all bad, you know. The trouble is that he inherited the title at far too young an age, and what with one thing and another, has always had too many people trying to toad-eat him and too many caps set at him. I'm afraid the truth is that he has been sadly spoiled. I know he is sometimes autocratic and arrogant and ill-mannered, but I'm really quite fond of him. You will no doubt say that I am naturally prejudiced in his favor!"

It was impossible not to like this frank creature with the engaging twinkle. Dominique extended her hand, saying apologetically, "Please forgive me, Lady Sarah. I fear my temper is nearly a match for your brother's!"

Lady Sarah laughed delightedly. "With that hair I hoped as much! Please call me Sally. I have a feeling we shall be great friends."

Dominique met her eyes frankly, her color a little high. "I know you must consider this whole thing a ramshackle business. I do myself. Nor can I excuse my part in it. But I assure you it was never my intention . . . I—I did not wish . . ."

Lady Sarah took pity and rescued her before she became wholly lost in her convoluted sentence. "My dear," she said quietly, "it is clear that you don't yet know me well. I think you'll be the making of Vidal!" She reached for Dominique's hand and clasped it, a smile deep in her eyes.

At that moment Vidal strolled in with Miss Mabington, his eyes resting lightly on their clasped hands. "Ah, Sally," he said, "I see you have made the acquaintance of my wife, and have no doubt been regaling her with highly improper and probably false tales about me!" He kissed his sister's cheek. "Now may I make Miss Mabington known to you? She is a very old friend of Dominique's."

It was a gay meal that followed. Lady Sarah kept them all in whoops with her bright, highly-spiced chatter, and Dominique saw a side of Vidal she had never imagined. High in the instep he might be, but he obviously had a soft spot for his sister. He laughed at her sallies, told several amusing tales himself, and gently teased them about the projected shopping tours.

When Lady Sarah left soon after eleven it was with the promise to return first thing in the morning to escort Dominique on the first of these expeditions.

"I vow I have not had this much fun in years!" She kissed Dominique on the cheek and whispered in her ear, "How glad I am to have you in the family, my dear!"

Dominique retired shortly afterward, pleading fatigue to avoid the nightly chat Maby so loved. Her mind was in a turmoil. She could not help liking Lady Sarah, but that almost made things worse. She had had ample time for reflection in the past weeks, and she had been forced to accept the fact that she was indeed inexorably married. But nothing could alleviate the galling knowledge that she had forced an unwilling marriage on the most sought-after bachelor in the country.

To be truthful, of course, he had forced it upon her, but that was mere quibbling. Vidal could only despise her for her part in the circumstances surrounding the affair, however good a face he attempted to put on the matter. For someone with her pride and spirit it was an untenable position.

Nor was it helped by the knowledge that had circumstances been different, she could have liked Vidal very well. Indeed, she had discovered that she did like him. He had a lively sense of humor. He showed a marked kindness toward Maby, and indeed treated his servants with a tolerance she would not have expected. They, in turn, seemed to hold him in considerable affection.

There was even a certain exhilaration in crossing swords with him. To his credit he never seemed to be shocked by her outrageous sallies, no matter what her unruly tongue led her to say. And he could on occasion be kind, in his own careless way. A hazy memory intruded, perhaps half-dreamed, of warm arms enfolding her, soothing softly in French, only to be thrust swiftly away.

Circumstances were not different. She sighed and began preparing for bed. There was still, however, the problem of the proposed shopping tours. Her pride longed to refuse to accept anything from Vidal, but her common sense told her she could only appear foolish by such a stand. And she had enough experience of Vidal to know he would go to any lengths to get his way, even to ordering gowns for her and seeing that she wore them.

And since, if she were honest, it played little part in her plans to remain the mousy creature he so obviously thought her, at last she allowed her objections to be overborne, and drifted to sleep with gratifying images filling her mind.

When she descended the stairs the next morning she found Vidal in the hall.

"Ah, there you are, my dear." He drew out his pocket book and withdrew several notes. "You will need some pin money, no doubt," he said easily. "I have arranged an account for you to draw from. Apply to Charles Hastings when you need more funds."

Under the eye of the butler she could do nothing but

accept the bills he proffered so carelessly. He bowed and left her.

A few seconds later he entered the office where his secretary sat at a desk piled high with papers. He raised his quizzing glass. "Why, Charles, surely I cannot be working you this hard?"

Hastings, a likable young man with an open face, colored and laughed. "No, no, sir! Quite the contrary. I was merely going through the files on the jewelry in the vaults. You will no doubt wish to have them returned from the bank now, sir."

"Ah, yes, how remiss of me." Vidal idly leafed through the file. "Hmmm . . . the emeralds, I think. Yes, and there is a ring as well, if my memory serves, that belonged to my grandmother."

Since the Waincourt family jewels were renowned for being as vast as they were magnificent, Hastings seemed at somewhat of a loss.

"Yes, and now that you put me in mind of it, make an appointment for me with Rundle."

Rundle and Bridge were the most fashionable and expensive jewelers in London. They had enjoyed an extensive and highly profitable relationship with his grace for many years, since the high-flyers he had had in his keeping over the years had been as famed for their rapacity as their beauty.

Vidal did not look up. "And wipe that smirk off your face, my boy. I am purchasing a present for my wife."

Hastings' smile broadened. "Yes, sir. Oh, sir, I have received the documents from your lawyers. They need only your signature and that of her grace."

"Excellent. Now was there not something else I wished to speak to you about? My wretched memory . . ."

Since Charles had reason to know that his grace's languid air and lazy eyes masked an extremely shrewd brain, he appeared unmoved by this speech.

"Ah, yes! Now I have it! If you are quite certain you have completed the settlements, I wish you to take a little trip."

His secretary's eyes widened, but he said nothing.

"Yes, I think you deserve a holiday, my boy. Shall we say . . . France?"

Hastings' face was suddenly impassive.

Vidal surveyed him for a moment, then nodded. "Good. I wish you to find out what you can about a certain family. I believe the name is de St. Forêt. I must return to Wain Court in the morning. You will make the necessary arrangements."

Chapter Nine

The next week Dominique spent in a jumble of fittings, shopping expeditions and conferences with Mme. Le-Camier, the outrageously expensive modiste presently enjoying the patronage of fashionable London.

She could not help being delighted to be in possession of lovely new gowns in the latest mode, but it soon became apparent that Lady Sarah's notion of the number of morning dresses, walking costumes, evening gowns, habits and cloaks, to say nothing of slippers, kid gloves, silk shawls and other such furbelows necessary to the wardrobe of a lady of quality, did not match Dominique's determination to be as little under obligation to Vidal as possible.

She herself knew her position to be an indefensible one, for she was already so deeply in his debt that she could never hope to repay him. But she could not resist the opportunity to try again to make Lady Sarah understand her feelings. They were in Dominique's bedchamber inspecting the latest gowns sent from Mme. LeCamier's elite shop in Bond Street when she again broached the subject.

Lady Sarah merely laughed. "You are talking nonsense, my love! Now which bonnet do you think with this green walking dress? The chip straw is ravishing, but—" she smiled at Dominique's impatient exclamation. "Yes, I know, my dear, you would rather not be beholden to him! But nothing is going to change the fact that you are his wife."

"Yes, but Sally," Dominique said desperately, "he cannot approve of my spending all this money! I shudder to think of the total of the bill from Mme. LeCamier alone!"

"Exactly what he deserves, my love!" Lady Sarah said airily. "He is odiously wealthy, you know." Her eyes twinkled. "I assure you this is but the beginning. We are going to make you the rage, my dear! Now which bonnet—?"

After a moment Dominique gave up and turned her attention to the respective merits of a chip straw over a green silk with high poke front.

During the past week they had become fast friends. Lady Sarah, if prepared to like Dominique for her brother's sake, very soon ended up being genuinely fond of her. She liked her quiet dignity, her quick mind and her lively sense of humor. And she had perceived with relief upon their first meeting that there could be no doubt of Dominique's breeding or her qualifications to fill the position so abruptly thrust upon her.

Lady Sarah had expected to be called upon to guide Dominique in her choice of wardrobe, but she soon discovered that Dominique had excellent taste and an unswerving instinct for what would best complement her unusual coloring. Lady Sarah had told the simple truth. She had no doubt that Dominique would take the town by storm.

All in all, Lady Sarah thought complacently as she shook out a lovely gown of amber silk, things were going extremely well. Extremely well indeed.

The all-important ball was rapidly drawing near. Dominique, despite her misgivings, found herself caught up in the excitement of preparations. It had never been her desire to cut a figure in society, and she had always rather looked with contempt upon those who did. But despite her basic honesty she was strangely loath to examine her feelings too closely in this matter. She only knew that Vidal should not be ashamed of her.

Vidal himself was not due to return from the country until the afternoon of the ball.

"Just like a man to abandon us like that!" Lady Sarah grumbled to Dominique as the preparations for the ball, fittings and shopping tours kept them busy from morning to night. "They hate a house in an uproar! Ambersley always retires to his club at the first sign of a caterer."

Dominique had made the acquaintance of Lord Ambersley, and found him a quiet man, very much in love with his wife, and a little in awe of her boundless energy and inconsequential chatter. She liked him. He, more than anyone, seemed to enter into her feelings a little, and made a genuine effort to check his wife's more extravagant efforts on Dominique's behalf.

"Well, my love, I perfectly understand the need for a

wardrobe, although I must agree that two fur-lined capes seems a little extravagant at this time of year!" he teased. "But I do think Vidal will strongly object to the addition to his household of three Russian wolfhounds."

This idea had been advanced by Lady Sarah the night before the ball as the three of them sat over tea after dinner. Dominique had become a frequent guest in their house in Curzon Street and was a decided favorite with the two scions of the house, at present still in the nursery.

"But love," Lady Sarah insisted, "you know that Russian countess was stunning, and she went everywhere with her two dogs." She paused and added reflectively, "Though I must admit I could not like her! Even the dogs seemed to be nasty-tempered brutes!" She smiled in sympathy at their whoops of laughter.

"Very well, but you will not deny that Dominique looks magnificent!" she said, justly proud of her efforts.

It was true. Dominique had never been plain, even in her dowdiest gowns, but dressed in the latest style and with her hair expertly dressed by the expensive but talented dresser they had employed, she was breathtakingly lovely.

Dominique blushed and turned the subject, but she was honest enough to feel extremely pleased with her appearance. She was not impressed by her beauty and had been known to grumble about the shade of her hair, but even she was pleasantly surprised at the difference a change of wardrobe could make.

She had never worried too much about how she looked, and had steadfastly refused to think about clothes at all for the last few years. There had been too many other demands on an always too-slender purse. But there was a very real reason now why she longed to look her best. And he was going to be very much surprised indeed!

The morning of the ball Dominique spent in consultation with Alphonse, the extremely Gallic and voluble genius that presided over the kitchens. He had embraced her as a fellow countryman, the only sane member in this mad English household, and it had fast fallen to her lot to soothe his often-exacerbated sensibilities.

At present he had been incensed at the invasion of his domain by what he succinctly termed *canaille,* the caterers hired to supplement the staff for the ball. It had taken all her persuasive powers to keep him from flinging off his apron and instantly deserting his post.

"For I tell you plainly that this is not the treatment I am used to!" Alphonse exclaimed in righteous indignation. "I had thought *Monsieur le Duc* to be a man of sensibilities and taste. But I discover of a certainty that I am mistaken! It is only for you, *chère* madame, that I do not leave this instant!"

She had managed to placate him and escaped from the kitchens at last, only to encounter Vidal in the hall. She sighed and mentally surveyed her simple cambric morning gown, smoothing back a wisp of hair that had escaped.

"Ah, your grace, you are returned. I hope you had a pleasant journey?"

"Very pleasant, thank you, ma'am. Will you give me a moment of your time?"

She frowned a little, but hesitated only briefly before allowing herself to be ushered into the library.

He crossed to his desk and picked up a large cask. "These are the Waincourt jewels, ma'am. I would have given them to you sooner, but they have been at the jewelers being cleaned and repaired. Mrs. Billings will show you where the vault in your room is located."

Her eyes darkened and she opened her mouth impulsively, then bit back her hasty words. She accepted the cask silently and moved toward the door.

"Dominique!"

She turned back slowly, her face set and pale. He took the cask from her and set it carelessly on a nearby table. Then taking a ring from his pocket he slipped it on her finger.

She tried convulsively to pull her fingers away, but he held them firmly and regarded the ring he had placed on her hand. It was an exquisite, almost barbaric thing, composed of immense emeralds circling a wide, intricately carved band.

"It belonged to my grandmother," he remarked. "I thought it would suit you."

When she remained silent his fingers tightened and there was a frown deep in his eyes. "You hate to accept anything from me, don't you?" he demanded.

She had been angry at first, but now her anger deserted her, and she only knew herself to be miserably unhappy. She sighed and would have turned away, but he grasped her chin with hard fingers and forced her head up.

At that a spark of her anger returned and she met his eyes, her own proud and resentful.

He regarded her for a long moment, then gave a bark of laughter and released her. "Well, ma'am! You are certainly different in that at least from any other female of my acquaintance!"

He drew from his pocket a wide jeweler's case and opened it. On the velvet rested a necklace, bracelet and earrings of flawless emeralds spun together by a golden chain so fine as to be almost invisible.

"These were my grandmother's also," he said negligently. "I have had them reset." He snapped the case shut and handed it to her, then turned away.

Back in her room she tossed the case furiously on her dressing table. But in so doing her eyes were caught and held by the ring on her finger. Slowly she sank down on the chair.

When Maby came to find her sometime later she was still sitting as if mesmerized, emeralds dripping from her fingers.

"My dear! I have never seen anything so magnificent!" Maby breathed.

Dominique slowly replaced the emeralds in their case, then unfastened the clasp of the cask and opened the lid. Stones of every color and brilliance glittered back at her.

Maby stared in frank fascination. "The Waincourt jewels! They are famous throughout the country. Whatever can he be thinking of to have them in the house? They must be worth a large fortune."

"There is a vault in my room," Dominique said dully.

"Then for heaven's sake put them there! They make me nervous!" She eyed Dominique's drawn face with concern. "You will be exhausted before the ball even begins, my dear."

She bullied and cajoled until she saw Dominique laid down on her bed. "I will call you at seven!" she whispered as she tiptoed out.

Bates was just putting the finishing touches to Dominique's burnished curls when there was a light tap at the door and Lady Sarah stuck her head in.

"May I come in, my dear? I couldn't resist a final peek!"

She expertly surveyed the coppery curls. "Yes, I think we were right not to put anything in your hair." She spied the emeralds in the open case. "Ah, the very thing! Did Vidal have them reset for you?" There was a secret little smile in her eyes, but she said nothing more.

Bates lifted the gown reverently and whisked it over Dominique's head, then stood back to survey her handiwork.

After a long debate they had settled on an artlessly simple gown of emerald crepe. Dominique had protested that it was cut too low, but she had given in when she saw the effect of the brilliant green against her clear skin. The gown was unadorned and fell from its high waist in graceful folds about her feet.

Lady Sarah fastened the emeralds around her neck, then stood with her head cocked to one side. At last she broke into a broad smile. "I knew it!" she cried delightedly. "You will break hearts tonight, love!"

Dominique laughed and tried to hush the elated cries of Bates and Maby, but allowed them to draw her to the mirror. She surveyed her reflected image almost in wonder for a brief moment, then smiled with a touch of self-mockery. "Well, you have certainly succeeded in turning me into a swan for one night, at least!" she admitted.

She drew on the long kid gloves Bates handed her and allowed Maby to clasp the emerald bracelet on her wrist. "You are looking in particular bloom tonight, Sally. Is that the gown you had last week from Mme. LeCamier?"

"Oh, my dear, I am postively hagged tonight!" Lady Sarah cried, perfectly aware she was always turned out in high style. "But it matters little what I am wearing. No one shall be looking at me. Come, we'd best go down. I forced poor Ambersley to bring me a full three quarters of an hour early! Although I don't doubt he's forgotten my existence by now. I left him and Vidal in the library with a very old bottle of claret Lymings had just discovered in the cellars."

Dominique laughed and led the way downstairs. She had just reached the bottom steps when Vidal and Ambersley came through the library door. Ambersley smiled and gave her an elaborate bow, and Vidal came toward her and took her hand, a mocking light in his eyes.

"Well Justin? Is she not lovely?" Lady Sarah demanded archly.

Vidal retained his light clasp on her hand. "Certainly, my dear. But you know," he added musingly, "I almost believe I preferred her in her breeches."

Lady Sarah gasped and Dominique's eyes flashed for a moment. Then her mouth curved in a reluctant grin. "I might have known! You are abominable, sir!"

His amused voice reached her ears softly. "Did you think to dazzle me, my dear? I assure you I have always known how lovely you are."

Her eyes held a sudden question as they met his, but the first of the guests began arriving and there was time for no more.

A few particular friends had been invited to dine before the ball, and it was a small but select party that sat down to dinner some half an hour later. Dominique turned to find herself being surveyed by the merry blue eyes of the gentleman on her left. He was a young man dressed in a style that strongly suggested the dandy. His shirt points were almost excessively high and the arrangement of his neckcloth was a little complicated for her taste. She could not help comparing his attire with the exquisitely plain raiment Vidal wore. But then Vidal always looked carelessly elegant and dignified.

Then she started guiltily. "I beg your pardon, sir! What was it you said?"

"Ah, your grace!" He gave an exaggerated sigh. "I was saying that Justin has always had the knack of discovering the most beautiful women, but he has positively outdone himself this time! Where, pray, has he been hiding you?"

"In truth, sir," she said lightly, "we met but a brief time ago in the country."

"The country!" He groaned disgustedly. "Just like him! All *I* ever meet in the country are fresh-faced damsels who have been enjoying rather too much of their own butter and cream!" His eyes danced. "I declare it is too bad in him! Only one circumstance keeps me from calling him out on the instant."

Dominique had to smile at his absurd manner. "And what is that, sir?"

"He is a much better shot than I," he said sadly. At her peal of laughter Vidal's eyes strayed to her animated face for a brief moment before returning to his partner.

"That is certainly shabby of you, Mr. Linville," she murmured teasingly.

"Cow-hearted!" he admitted frankly. "But I am greatly heartened that you at least recall my name! I shall not despair!"

She laughed again and turned to the gentleman on her right, a quiet man with dark eyes and a military bearing.

"You must pay no attention to Linville," he said, smiling. "He is a sad rattle. I am Carleton, you know."

"Certainly, my lord. I believe you have known my . . . husband for a great many years?"

If he noticed her slight hesitation, he did not betray it. "Oh, yes! I have known Vidal anytime these past eighteen years, ma'am. We were at Oxford together, you know, although I'm afraid I was not up to his lead."

She returned a polite answer, but her eyes were slightly puzzled. She found herself liking this quiet man with the calm demeanor, but could find little that he and Vidal would have in common.

"He took Honors, you know, he added quietly. As her eyes widened, he regarded her for a moment, then said frankly, "You are wondering at our friendship, ma'am. I hope you will not be fooled by his reputation and his frivolous manner. The truth is that there is no one I would rather count my friend, or for that matter have behind me in a tight corner."

Someone addressed a question to her then and the conversation became general, but she found her eyes returning several times to quietly study Vidal's face.

At ten o'clock the first of the ball guests began arriving. Dominique's head was soon swimming with elegant faces and names. When, an hour later, they at last left their post at the entrance to the ballroom it was very apparent that the evening was to be accorded the highest accolade—a sad crush.

Vidal led her down the stairs, murmured, "Shall we, my dear?" and swung her into the waltz. She was momentarily grateful for the many hours of lessons from the junior officers in Madrid and Vienna as her steps fitted themselves perfectly to his.

After a moment he remarked softly, "You dance beautifully, my dear. You failed to include that in your catalogue of virtues."

She blushed but refused to be drawn.

"You are, however, I believe, supposed to look at your partner." His amused voice brought her eyes indignantly to his. "Ah, that's much better. I can see I am the envy of every other gentleman in the room."

The scene that afternoon might never have been. Her eyes were suddenly suspicious. "You are not by any chance flirting with me, your grace?" she asked lightly.

His arm tightened around her waist and he pulled her nearer. "And if I were . . . ?" he murmured provocatively against her curls.

She made no answer, but allowed herself to relax in his arms.

When the dance ended he lifted her hands to his lips for a long moment, then bowed and left her. Only then did she become aware of the number of eyes upon them. She realized that he had done exactly what he had set out to do: convince the world that he was more than content with his marriage.

She was surprised and even rather touched. She had not looked forward to this evening. She was well aware that there was bound to be a great deal of speculation about Vidal's sudden marriage, most of it probably uncomplimentary to her. Vidal, after all, might be somewhat disliked, but he was a duke and had been until his hasty marriage the most sought-after of bachelors, while she was unknown to them and even a foreigner. She had expected to encounter a great deal of suspicion, if not outright hostility.

But although one or two conversations were ended abruptly when she drew near, and she was conscious of a great many eyes upon her, not all of them friendly, no one was anything but charmingly polite to her. Where Vidal, an acknowledged leader of fashion, bestowed such patent approval, few dared not follow.

She lifted her head proudly. She did not care what they thought of her in private. Indeed, she would have been less contemptuous if they had dared to show her their true feelings. But they did not, so she would play the game as it had been laid out. She smilingly accepted the arm of her next partner and accepted his effusive compliments with a charm only slightly touched by her cynicism.

Vidal, his eyes on his bride, only nodded when Carleton came to join him. They both stood there for a moment, watching her take her place gracefully in the country dance.

"She's very lovely, Justin," Carleton said quietly. Then his slow smile appeared. "I am sure you know what you have just done."

Vidal smiled rather grimly. "Oh, yes!" he said carelessly. "I have no doubt it will be common knowledge by tomorrow that Vidal has been brought to heel at last by a beautiful face!"

Carleton, who knew nothing of what lay behind Vidal's marriage, but like a great many others had his suspicions, merely clasped his friend's shoulder and moved off at the imperious signal of Lady Southhampton.

The rest of the evening for Dominique passed in a kaleidoscope of colors and ever-changing partners. And if she did not quite enjoy herself, at least she made a very good show. She was not shy and was able to meet people with a relaxed, easy manner, and not by the slightest sign did she betray her awareness of the undercurrents of the evening.

At one point Lady Sarah whisked by to squeeze her hand and whisper in her ear. "That's showing them, my love!" and Dominique was forced to laugh. Indeed, all of the faces were not polite only. There were several in her myriad of partners she liked: Carleton, and even the absurd Linville, and of course Lord Ambersley, and several other quiet gentlemen. Even a few of the ladies seemed inclined to swing their suspended judgment slightly in her favor.

Only one incident occurred to mar the proceedings. Vidal danced very little, and at one point her eyes found him standing in the corner with a voluptuously beautiful brunette in clinging crepe. The brunette had her fingers on his arm in an intimate manner and appeared to be whispering something in his ear.

Vidal suddenly lifted his head and his eyes met hers across the room. Dominique quickly turned away with a dazzling smile for her partner, whose face she was never afterward able to remember.

During the next interval she found Vidal at her elbow with a glass of champagne. "Here, drink this." His eyes surveyed her heightened color. "You are doing very well, my dear," he remarked softly.

Her hand was then claimed for the next dance and she saw little more of him. He did not dance with her again.

It was very late before the last of the guests departed and she could retire to her room. She smiled ruefully at her reflection and adjured her sleepy dresser to go to bed. She was well used to looking after herself.

At nine o'clock the next morning she entered the breakfast room to find Vidal there before her calmly eating a sirloin and reading the morning papers. She checked slightly, then took the chair he held for her.

"You surprise me, my dear," he commented. "I had not thought to see you before noon today."

"I am always an early riser, your grace."

He raised an eyebrow. "Very commendable, my dear. Do you care for coffee or shall I ring for a pot of tea?"

"Coffee is fine, your grace." She accepted the cup he poured for her and helped herself to bread and butter.

He surveyed her very elegant habit of black velvet and the rakish hat tilting over her left eye. Its severity suited her and showed her excellent figure to advantage.

"Most becoming!" he observed sardonically. "I believe I must compliment you on your *succès fou*, my dear. It would seem you have taken the town by storm."

She thanked him in a polite voice. His eyebrows rose again. "You appear to be unimpressed by your achievements."

She smiled a little derisively. "I doubt, sir, that I would have been the *succès fou* you term me as other than a—*duchesse* and your wife."

"Then you are mistaken, my dear. You are far too beautiful to be ignored."

Her color rose, but her eyes were serious. "I think you know better than that, your grace," she said quietly. She hesitated, and then added stiffly, "Nor am I—unaware of what you did last night. In any event, my beauty, as you choose to call it, stood me in little stead as a governess."

She felt his eyes on her and shrugged lightly. "Oh, you are right. I was not ignored." Her smile was bitter. "But neither the men nor the women could forget that I was a governess and . . . pretty. My station and my appearance were deemed incompatible, and nothing could alter their opinion."

His fingers closed suddenly about her wrist. Her eyes flew to his, a startled question in them. "Very probably, my dear. Don't be such a romantic!" he drawled.

Angrily she sought to pull her wrist from his grasp.

"Oh, no! You'll listen to me! You are angry because people who would not have you in their house as governess now fawn upon you as a duchess. Well, that's the way of the world, my dear." His eyes held hers. "But don't you think you are being rather foolish to condemn a whole class because some of its members are admittedly shallow and stupid?"

He smiled a little grimly. "Well, my dear, there are snobbish people in any class of society. But if you believe that what you are would make the slightest difference to people like my sister and Ambersley, or Carleton, or anyone else that matters, once they knew you, then you are the snob, my dear!"

She was very pale. He released her wrist gently and stood up. "You were to ride this morning, my dear? May I accompany you?"

She rose too. "If you wish, your grace," she replied indifferently.

His eyes twinkled in sudden amusement. "Ah, no doubt that was meant to be a snub. But I am notoriously immune to snubs! Shall we go?" He held the door for her.

She chatted easily enough with him as they cantered through the park, but her eyes were preoccupied.

"Are content with Serena?" he asked suddenly.

"What? Oh, yes, your grace! She is a beautiful little lady with excellent manners."

His lips quirked. "You are certainly the first to say so. I believe I complimented you once before on your seat, ma'am. I don't believe I've ever seen a female ride as well as you do."

"Why, that is praise indeed! I warn you, you shall turn my head, sir. My riding is the one thing I pride myself on," she said lightly.

"You are too modest, ma'am. Unless my memory fails me you recently regaled me with a much longer list of your accomplishments."

Her color deepened. "I did no such thing! At least— you must know I was not serious—! Oh!" as his grin broadened. "You are abominable! Why do you delight in making me lose my temper?"

"Because it is so easy," he replied promptly.

She bit her lip to keep from laughing.

"That is better, child. I did not mean to put you in the mopes," he said gently.

She stared up at him for a moment and he took the opportunity to study the effect of the sun glinting on her copper hair. "You know, I have always had a penchant for Titian hair," he uttered soulfully. "Although yours is almost copper in this light," he added reflectively.

She laughed suddenly. "What a fib! I have it on the best authority that you have always been distinctly partial to blondes!"

"Yes, but I had never seen hair the color of yours before."

She merely laughed and cantered ahead.

After several moments he spoke again. "Ah, now that I think on it, did you not mention you included driving among your myriad skills? I shall have to take you out one day and see how you handle the ribbons. Perhaps I will purchase you a carriage and pair."

"Will you let me drive the bays?" Her glance was a challenge.

"Certainly not."

"Then no thank you! I prefer to make my own arrangements. Mr. Linville was telling me last night about a charming pair of chestnuts that have just come on the market. He promised to take me to see them."

"Not Wibbley's breakdowns!" His mouth was suddenly firm. "They are a beautiful pair, but completely unsuitable for a female." He spoke with the finality that clearly indicated he expected to hear no more of the matter.

She bit her lip, but maintained a discreet silence as they turned from the park and rode the short distance to Berkeley Square. When he helped her from the saddle she merely thanked him politely for the pleasant ride and left him at the door.

Maby at that moment came from the back of the house. She stood regarding Vidal in silence as he watched Dominique climb the stairs.

"Ah, Maby! Are you recovered from the dissipations of last night?" His eyes quizzed her. "I quite believe you made a conquest of old Colonel Williams!" Vidal and Maby had long ago reached an excellent, if silent, understanding.

Maby laughed, but her eyes were serious. "Have you been quarreling again, sir?"

Vidal smiled ruefully. "Why, as to that, Maby, I'm afraid I delivered a lecture over the breakfast table on the evils of snobbery!" He gave an exaggerated sigh. "It is clear that I shall end in Bedlam before long."

He held the door of the library open, a question in his eyes, and after a moment's hesitation she entered.

"Yes, I did wish to speak to you," she said bluntly. "Dominique won't thank me for sticking my oar in, but I know she will tell you nothing, and I would like you to understand a little why she behaves as she does."

Vidal looked a little surprised, but asked gently, "How long have you been with her, Maby?"

"Since she was twelve, your grace. And a more beautiful, gallant little thing I've yet to see!" Her usually frank eyes were soft and distant. "She had been taking care of her father for nearly four years when I came, and I mean that literally, sir. There had not been a nurse or any other female in the house in all that time. And no telling where all he'd dragged her, either!"

Vidal made no comment and after a moment her eyes met his. "I don't know what to tell you about her father, your grace! He was a kind man, a gentle man in many ways and fond of Dominique in his own way. He kept her always with him, although if she had been a nuisance I don't doubt he'd have made other arrangements. He taught her the classics, how to ride, shoot, fence . . . treated her more like a son than a daughter and encouraged her to be fearless and proud.

"But he was a gay, careless man, and he never allowed her to interfere in his pleasure." She hesitated. "She always has had to be very independent, your grace. That is why her position now is so hard for her to accept."

There was a long silence. At last Vidal inquired quietly, "And her mother?"

"Why, I know very little, sir. She died when Dominique was a tot. I believe there was some upset over the marriage. Her mother was Scots, you know, and of another faith, and both families disapproved. I don't know what happened to her family, but he was disinherited by his father."

"Do you know the name of her mother's family?"

"No, sir, I'm afraid I don't. Annemarie was seldom spoken of and never by Dominique's father."

He hesitated. "Dominique has said that they traveled around a great deal. How did they manage?"

"On their wits!" she said bluntly. "Gerard did a little of everything. He taught fencing at one time. And then he was attached to the British troops during the war as an advisor. After the war he could have gone back to France, of course, but he'd grown used to wandering around. And he gambled, sir. Usually his luck was quite good. But toward the last it seemed to be consistently against him.

"There was never any money by then, and no servants. I would never have left Dominique, whether I was paid or not, but my sister became very ill and needed me, and Dominique insisted I go to her."

She brushed a hand impatiently across her eyes. "I should never have left her. I don't excuse myself, nor will I ever forgive myself. She had old Jacques, of course, but she should have had me too!"

She saw his questioning look. "He became ill, you see. I knew nothing until she wrote to tell me he was dead. Thank God Jacques had enough sense to bring her to me!"

She angrily shook her head and her tones became brisk again. "That was just a little over six months ago, sir. She had it in her head that she could not be a burden on me and that she must take a position as a governess. I tried to dissuade her, of course. I knew, if she did not, what her life as a governess would be. I had almost begun to hope she wouldn't find a position—few women will have a governess that looks like Dominique—when that wretched Lady Thornton engaged her sight unseen. That was when she hit upon the notion of dyeing her hair."

She met his eyes squarely. "You will think I am a stupid old fool to have let her do such things, and you are right, your grace."

"No, Maby, I don't think that. I am well aware you could not stop her once she takes a notion into her head." His voice became firm. "But I can. You need not worry about her anymore."

She studied his face for a long moment. "Yes, your grace, I believe you can," she said simply, and moved to the door.

"And Maby?"

She turned her head.

"Thank you for telling me these things," he said quietly.

Since Dominique spent the remainder of the day in her room and Vidal dined at his club that evening, she did not see him again until much later. It was past midnight when she heard him come in. She had been idly turning over the pages of a periodical in the small sitting room, but she could not have honestly been said to have gained much knowledge of the beauty hints to be found in its pages.

Vidal had just removed his hat when she appeared in the dimly lit hall. "May I have a word with you, sir?"

His mobile brows rose but he opened the library door for her and said calmly, "Certainly, my dear."

He poured her a glass of sherry and handed it to her. "What is the trouble, Dominique?" he asked quietly.

She looked up from her intense absorption in the contents of her glass and colored a little. "Not trouble, precisely, sir. It is just that I wish to offer my apologies to you."

"Good God! This is a new come-out!" His comical expression of amazement caused her to smile, but it did not reach her eyes. "I assure you there is not the slightest need for any apologies, my dear. It's far more likely the shoe's on the other foot! You had much better rail at me instead!"

She said frankly, "You are rude, overbearing, autocratic and without the slightest interest in anyone's wishes but your own. But I have not come to pick a quarrel with you. I—I—" She clasped her hands tightly and drew a deep breath. "I have thought a great deal about what you said to me this morning. You are right, of course." She was very pale.

"For—various reasons—I have been used to think contemptuously that the nobility are heartless and—stupid." She regarded her clasped hands steadily. "But I have met with nothing but kindness since coming here. I am very fond of Lady Sarah and Lord Ambersley, of course. And you also, although we are never likely to agree upon the reasons for my being here, have behaved toward me with—with—"

"Come, child! You will have me thinking you are on the brink of a decline if you continue in this unnatural vein!" he said lightly.

She laughed at that. but shook her head. "No, no. What I really came to say is that I have not behaved very well, I know. I hope you will accept my apologies and my promises to try to do better in future."

He came forward and lightly taking her hands, drew her to her feet. "If you mean we can cry friends, I shall be very glad. But if you mean to go on in this subdued manner, I shall very likely be forced to violence before the week is out!"

She raised her eyes to his face, suddenly a little shy. He slowly lifted her hands and placed a light kiss in each palm.

"Now go to bed, you absurd child."

When the door closed behind her he poured himself a glass of brandy and stood staring somberly into the fire. He straightened suddenly, drained his glass, and cursed himself for a fool.

Chapter Ten

This pax lasted exactly a fortnight. But since Dominique was immediately caught up in the constant rounds of routs, card parties, assemblies and balls that signified the London Season in full swing, it could not be said they had much opportunity for testing their new understanding.

Then Dominique attended a ball at Waverley House. Halfway through the evening she ripped her flounce and retired to the dressing room for repairs. A maid was busily pinning it up for her when the ripe brunette she had seen chatting so intimately with Vidal at her own ball entered.

The brunette halted with narrowed eyes at sight of her, then entered slowly and looked Dominique up and down in a measuring way like a distinct slap in the face. "Allow me to introduce myself," she drawled. "I am Caroline Graham. Your husband and I are—very old friends." She lingered over the words.

"As such, perhaps you'll allow me to give you a piece of advice, my dear. I don't know why Vidal married you, though I can hazard a guess. No doubt you think yourself very clever. But I would not make the mistake of thinking you mean anything to him." She paused. "Or of thinking he has given up any of his old . . . friendships . . ."

Dominique had stiffened, but she forced herself to speak lightly. "Vidal has told me about a great many of his . . . old friends, but I don't believe he mentioned your name. Perhaps he placed less value on the—er—friendship than you," she said quietly and swept out.

Later, catching sight of Lady Caroline across the room, Dominique asked Lady Sarah about her. The titters of several ladies standing within earshot and Lady Sarah's hasty attempt to change the subject told her all she needed to know.

Actually, if Dominique could but have known it, it had been spite not unmixed with desperation that had prompted Lady Caroline to speak to her. Lady Caroline, the daughter of a penniless peer, had at an early age contracted a marriage to a man many years her senior. That he had died within five years of their marriage she considered to be only the decent thing he had ever done.

But that she had been bitterly misled about the size of her widow's portion became swiftly apparent to her. She was forced to exercise the strictest economies to maintain the facade of the beautiful and wealthy widow she chose to convey. She had, therefore, set about her to find herself a second, and hopefully more congenial husband. Not unnaturally, her choice had settled upon Vidal.

Vidal had quite easily succumbed to the invitation of her beauty, but he had had a great many mistresses over the years, and she wanted a good deal more than that. But if her move had been calculated, she was, in her own fashion, truly in love with him.

She had been well aware that the betting was heavily against her at Whites, the general opinion being that when Vidal took a bride at last, as he surely must do, he would choose a girl of unexceptional birth and unsullied reputation. But she knew exactly how much Vidal despised inexperienced and immature girls and she did not despair.

Then the notice of his marriage to the little nobody was announced, and it had taken all her courage to pretend she had known about it all along. She had not, and it had been a blow to her pride, if not her heart, that he had seen no need to even apprise her of his intentions.

The next time they had met she thought she had her emotions in hand and had even chaffed him a little about his sudden marriage to the charming incognita. But he had made it very clear that he did not discuss his wife with his mistress, and she had come very close to ruining everything. To be sure, she had manged to smooth things over, but their relationship had never quite regained its old footing. His visits were less and less frequent, and she knew inexorably that she was losing him.

She did not hesitate to place the blame squarely where it belonged, and her hatred was fierce and implacable. She would willingly have done Dominique any injury she could. Failing that at the moment, she must be content with mere malice.

Unfortunately Dominique knew nothing of this, and Lady Sarah, who perhaps understood a little more, did not think it was her place to speak of it. She had a fair notion which way the wind lay, and she would not have hurt Dominique for the world.

Thus it was that Vidal, walking with his friend Lord Carleton a few days later, was privileged to see his wife seated in a racing curricle and driving a beautiful pair of chestnuts down the street at a spanking pace. The fact that she was handling a very difficult pair with considerable skill appeared to offer him no gratification whatsoever.

"Good God! Isn't that—" Lord Carleton exclaimed before he could check himself. He glanced ruefully at Vidal's black visage and shook his head. "Impossible, of course. But by God can she drive!"

"You will excuse me if I fail to share your enthusiasm!" Vidal rasped and strode off without another word.

His temper was not improved by being forced to cool his heels for three quarters of an hour before he at last heard her voice in the hall. During that time his servants, well acquainted with the implications of that black frown, had taken great pains to remain out of his vicinity. And when Lymings, secure in his privileged position, had ventured to suggest a glass of claret, even he had been roundly cursed for his pains.

As Dominique crossed the hall Vidal thrust open the library door. "A word with you ma'am!" he grated.

Her eyes were startled, but she walked into the room and stood lightly drawing her kid gloves through her fingers. "Well, your grace?"

His black brows met in an ominous line over his eyes. "Perhaps you will have the goodness to explain yourself, madam!"

A slight frown marred her forehead, but she answered equitably enough. "I must suppose you to be referring to my new carriage and pair, but I do not believe there is anything to discuss."

A harsh laugh broke from him. "Oh, very cool, ma'am! It had no doubt slipped your mind that I forbade you to purchase that very team little more than a week ago!"

"Forbade—!" Her eyes glittered greenly and she controlled herself with an obvious effort. "We will continue this conversation later, when your temper has had time to cool!" She spoke coldly and turned toward the door.

His fingers bit into her arm, and he jerked her around to face him. "You will stay until I give you leave to go!" He did not loose his hold of her arm.

At that her own temper flared. "How dare you!" she cried furiously.

"How dare you, madam! I have no doubt it was your intention to make a laughing stock of me! You have taken no pains to hide what your feelings are toward me!"

At that some of the anger died from her eyes. "A laughing stock? Why I know it may be a little unusual for a lady to drive her own carriage, but I know of at least two women who do so."

His lips curled. "Do not try to gammon me, my girl. You bought that team with the express intention of angering me!"

She blushed a little, but drew herself up proudly. "And if I did, sir, it was to teach you that I am not to be ordered about like a serving girl!"

"I will remind you that you are my wife, madam! If I expect nothing else, I expect obedience!"

"Your wife!" she cried, her breast heaving. "Good God! I am not your wife! I am an inconvenience! And I acknowledge obedience to no one!"

"An inconvenience—!" Vidal repeated in a thunderstruck tone. Suddenly there was a strange light in his eyes and his lips curved as he pulled her slowly to him. When she would have jerked away he took her chin in his fingers and forced her head up. His eyes played over her heightened color and slightly parted lips.

She stood stiffly under his hands. "Unhand me, sir! she said coldly.

His arms tightened. "I think it is time I made your position in my house clear, my dear," he drawled. His eyes glittered as he lowered his head to hers.

She struggled against him, but he held her firmly and after a moment she grew very still. When he at last lifted his head her eyes were very dark and her breath came rapidly from between her parted lips.

His finger lifted to lightly caress her cheek, then moved to her throat. He lowered his head again and his lips moved with aching sweetness against her cheek, the corner of her mouth. Her sigh was lost as his lips again claimed hers.

This time when he lifted his head his breath had quickened too, and his eyes were heavy-lidded with passion. Then he shook his head slightly and slowly smiled, a note of mockery in his eyes. "You surprise me, my dear," he murmured.

She gasped, and tears of anger and humiliation stood in her eyes. "Are you satisfied, your grace?"

"Satisfied? No, child, I am not satisfied," he said softly. "Nor am I hypocrite enough to apologize. But remember this the next time you think to try me too far."

When he released her she walked with restraint toward the door. She had just reached it when his quiet voice stopped her. "You will, of course, give me the bills for the chestnuts and curricle. I believe they shall be my wedding present to you." His light laugh followed her as she slammed the door behind her.

In the privacy of her bedchamber she sank into a chair and put up her hands to cool her fevered cheeks, her mind in a turmoil. At first she raged fiercely against him, but her innate honesty soon forced her to admit that she was as much to blame as he. She *had* bought the chestnuts to make him angry. And she had done it out of the worst possible motives: to get back at him because he thought so little of her he openly maintained his relationship with his mistress.

She was no prude. She knew well enough that a man like Vidal would have a mistress. Only a fool would expect him to change his life because he found himself in possession of an unwanted wife.

And she was neither naïve nor a fool. He had made no demands upon her. If he had done so, she would have repulsed him furiously. She could not expect him to lead a celibate life. Nor should it matter to her what he did.

But it did matter. And to know that he was spending his nights in the arms of that—! She used an expression that would have shocked Maby.

Then she smiled in bitter amusement, only to have the smile die as she remembered the ending to the scene. Useless to say it had been typically arrogant of him to kiss her. And equally useless to deny that she had not allowed it and even enjoyed it. She might just as well have thrown herself at his head!

A hand stole to her cheek as she remembered again his arms around her and his lips, expert and demanding. Then she shook herself angrily.

She had long been aware that she could like Vidal very well. Indeed, she had never met a man she liked as well.

He might be autocratic and too set up in his own conceit, but he treated her as a human being, not as a piece of Dresden china. His temper might be abominable, but her own was fierce, and to his credit he did not hold a grudge and readily admitted it when she had got the better of him.

And if he was cynical, why his sense of humor led him to laugh at himself as often as he laughed at others. Dominique's own deplorable levity often betrayed her at most inopportune moments, but she found she could always count on Vidal to be enjoying the jest as well. And to meet his eyes across a room when some absurd thing occurred, like that ridiculous young Mr. Ffoliott spilling lemonade over his exquisite flowered waistcoat and theatening to call out poor Lord Wainscott, who was as deaf as he was stout, and couldn't understand a word of the ensuing scene. Well, she had soon discovered that without Vidal most entertainments proved sadly flat.

Yes, she liked him very well. But it went no further than that. It *could* go no further than that, she thought in quiet desperation, and resolutely went to find Maby.

When she came downstairs the next morning it was to find Charles Hastings in the hall, his luggage being carried in by the footmen.

"Why, Charles, you are back. Did you enjoy your holiday?"

"Yes, your grace, thank you. I spent most of the time in and about Paris, you know."

She stopped to chat for a few minutes with him about France, which in truth she knew very little better than he did. She liked the open young secretary and had had several enjoyable conversations with him before he left.

As she turned to go he asked if she could spare him a few minutes in the office at her convenience. "I have some documents I need your signature on, ma'am. It won't take much of your time."

She promised to meet him in the office at noon and left him.

A few seconds later he tapped on the library door and entered at Vidal's drawled invitation.

"Ah, Charles. How did you find Paris?" Vidal's lazy eyes twinkled. "Did you enjoy your holiday?"

Charles grinned, but almost immediately sobered. "I hope I've been of some help, sir. It's a pretty complicated situation. The present Marquis de St. Forêt was the youngest of three brothers and only recently came into the title. From what I can gather, the old Marquis was a remarkable old gentleman. Fled during the revolution and succeeded in getting most of his valuables out. Even regained his estates after Napoleon relented and invited the nobility back. But he doesn't seem to have been popular. Village gossip is that even the sons hated him.

"The heir died a few years ago in a hunting accident. The middle son seems to have marrried against the old man's wishes and been disinherited. When his wife died soon after, he took himself off and was never seen again. The old Marquis died last year and the youngest son inherited everything as the last surviving son."

"I see." Vidal's voice was quiet. "Was nothing more known about the disinherited son?"

"Well, the whole thing is rather odd. There seems to have been something strange about the wife's death, though I couldn't find out exactly what. Probably just village gossip. But the old gentleman apparently had a change of heart shortly before he died and tried to find his lost son. Knew he would inherit the title, I guess, and wanted to keep the estates and fortune with it. But he doesn't seem to have had any luck. The man was probably already dead."

"Hmmm." Vidal glanced up. "Very good, Charles. Thank you. I may be forced to give you a real holiday now."

"Yes, sir." Hastings hesitated. "There's one other thing, sir, I think you should know. Someone became very upset by my questions and sent a couple of ruffians to warn me to keep my nose out of business that was no concern of mine. Probably nothing, but I felt I should tell you."

Vidal frowned. "You were quite right." He toyed with his quizzing glass for a moment, then came to a sudden decision. "I think perhaps we should learn a little more about the present Marquis de St. Forêt. See if you can search out a reliable investigator, Charles."

It was shortly after noon that Dominique burst into the library, surprising Vidal at his desk. He looked up calmly, his gray eyes noting her flushed cheeks and sparkling eyes. "Yes, my dear?" he inquired politely.

"Your grace! What is the meaning of this?" She waved a sheaf of papers in agitation.

One eyebrow rose. "Come, ma'am! Control yourself and

tell me what the devil you are in such a temper about!" he said bitingly.

His words had the desired effect. She glared at him, but ceased her restless pacing. "Very well! I wish to know what all these legal documents mean?"

"They are Marriage Settlements, my dear, as you no doubt very well know."

She bit her lip. "I know that! But why?"

"It is usually customary, my dear," he drawled.

"I don't care! I will not have it! I will not! I will refuse to sign!"

She seemed so genuinely upset that he came to her quickly and took her hands in his hard grasp. "Dominique!" He eyed her intently.

"No, no! You will not talk me around this time! I do not want your money!"

His eyes were suddenly bleak. "I am well aware of that, madam!" He almost threw her from him and strode from the room.

She stood in despair in the middle of the room for a very long time. Finally she straightened wearily, glanced almost in surprise at the documents strewn about her, and bent to pick them up. She glanced through them, her face expressionless, then signed them and left them in a neat stack on his desk before slowly climbing the stairs to her room.

Chapter Eleven

Dominique had been correct in assuming that there would be a great deal of speculation about Vidal's sudden marriage to the unknown beauty. But although many sensed a scandal, the truth of the case was kept so well hidden that the majority of the rumors became so fantastic as to be wholly unbelievable, and the talk at last died down for lack of fuel.

Of course the Duchess of Vidal had entree everywhere; every hostess of the Season was eager to obtain her presence. And if some of them were tempted to be a little patronizing to a young lady no one had heard of a month before, they seldom repeated the offense. Lady Sarah saw with relief that Dominique was well able to take care of herself.

Lady Sarah had kindly taken it upon herself to accompany Dominique to these early functions, but she soon saw she might have spared herself the effort. Dominique did not need her support. She met sly innuendoes with unruffled calm, and was fully capable of greeting outright rudeness with a cold hauteur that perfectly conveyed her contempt for such ill-bred behavior. Lady Sarah, full of quiet admiration, thought Vidal hardly deserved his luck.

She worried a little, however, that Dominique might be nursing a secret unhappiness, no matter how good a face she put upon the matter, for Lady Sarah was well acquainted with her sister-in-law's pride and spirit. But when she broached the matter, Dominique only laughed and assured her that she did not mind in the least.

She then grinned impishly and added, "In truth, Sally, it is a lowering thought, but I find I am rather enjoying myself! My wretched sense of humor, you know!" She gave a mock sigh. "I fear I am growing nearly as cynical as Vidal."

As a matter of fact, Lady Sarah very soon discovered that her self-imposed task was not one of unmixed joy. Dominique's manners were just as they should be, and she had a pretty, easy address, but her deplorable levity was apt to surface at the most unexpected times. Lady Sarah began to live in lively dread of what her irrepressible relative would next say.

She could not help being delighted when Dominique was led to give that wretched Mrs. Coombes a much-deserved set-down, for really, she was a dreadful, encroaching woman and had adopted a coy, condescending manner toward Dominique that had even aroused Lady Sarah's gentle temper.

But when Dominique remarked to the Princess Esterhazy, when that lively lady had been kind enough to compliment her on her horsemanship, that she considered the sidesaddle a ridiculous invention designed to break women's necks, and always rode astride in the country, Lady Sarah began to perceive that her position was not going to be an easy one.

Fortunately, the Princess had only been amused and had told Lady Sarah later that Dominique was a delightful young minx. But Lady Sarah feared what her unpredictable brother would have to say if he came to learn of his wife's conduct. He was so lax in his own manners that he might only be amused, but it was also entirely possible that he would expect quite different conduct from his wife and hold Lady Sarah responsible for her lapses.

Lady Sarah, who had held such high hopes for the match, was obliged to admit she did not know what had gone wrong. Dominique, normally the most delightful of companions, took on an intractable look and refused to speak of Vidal, and although Vidal remained outwardly the same, his eyes had assumed a hard look that Lady Sarah did not remember. They seemed to see very little of each other, although Dominique was invariably surrounded by so many admirers that Vidal's absence was hardly noted.

Then one evening Lady Sarah fled from the ballroom at Manton House only to encounter her brother just arriving. She started in dismay and sought to control her features.

Vidal lifted one eyebrow in amusement. "Well, Sally, where are you away in such a hurry? Have you an assignation?"

"Certainly not! I have torn my gown and must repair it."

Vidal looked slowly at her immaculate toilette, and lifted his eyes to her slightly heightened complexion. "Sally, Sally," he said sadly. "Surely you cannot be deserting the field? I had thought better of you." As her lids came down hurriedly to veil her betraying start, he added idly, "Just what has Dominique said now?"

She eyed him in consternation for a moment, then said bluntly, "She has just told Lady Jersey that her father was a fencing master."

She watched his shaking shoulders. "It's very well for you to stand there laughing," she said with considerable asperity, "but really, Justin! What am I to *do* with her!" She paused and then her own lips curved. "Well, I own it w-was funny! I have never seen poor Silence so at a loss for words!"

She dwelt on that pleasing spectacle for a moment, then brusquely recalled herself to a sense of duty. "But Dominique shouldn't have done it. I've no doubt it will be all over town by tomorrow!"

Since Vidal seemed unmoved by this possibility, she started away in irritation, only to turn back as a new thought struck her. "Justin, exactly who *was* Dominique's father? I've often wondered."

"Why, Sally, she told you," Vidal said gently, an unholy light in his eyes. "A fencing master." He strolled away.

Vidal himself was privileged to be present the next time his wife's imp of mischief compelled her. He entered the drawing room of his sister's house unannounced one afternoon, to find several other people seated there.

Lady Penkridge, a large woman given to portentous statements, was just saying that she had never been so relieved in her life as at the news that that Monster Napoleon had been secured at last.

"Although I doubt I shall really feel safe again until he is dead! I don't think any Christian lady dared sleep soundly in her bed knowing that he and his monsters were loose again! Penkridge armed all the servants, and himself kept watch during the height of the danger."

She was extremely proud of her only son, a staid and rather conventional young man, and spoke with maternal complacency. "I don't know what I would have done if I had not had him to lean upon."

Miss Penkridge, a lively young lady in her first Season, made the mistake of blurting, "Yes, and Soames nearly shot him one night mistaking him for a French soldier!" and received a quelling look from her mama.

"I know *you* must agree with me, dear Duchess," Lady Penkridge said with an arch look for Dominique.

Dominique shrugged. "Why, certainly, ma'am. I have been places, however, where it scarcely mattered what uniform the soldiers wore."

Lady Penkridge smiled coyly. "You cannot mean, I am persuaded, that the people were not happy to see *our* soldiers arrive?"

"Why, I suppose they were. But to the poor people and the peasants, it makes little difference who wins the war, you know. Their fields are trampled and their food stolen no matter which troops are marching through."

Lady Penkridge bridled. "I do not think you mean to imply that British soldiers did such things!"

"All troops are hungry, ma'am," Dominique said gently. "And they are hardly particular where they conduct their battles or how many civilians may be accidentally harmed. You here in England can know little of war, I think. And I hope you may never have to."

"And I suppose you do, dear Duchess?" Lady Penkridge tittered angrily.

Dominique glanced up at that moment to find Vidal's eyes upon her, and she colored a little, but lifted her chin. "Yes, I do, Lady Penkridge. I was in Portugal and Spain during the war, and the people welcomed the British soldiers as they had done the French before them, but they still buried their valuables and hid their daughters."

Lady Penkridge's face was alarmingly red, but her daughter, blithely unaware of her mother's mood, said breathlessly, "Why, ma'am! You were actually in Portugal? Did you see the Iron Duke?"

After a moment the fire left Dominique's eyes, and she answered calmly and even told several amusing stories about Wellington and the troops in Lisbon, and the moment was glossed over.

The guests left shortly afterward. Lady Sarah looked from Vidal to Dominique and made a valiant effort to engage Vidal's attention.

He answered her readily enough, but as soon as there was a lull in the conversation, said, "Are you leaving now, my love? I will escort you home," and bid a polite but firm farewell to his sister.

He helped Dominique into his phaeton without a word and climbed in beside her, then signaled Hollings to stand back. She did not miss the significance of that and said flippantly, "Oh, very wise, sir! It is always difficult to do proper justice to your feelings when there is a third party present!"

"I would advise you not to attempt to vent your temper on me, my girl!" he said drily. "I am not quite as easy a mark as Lady Penkridge."

She bit her lip in vexation and glanced at him out of the corner of her eyes. After a moment she said frankly, "Very well, sir. I admit that was ill done of me. I am sorry if I embarrassed Lady Sarah. I will try to guard my tongue in future."

He smiled quizzically down at her. "I hope not too closely, little one. I would find life very dull then."

She stared suspiciously at him, but he only laughed, and after a moment she lapsed into silence. As he helped her down from the carriage, though, he retained his light clasp on her hand. She looked up a little shyly.

"I hope someday you will tell me about your travels, Dominique. I would enjoy it very much," he said quietly, then bowed and left her.

Despite these occasional lapses, it soon became apparent that Lady Sarah's prophecy had been exactly right. Dominique quickly became the most talked about beauty in London. Her simple good taste was almost universally applauded, and she was credited with causing at least several in the ranks of the young ladies to reduce the number of ribbons, lace and jewels used to bedeck their gowns. And if she rode rather too dashing a mount, and drove herself in a racing curricle, why it was generally acknowledged that she was a nonpareil, and gentlemen clamored for the privilege of being taken up beside her for a turn about the park.

To be sure, there were certain ladies who considered her fast, and complained of her frank manners and odd humor, but they no doubt had been put out of countenance by her marriage and meteoric success. The general consensus held her to be a beautiful young woman with spirit and dash, all of which she would need to keep Vidal in line.

Dominique herself was forced to admit that, whatever their reasons, people were wondrously kind to her. Her time was filled from morning to night with entertainments, and the number of admirers seeking to drive out with her or leaving floral tributes with an impassive Lymings increased daily.

And if she sometimes grew a little tired of the ridiculous flattery and the idle people about her, and longed for her simple life and the freedom of her breeches, why it was only very occasionally and did not last long. For the moment she was content not to delve too closely into her feelings or her future.

Vidal was at last moved to complain lightly to his friend Carleton that he could never enter his house anymore without being accosted by some love-sick puppy with a billet-doux wrapped up in ribbons.

Carleton laughed. "Yes, she is certainly the rage. Several ladies have been moved to emulate her skill with the ribbons, with disastrous results, and there's no getting near her at balls. It has become a mark of distinction to be taken up beside her in her curricle. Even Lady Jersey told me she found her delightful and considered her the freshest personality to hit London in years." He grinned. "I am only thankful I can trade upon my position as an old family friend, or I should be quite cut out!"

"So she's bowled you over too, eh, John?"

Lord Carleton's eyes became suddenly serious and he did not rise to his friend's bantering tone. "I am very fond of her, Justin," he said quietly. "I—" He colored slightly. "I know you will tell me to go to the devil, with justification, but I feel I must speak. Don't you think you're letting this thing go too far?"

He ignored Vidal's stiffened posture and went on doggedly. "There is bound to be talk when you allow your wife to be always surrounded by love-sick puppies, as you call them. I think Dominique is very careful to single no one out so there can be no real food for gossip, but I think it's time you sent most of those puppies about their business and paid a little attention to your wife," he said bluntly.

Vidal gave a crack of laughter. "Would you have me compete publicly for my wife's affection?" he snapped.

"I think you should know her better than that," Carleton said quietly.

Vidal's eyes narrowed. "Good God! She *has* bowled you over!"

Carleton regarded him steadily, and his tone was hard.

"You insult us both, your grace!" He turned on his heel and left him.

Vidal's mood was not improved by encountering Lady Sarah emerging from a shop a few minutes later.

"Oh, Vidal! The very person I wished to see. I must tell you I have been considering giving a Venetian breakfast, but Ambersley says he will refuse to attend anything held at such an ungodly hour! Now isn't that just like him! I depend upon you to talk him around."

"You had much better depend upon my wife!" he uttered savagely. "She appears to have the whole town in her hip pocket! Your servant, ma'am!" He bowed and stalked off.

Lady Sarah watched him go, a smile deep in her eyes, and hurried home to tell her Richard that Vidal was caught at last.

Ambersley had to smile at his wife's obvious delight in her brother's fate. "But I think you are too optimistic, my love," he said. "I agree he likes her well enough—how could he help it? But I can't say he appears to have reformed in any way." Lord Ambersley knew well the sacrifices entailed in marrying a loving and determined woman, and thought Vidal might still be a bachelor for all the concessions he had yet made to his married state.

"You mean Lady Caroline, no doubt! Of course he has refused to change! And it's got him in such a temper I thought he would snap my nose off just now!" Her eyes twinkled merrily. "I knew Dominique could handle him!" she added cryptically, and went off into peals of laughter at his bewildered expression.

Whatever Vidal's thoughts were on the subject, it was suddenly to be seen that he could be found at a number of events he might normally have been expected to scorn. On the first of these occasions he entered a ballroom to find his wife the center of a laughing circle disputing the right to lead her to the floor for the waltz.

Her suddenly self-conscious swains gave way before him and he clasped her wrist lightly. "My dance, I believe, my dear."

Her color was slightly heightened, but she allowed him to lead her to the floor.

He surveyed her gown of golden silk that showed to advantage the lovely swell of her breasts and her creamy shoulders. "Very lovely, my dear. You always know exactly which color will set off your hair and eyes and skin to perfection."

She blushed, but lifted her eyes to his. "Why, thank you, sir," she said lightly. "I believe you are generally held to be an arbiter of female beauty. I am flattered indeed.

"I do not usually see you at affairs of this type," she continued easily. "Are you by any chance assuring yourself I am behaving properly, your grace?"

"Not at all, my love," he answered gently, and pulled her closer.

When the dance ended, he thanked her politely and left her. He stayed a moment to drink a glass of champagne with his hostess, then quietly left.

Dominique soon became accustomed to finding him at such events. He seldom stood up with her more than once, or remained long at any of them. But she had often to chide herself for the sudden joy she experienced at the sight of his tall figure coming toward her, and stifle a pang when her eyes could no longer find him in the crowded room.

He began to accompany her occasionally on her morning rides as well, and people became accustomed to seeing his dark head bent to hers in the park, or riding in her curricle. Some took malicious delight in seeing the notorious Vidal humbled at last, while others, who had perhaps cherished secret hopes of their own, deplored the bad *ton* of a husband and wife carring on in such a disgusting manner in public.

But although Vidal found Dominique very willing to dance with him, walk with him, ride with him and not even averse to a light flirtation, she maintained a reserve he could never quite break through. She let him see she found pleasure in his company, but did not seem to prefer it to any of a dozen others of her court.

He commented upon this one day as they drove toward Richmond in his phaeton. He had only prevailed upon her to come by promising to let her tool the bays. When they had reached the outskirts of London he handed her the reins, remarking, "Mind the off-horse. He has a tendency to shy at gateposts."

She wisely ignored this reflection on her driving skill and concentrated on controlling the spirited team.

"You are a strange child, Dominique. Are you this elusive with all your beaux?" His eyes on her lovely profile.

She merely laughed, her eyes busy on the road ahead.

"Why do you come out with me?" he asked curiously.

"Why, your grace, my reputation, of course," she replied promptly. "My credit could never survive it being said I could not hold the attention of Vidal! Were you seen to have grown tired of me, I would not boast one admirer inside a week!"

"Surely you underestimate the devotion of your followers."

"Why as to that," she answered lightly, "I believe there are some who are genuinely fond of me. But since I am considered very fashionable at the moment, you must know it lends considerable cachet to be numbered amongst my court!"

She glanced at him out of the corner of her eye. "I am perfectly aware you have taken it upon yourself to reduce my . . . er . . . following, sir. But you need not have worried. In six months' time society's fancy will have lit upon someone else and I shall be relegated to the ranks of the matrons. So you see," she added kindly, "you can go back to your clubs."

But for some reason Vidal did not avail himself of her kind permission. They were often to be found together, and Dominique gave herself up to the pleasure she found in his company, but kept herself tightly in check.

On one such occasion Lady Caroline was among a party of horsemen when the Duke and Duchess of Vidal rode past. Dominique was looking particularly enchanting in a habit of dark green velvet, and he was laughing at something in a way that changed his saturnine face for a moment, making him appear younger and almost gay.

"By Jove!" young Wentworth exclaimed. "Don't they make a pair!"

"Oh, aye," someone else said. "Whoever'd thought we'd see Vidal dance attendance on any female, let alone his wife!"

There were several other ill-natured jests and not a few sidelong glances at Lady Caroline. She, well aware of those looks, managed to laugh with the rest and temporarily allay a few suspicions. But her position just now was not an easy one.

It had been an open secret in London that she intended to marry Vidal, and since she was not universally popular, a great many people were taking malicious delight in her present discomfiture. It was but another payment she owed Dominique, and she was keeping very careful score.

Their party had dismounted and were engaged in conversation with a walking party they had encountered, and for a moment she allowed her eyes to rest on the retreating backs of Vidal and his wife.

A charmingly accented voice spoke in her ear. "Somehow I do not think you join in the general appreciation of my young countrywoman, Lady Caroline."

She turned sharply to survey a man of medium height and build whose clothes conveyed a slightly tendency toward dandyism. There was nothing of that in his face, however. He wore a slightly weary air that was not unattractive, and although she guessed him to be in his mid-forties, he was still a very handsome man. She smoothed the frown from her face.

"You know my name, sir, but I do not believe we have met . . . ?" She allowed a slight question in her throaty voice.

He bowed with great charm. "Alas, no, madame, but I have been at your feet since first I saw you."

She was no fool, and her eyes narrowed. He spoke with practiced gallantry, but there was something in his eyes that told her his thoughts were elsewhere. She took a closer look at him. "But there is something very familiar about you, monsieur. Perhaps we have met after all?"

"No, I do not think so, *ma chère madame*. I could not have forgotten such an occasion." He proffered his arm, a questioning look in his eyes. "Shall we walk?"

She hesitated, then gave her reins into her groom's hands and accepted his arm. After a moment she remarked idly, "Perhaps you know her family, sir? You must know there is a great deal of speculation about our charming but somewhat mysterious new duchess."

He laughed softly. "Let us say that I am not unfamiliar with her circumstances, dear ma'am."

She could get no more from him. He led her to a bench set a little apart and somewhat shaded by hedges, and seated himself beside her.

She laughed drily. "Somehow, monsieur, I do not think it is to enjoy the pleasure of my company that you have led me to this somewhat . . . clandestine spot. Just what is it you wish of me?"

He smiled, his eyes intent upon her. "My dear Lady Caroline, you do yourself an injustice. You tempt me very much indeed. Almost I wish—but no, it cannot be!" He sighed and shrugged his shoulders in Gallic regret. "Then let us talk business. I can see that you are a very *perspicace*—how do you say?—a very shrewd young woman, my dear. I think perhaps we can be of assistance to each other."

She raised delicate brows. "Why, sir, you surprise me. I was not under the impression I needed any assistance."

"Come, Lady Caroline!" A smile played about his mouth. "I think we understand each other very well. I do not think it would displease you if a certain young lady were to . . . let us say . . . return to her own country," he suggested softly.

She lifted suddenly hard blue eyes and did not pretend to misunderstand him. "I do not think that would accomplish a great deal from my standpoint, sir. Perhaps you are forgetting that they are married?"

There was genuine admiration in his eyes. "Ah, yes. My compliments, Lady Caroline. I had somewhat underestimated you. Let us say, then, that perhaps an accident might befall her. So very sad for such a beautiful young woman, but these things do sometimes happen. I have no doubt the grieving husband would very soon turn to his former love. Hmmm, Lady Caroline?" His eyes were mocking.

She smiled provocatively. "And just what is your interest in this, monsieur?" Then as his smile broadened she added in a very different tone, "Come, let us cease this game! I am sure it has occurred to you that as Duchess of Vidal I would naturally be very rich. But it seems to me you would be taking a considerable risk on an outcome that I'll admit is probable, but by no means certain. I have no doubt you are thoroughly familiar with my affairs, so you must know *I* have scarcely a penny to my name!" She smiled derisively. "Nor do I think you would undertake such a . . . er . . . commission . . . for the sake of my *beaux yeux*. I repeat, monsieur, what have you to gain?"

"Ah, what a pair we would have made, *ma chère!* I think I must be a little jealous of the noble *Duc*." He was laughing openly at her now and dark color stained her cheeks.

He lifted a careless finger to caress her chin. "Do not be angry with me, *petite*. I think I shall keep my secrets. Let us say only that the fair Dominique is a distant relation I would . . . er . . . prefer not to recognize, hmmm?"

She smiled spitefully. "Perhaps not so distant, after all. I believe I have already remarked on the resemblance!"

"My compliments, *chérie*. You continue to amaze me. I think . . . hmmm? . . . that we shall deal admirably toogether. Allow me to introduce myself. Gervaise, Marquis de St. Forêt, at your service!" He raised her hand to his lips.

Chapter Twelve

And so the weeks passed. Vidal continued to seek out his bride in public, seemingly impervious to the gossip he was arousing, and she alone knew how little there was to the rumors. Indeed, she sometimes suspected that his vanity had been wounded, and he had deliberately set himself to make her fall in love with him. But since she had no intention of accommodating him on that score, however easy it may have been to do so, she kept a tight rein on her emotions and refused to give in to his undeniable charm.

It was perhaps fortunate for her peace of mind, however, that while Vidal's manner was attentive, teasing and even provocative on occasion, and he had begun to allow his eyes to rest upon her in a lazy intimacy that was difficult to resist, he made no attempt to change the terms of their relationship. She, who had set those terms, might sometimes suspect that the initiative had passed to him and he would alter them exactly when it suited him to do so; but she had nevertheless to be thankful for his unexpected forbearance.

But despite every resolve to show Vidal how very little her happiness depended upon him, the Season began to pall on her after a very little while. She was an acknowledged Toast, her admirers grew apace and she often had the felicity of choosing between half a dozen cards of invitation each night. But, perversely, she found herself oddly discontent and more than a little bored. A small unwelcome voice whispered to her that were she not little more than an impostor foisted upon Vidal—and the world, as well—under totally false colors, things might have been very different.

But they were not, so that even the novelty of hearing her beauty praised endlessly in bad poetry and having verses dedicated to her left eyebrow soon lost the power to amuse her. If she could only have shared such ridiculous flights of fancy with Vidal, for she had a pretty shrewd notion what his opinion of such nonsense would be—! But of course she could not. They were not on such terms of intimacy that she might share the jest of poems about the green of her eyes with Vidal, however tolerant he had shown himself to be.

There was the ball at Lady Sefton's tonight. She found herself dreading it. She was just a trifle moped, of course, and it had nothing whatever to do with the fact that she knew Vidal was not to be there. Nevertheless, when Bates inquired about the gown she desired that night, she found herself telling Bates she did not mean to go. She had a slight headache and was not in the mood for dancing. She would go to bed early with a book.

Thus it was that at a quarter after eight Vidal entered his library to find her perched halfway up the library steps, turning over the pages of a novel.

She started as the door closed quietly behind him. "Oh! You startled me. I did not expect to see you this evening, sir."

He observed her simple muslin gown. "Are you not going out this evening, my dear?" he asked in surprise.

"Well, in truth, I was just a little bored with everything and thought I'd spend a quiet evening at home, for a change," she said lightly.

His eyebrows rose. "Have your conquests palled so quickly, my dear?" Then when she colored he said suddenly, "No, forgive me. It is an excellent idea. May I not join you?"

She regarded him in sudden confusion. "I believed you were engaged to dine elsewhere this evening."

"I am! But I'll gladly consign 'em to the devil if you'll join me for supper here before the fire," he replied promptly.

She laughed, but her eyes were wary.

He moved to stand below her and held out his hand, his eyes quizzing her. "Coward!" he chided softly.

She hesitated a moment longer, then laid her fingers in his. "Shall I change, sir,"

"Oh, by all means. Shall we say . . . nine o'clock?"

She chose to wear a new soft white gauze she had been saving for a special occasion. The gown clung revealingly to her figure and gave her a deceptive air of fragility. She studied herself in the mirror and firmly refused to examine her motives. When Bates produced the emeralds she hesitated only a second before defiantly allowing them to be clasped about her neck. Then she smiled a little grimly and descended the stairs.

Vidal was awaiting her at the foot of the stairs. His eyes rested on her for a moment before he smiled and drew her into the library. As he had promised, a small table had been set before the fire, but he poured her a glass of champagne and did not seat her yet at the table, but in a wing chair instead.

"Let us talk a little first," he said lightly, lifting his glass to her in a silent toast. "I must admit I have always thought the worst thing about marriage was that two people soon grew so intolerably bored with one another, but it seems we seldom see each other. Or have you been avoiding me?"

She had, a little. She laughed quickly, a tinkling, not very genuine sound. "Ah, your grace, I must take care you continue to feel so. Wives, I understand, are like caviar: They become quickly surfeit. Your sentiment, is it not? Or have I the quote wrong?"

If she expected to discomfit him she was disappointed. He bowed. "Your hit, I believe, my dear!" His eyes were full of laughter.

She too smiled a little recklessly and drank more of her champagne.

He refilled her glass. "I am sure I need not tell you that you have proven me completely wrong," he said softly. "You must know how much pleasure I derive from your company."

She lifted her head sharply. She was on edge, distrustful of him in this softened mood, and very much on the defensive. "But then you have always enjoyed a challenge!"

He raised his glass in acknowledgment. "I think we have that in common," he said. "Did I tell you how beautiful you look tonight, my dear? But then you always do, don't you? I think you must be well aware that half the men in London are in love with you."

She frowned lightly. "Ah, but you Englishmen think very little of love! You make a plaything of it, a pleasant way to occupy a few weeks only. Then it is forgotten."

"And are you different, Dominique?"

"Yes," she whispered, almost to herself. Then she caught herself and lifted her head. "Do you wish to know if I have taken lovers, your grace? You must have wondered.

The French are notorious for their amours, are they not?" She spoke flippantly.

"I do not have to ask, my love," he said quietly. "I know you have not."

Despite herself her eyes searched his face. "Y-you cannot know that, sir."

He smiled a little whimsically. "My love, why do you persist in thinking me a fool? I have only to look into your eyes to know you have no lovers." When she would have looked hastily away his fingers lifted her chin and he laughed softly. For one timeless moment she was held in his gaze, her breath coming unevenly. Then he released her negligently and said in a quite different voice, "Are you enjoying the Season, my dear?"

So. The game was to go on. She managed to reply in a tone that matched his own. "Why, certainly, sir. I would be very difficult to please indeed if I—" She broke off abruptly at his sharply indrawn breath. "What is it, sir?"

He sighed. "Nothing my dear. Only I have the strangest wish that one night we might dispense with the forbidding Miss Forrester of my earliest acquaintance, and the very charming but equally forbidding Dutchess of Vidal, and I might have instead my scapegrace Dominique back again." He eyed her suddenly still expression. "Are you afraid of me, Dominique?"

"I—Yes, sir," she said simply.

His expression was unreadable. "Of me, or of both of us?" he asked quietly.

But that she would not answer. She kept her eyes firmly on the bubbles in her glass.

"Very well, my love!" He was laughing at her. "Let us have Miss Forrester back again, then. Of the two I think I prefer her. She is proud and stubborn and has an abominable temper, but she at least is not polite and sophisticated and wholly unapproachable."

She looked up in dismay. "Have I been as bad as that, sir?"

"No, child. Perhaps only to me because I know you so well. You see, I could not help longing for my old Dominique. And I do not think you have been very happy in your role of *femme du monde*."

She sighed. "No, sir."

"Is it that you still dislike the people?"

"I—I never disliked them, sir." She twisted the stem of her glass. "And everyone has been marvelously kind to me. Only sometimes it seems that they all have too much money and too little to do. I do not think many of them even like themselves very much, let alone each other."

"And do I fall into that category, Dominique?" he asked gently.

She drew a deep breath and raised her eyes. "Sally told me once that you have been frightfully spoiled, your grace, and I think it is perhaps true. You have everything you could possibly want, and so you do not value any of it very much. And you are bored."

"I do not have everything I want, my love," he murmured wryly. "Not everything . . ."

She glanced up, a question in her eyes, then colored. "I should not have said that, of course. Especially after my own behavior the past months. I wasted little time in adapting myself to luxury and pleasure." She smiled a little bitterly. "But Maby was right, all those years ago. Money cannot buy happiness. What a ridiculous thing to learn at my age."

He did not smile. "Is it our marriage that makes you unhappy, Dominique?" he asked quietly.

She studied her glass for a moment before proffering it for more champagne. "Ah, I have learned many things since coming here! Champagne for courage!" Her smile was a little crooked.

His eyes remained steady upon her. After a moment she shook her head and answered slowly, almost against her will. "I don't know, sir. I will not lie to you and tell you that I had any desire to become a governess . . ." She smiled momentarily at the sudden humor in his eyes. "I knew too, that I was not—not suited to the position. Nor can I deny that I like to wear beautiful clothes and jewels and be admired." She made an effort to lighten the conversation. "In fact, I have gained a very great deal! I think it is you that is unhappy."

"Will you believe me if I tell you that I do not regret our marriage?"

She shook her head and said frankly, "I hardly think it can be true, sir. You are only being gallant."

He burst out laughing. "Oh, Dominique! When have you ever known me to be gallant!"

Then he turned his head. "Yes, Lymings, we will eat now. Perhaps you might leave everything and we can serve ourselves later."

She had not heard Lymings enter, but then Vidal's servants were always so well trained one hardly knew they were there. She watched as the table was set and then accepted the chair Vidal held for her.

His eyes shone wickedly. "This is quite like old times, my dear. I can never quite decide when it was you first intrigued me most. The night in the cottage when you accepted me so trustingly and I put you to bed, or the next night when the candle made your hair copper as it is tonight and you defied me so fiercely, your eyes the color of emeralds." His voice had grown pensive.

Her color rose, but she laughed. "What a whisker! The first night you wished yourself anywhere else, though you strove valiantly to conceal the fact, and the next night you were resigned to your fate and scarcely saw me. And both nights you thought me a fool and despised me for the cause of your problems."

She had meant only to stop his ridiculous flattery, but his eyes darkened and he frowned a little, and she regretted her hasty words. "I am sorry, sir. I did not mean to—"

"But then perhaps it is true. I told you once that you have a very chastening effect upon me, my dear." He shrugged lightly. "But let us talk of something else. You promised once to tell me about your travels."

She was so glad to turn the subject that she talked less guardedly than she would normally have done. She told him several amusing anecdotes of her early scrapes and Maby's difficulties with the life of a vagabond.

She did not realize how revealingly she had spoken until he said suddenly, "But what about your father? He seems to have figured very little in your life."

She smiled. "Maby would agree with you, I'm afraid. She and my father never saw eye to eye on the responsibilities of a parent."

"You once called him *pauvre papa,*" he remarked idly.

She looked surprised. "Did I? When was that?"

He did not enlighten her, and after a moment she went on slowly, "Well, Papa and I had an excellent understanding, but he *was* rather like a child. He was gay and carefree, you see, and did not manage very well, so that

I learned early that I must take charge or things were apt not to be done. But he did not interfere too much with me, so we got along excellently."

If Vidal thought this was a strange relationship between father and daughter he did not say so.

She grinned suddenly. "I must admit that after Maby came we had meals on a regular schedule and I lost certain of my freedoms. But she was the closest to a mother I ever had, so I made the change willingly."

"Why did your father never marry again?"

"Papa enjoyed the ladies far too much! He was a shocking flirt, you know!" Her eyes twinkled merrily. "He almost did marry once, but the lady called it off at the last moment and he was so relieved he became quite a reformed character for nearly six months!

"I used to think it was because of *Maman,* and wove a great romance about them: that he was so heartbroken after her death that he could never love another woman. I suppose that was because he would never speak of her. But the sad truth was that he was forever falling in love with women, only to fall out of love with them in a fortnight. He did not seem to care for anything very much."

Her eyes became clouded. "I think there was only one thing he cared about, but I did not understand that until too late . . ." Her smile was twisted, but then she looked up abruptly and shook her head, saying self-consciously, "Ah, pray forgive me! It is very boring to hear someone prose on forever about people you do not know. Tell me about your family."

He laughed. "I don't think I dare after that."

"What—? Oh! You know very well what I mean!"

So he told her about his childhood at WainCourt; one of too many servants and too large a house and a rather stern father who died when he was nineteen.

His mother had died soon after Sally was born, and the difference in their ages had been too great for them to have been very good companions. Vidal had been sent to boarding schools at an early age, and it seemed to Dominique that his life had been composed of discipline and training to prepare him for the position he would one day hold, and very little love or warmth. She at least had had Maby, and she found herself feeling pity for the lonely boy he must have been.

Some of that must have shown in her face, for he said

wickedly, "Why, if I had known my past would have this softening effect upon you I would have told you long ago. Are you imagining me a young boy unloved and unwanted? It was quite otherwise, I assure you. My life was surrounded by people who placed my well-being and comfort uppermost. I often wished them at the devil and myself an orphan, believe me!"

/ She was not convinced, but said nothing more. And when a few minutes later the clock struck midnight, she looked up in surprise and excused herself shortly afterward. Vidal made no demur, merely lifting her hands to his lips, then watching her as she climbed the stairs to her room. She resolutely did not look back.

A sleepy Bates awaited her and she allowed herself to be undressed, but she could not sit still when Bates would have brushed her hair and sent her away. She moved restlessly around the room, her thoughts chaotic and disturbing, filled with a vague longing she did not understand. Or perhaps she understood it too well.

When the door opened she was standing staring into the fire. She lifted her head slowly, as if it were somehow inevitable that he should be there.

She did not move as Vidal closed the door behind him and came toward her. Only as his hands closed on her shoulders did she move, but by then it was too late. His hands pulled her inexorably to him.

She met his eyes. "Vidal—! Justin—! Please—?" She did not care that for the moment she was not too proud to beg.

His eyes searched her face for a long moment before he bent his head to hers. His arms held her ever tighter, and his lips parted hers as her body lost its tension and at last strained to his. When he lifted his head her eyes felt heavy and her lips bruised from his kiss.

His eyes played over her face and then moved slowly downward. He bent his head again and his lips caressed her ear, her throat, the hollow between her breasts. He buried his face in the mass of her hair and then his hand lowered the soft silk of her gown over her shoulder and his lips found her breast.

At that she regained some of her wits and tried to pull away. He held her and his eyes contained an expression she had never seen there before. Tenderness? "No, no, my darling," he said softly. "I have been very

patient, but now I think I must have you." His hand
swept the tumbled hair from her face and he laughed, a
bare whisper of sound. "I want you, and you are mine!"

She could only stare at him, her senses reeling from
the unexpected passion he had aroused in her. All her
carefully constructed defenses were nothing in the face of
this feeling between them.

"Ah, do not glower so at me with your witch's eyes!
Your body betrays you, my love!" he said triumphantly,
and swept her into his arms.

Then he looked down at her and his eyes grew serious.
"Yes, I know I am a brute to take advantage of your
momentary weakness. I know you will hate me in the
morning. But tonight you will love me . . .." He lowered
her to the silken coverlet.

Much later she woke to his touch again. But where
before he had been compelling and demanding, now he
was gentle and coaxing and caressing, moving her to
madness. She sighed his name and moved her body to
meet his.

When she awoke again it was late morning and he
was gone. But the pillow beside her still bore the imprint
of his head. She felt herself blushing like a silly schoolgirl
and reached hurriedly for her nightgown, now lying neatly
at the foot of her bed. She had certainly betrayed little
maidenly modesty last night!

On the tray with her morning chocolate reposed a
single white rose. The card held two words in Vidal's
black scrawl: "Until tonight."

Her hand threw the card to the table, but then almost
immediately picked up the rose to cradle it against her
cheek. Then disgusted with herself, she rose and rang
for Bates.

She spent the day in struggle with herself and grateful
that she did not meet Vidal. In an age where young ladies
were innocent and inclined to vapors, she had displayed
an ardor that surprised herself almost as much as it must
have surprised Vidal. She thought he must be disgusted
with her, and wavered between fear that he would come
to her tonight and fear that he would not.

That night she purposely kept Bates later than usual,
brushing and braiding her hair, selecting a gown for the
next evening, discussing the clasp to her pearls which was

becoming loose. But she might as well have spared herself the effort. When Vidal entered, his mocking smile was very much in evidence. "Thank you, Bates!" he said firmly, and held the door for her.

When the dresser, her eyes carefully downcast, had left the room he leaned negligently against the door, his eyes gleaming wickedly. "Ah, my love! Surely you did not think that would deter me!"

She glared at him.

He spoke softly. "You have only to tell me truthfully you do not wish me to stay."

"I do not wish you to stay!" she flashed.

"Little liar!" He made it a caress.

Her eyes widened angrily. "Why, yes! I should no doubt be flattered that you choose to come to me, even if it may be straight from the arms of your mistress!"

In an instant he had crossed the room to her and his hand had forced her chin up. "If you mean Caroline Graham, which I assume you must, I broke off my relationship with her weeks ago."

"Weeks ago! But—!" She quickly clamped her lips shut.

"You should pay less attention to malicious gossip, my dear!" he observed righteously.

"You flatter yourself, your grace!"

"You called me Justin last night," he murmured provocatively, giving it her French pronunciation.

"You are a—a—" Furiously she groped for a word.

His lips quirked. "A what? Cad? Rakehell? Libertine?" he prompted helpfully.

"Yes! All of them!"

His face was very near. "And shall I tell you what you are, my sweet torment?" he murmured.

Still she resisted him. And when he would have pulled her into his arms she stiffened and turned her head away.

Gently he turned her face to him, his eyes suddenly serious. "Do not ever be afraid of your response to me, Dominique," he said quietly.

She closed her eyes. "I—"

"Shh," he said, his lips against hers.

Chapter Thirteen

But Vidal, pursuing his elusive bride very much in earnest now—whether out of pique, or some other emotion— had very soon to acknowledge that he had once again underestimated her fierce pride. He could not regret their new intimacy since it had shown him a side of Dominique as captivating as it was unexpected; but if he had thought to force her into declaring herself, he was doomed to disappointment. She might continue to meet him in public with unimpaired friendliness, but he saw with chagrin that she had withdrawn into herself as surely as if she had closed a door in his face. She had been on her guard with him before, but now she was almost totally unapproachable, and treated him so politely when they met that he had difficulty sometimes in not giving in to the desire to shake her.

He did not, but only because it had long ago occurred to him that his tiresome love was not nearly as indifferent to him as she would have him believe. He knew her far too well to suppose she could have responded so enchantingly to his love-making if her affections had not been very much engaged. Nor had his critical eyes failed to notice that she seemed not to be enjoying her customary spirits.

But while he might be confident of the eventual outcome, he was aware of an increasing wish that she might trust him enough to tell him the truth at last. That she did not, despite every opportunity he had given her to do so, rankled more than he liked to admit. Nor could he help wondering whether it was pride alone that kept her silent, or some other, more compelling reason.

He had no problem in understanding how difficult it must have seemed to one of her spirit to admit, once the ring was on her finger, that she had lied to him from the very beginning. But he did not believe she was either a fool or a coward, and it must surely have occurred to her long since that to lie to your husband about such a thing was hardly excusable. He sometimes wondered cynically whether she ever meant to tell him the truth.

He might have been less concerned if he could have known that Dominique was every bit as conscious of the invidiousness of her position as Vidal could have wished. She had stopped even denying to herself that she was deeply in love with him, and it had long ago occurred to her that she might now be oddly content, if only it were not for the wretched pride that had prevented her from disclosing the truth when it might still have been possible to do so.

But now, however much she might wish she had never been led to embark upon such a course, it was far too late to turn back. She was not naïve enough to believe that Vidal was deeply in love with her. She knew he was not. But they got on well enough, and he was not indifferent to her. Indeed, what was perhaps more important in a man of Vidal's experience, she thought he liked her very well. While it was not the emotion she desired from him, it could have been enough.

But however much Vidal might like her, that liking would never survive his discovery that she had deceived him from the moment they met. He might in the end forgive her, but he would never trust her again, and any affection he had held for her would be extinguished forever. She thought she could endure almost anything except seeing his eyes, so often teasing and affectionate now when they rested upon her, assume that cold arrogant mask they had worn at their first meeting.

No, she could not tell him the truth. It only remained for her to make certain he never guessed exactly how much her heart had been involved.

So while Vidal might suspect that his bride was lacking her usual blooming color, she took very good care he should not know how close she was to being blue-deviled. She was not Papa's daughter for nothing, and she did not wear her heart on her sleeve.

And since she had only herself to blame for her misery, after all, it would have been nonsensical to allow herself to fall into the mopes. Hearts did not really break, however much they might feel like it, and life went on very much as usual. Even if she had been inclined to brood, she was given very little opportunity, between the routs and balls and theater parties, and Lady Sarah forever popping in with some agreeable scheme or another. Maby was even begining to complain that Dominique was burning herself to the socket with all this racketing around and had not spent two nights at home in weeks.

But Dominique, having no desire for the leisure in which to think, could only be grateful at being kept busy, and firmly refused to dwell on the future. And if she sometimes realized that she could not continue forever to hide her head in the sand, she managed to push that thought aside as well.

Not until the letter arrived did she at last realize how foolish she had been to think she could escape the past forever.

She had come down to breakfast a little earlier than usual one morning, having an engagement to ride in the park with Carleton. Carleton offered her a friendship that was as kind as it was undemanding, and more and more she had come to rely upon his escort in place of the more importunate of her admirers.

Because of the earliness of the hour, she had the breakfast room to herself, and she glanced through her morning's post while she sipped at her tea. Finding nothing there to interest her among the usual assortment of invitations and tradesmen's bills, she had nearly thrown it aside to take up the *Morning Gazette,* when her eye was caught by an envelope that had been placed on the bottom of the stack and had escaped her notice.

She frowned at her name inscribed in large block letters, and curiously picked it up. There was no return address and, since it had come through the medium of the penny post, nothing to betray the sender.

Puzzled, but by no means alarmed, she spread out the single sheet. Then as her eyes moved down the brief message, she started and the color drained abruptly from her face.

I feel certain her grace is aware of the number of persons who would be extremely interested in learning the true identity of the lovely new Duchess of Vidal. If her grace would care to take steps to avoid such an unpleasant eventuality, perhaps she would consent to meet me at No. 10 Maiden Lane at three o'clock today. She should be alone.

She stared blankly at the letter for a very long time, her brain numb. She did not even wonder how she had come to be found out after all this time. She had always known that there was the possibility someone would turn up sooner or later who had known her father and would recognize her.

It would almost have been laughable, of course, if it were not all so unbelievably dreadful. She had never cared whether the world should come to learn of her identity and enjoy a few weeks of scandal at her expense.

But Vidal must never find out the truth by hearing his wife's name bandied about on the lips of malicious gossips.

She was only recalled to her surroundings at last by a slight sound behind her, and then she barely had time to thrust the letter into the pocket of her riding habit before Miss Mabington came bustling in, apologizing for oversleeping, and full of her plans for the day.

Maby chatted throughout breakfast of household matters, and if Dominique was aware of very little that was said, she at least managed to respond sufficiently to keep from arousing Maby's suspicions. Maby had settled into her new life with amazing ease, and was frankly overjoyed at the opportunity to exercise her considerable housekeeping skills in Vidal's large and well-appointed household. She had become unflagging in her devotion to routing out pockets of neglect and was unimpressed by the credentials of Mrs. Bundy, Vidal's housekeeper.

That poor unfortunate might have been wary at first of Vidal's new bride, but she very soon learned who was her real rival. But since she was by far the weaker personality, she could only trail jealously along behind Miss Mabington, seeing her shortcomings exposed to the light of day and her routine overset, and mutter ineffectually under her breath about leaving a household where she was clearly not appreciated.

Since Maby had energetically embarked the morning before on what she termed "spring cleaning"—which mild name had disguised a Herculean task of turning out all the rooms and linen cupboards and seemed to necessitate the labors of all the upstairs housemaids and several stout lads from the stables as well, and had threatened to wholly disrupt the household—she failed to notice

Dominique's preoccupation. Only when she had discoursed at some length on the merits of linseed oil and
turpentine as a polish of fine wood paneling, and what
was the best mixture to use on windows grimed by coal
smoke almost as soon as they were washed, did she at
last become aware that her audience was not attending
to her very closely. She frowned, and shot a sharp glance
at Dominique, then at last shrugged and turned her attention to compiling a series of lists of the tasks still to be
done that day.

Dominique scarcely noticed when Maby grew silent.
She was struggling against a wholly unfamiliar feeling of
sickness in the pit of her stomach, and try as she might
she could not think what she should do in the face of this
new threat. Only when the clock struck the hour and Maby
reminded her of the time did she recall her appointment
with Carleton, and by then it was too late to send him a
message. In the end she could only excuse herself and
send to the stables for Serena.

Carleton was already waiting for her when she arrived
a quarter of an hour later with her groom. He greeted
her in such a normal manner that some of the shock she
had been feeling receded a little and she was able to behave almost naturally. Once they had taken the fidgets
out of their mounts, they cantered briefly then dropped
back to a more sedate pace, and by then she was sufficiently mistress of herself once more to carry on a light-
hearted conversation, never more grateful than at that
moment for his kindness.

At the end of an hour they turned back toward the
gates. When they halted to say good-bye, Carleton's eyes
suddenly narrowed over her head. In an instant he recalled himself and continued easily with whatever he had
been saying.

Curious, she turned her own head, and was just in time
to see Vidal and Lady Caroline disappear down a side
path in Vidal's phaeton.

Carleton glanced at her face, then put out his hand to
cover hers and said in deep chagrin, "I'm sorry, my dear!
That was very clumsy of me!" At the expression in her
eyes he added quietly, "I can see you've heard the gossip.
But you really mustn't think anything of them being together, you know." He attempted a smile. "After all,
you're with me, and you don't expect Vidal to be jealous."

Dominique, who had reason to know the cases were not at all similar, and who had moreover been naïve enough to believe Vidal's assurances on that subject, lifted her chin and said coolly, "Vidal is perfectly free to see whomever he chooses! It has nothing to do with me."

When Carleton looked as if he would have liked to argue the point she quickly held out her hand. "I'm afraid I must go! Thank you for the gallop. Will I see you at Lady Fairley's tonight?"

In the end he took her hand and made some reply, then watched her ride away, a touch of impatience in his face.

But that unfortunate encounter had served one useful purpose. It had hardened her resolve that while they were still so very far apart, Vidal must not learn of her own deceit. His pride would not stand the scandal of an open break, but he would nevertheless despise her, and there would be an endless succession of Lady Carolines. It was not to be borne.

But the alternative seemed equally unthinkable. She was certainly intelligent enough to know that if she gave in to the demands of a blackmailer, she would never know a moment's peace again. She closed her eyes briefly, then rode home a little blindly, overcome by shame. That she—*she*—could be reduced to contemplating paying a blackmailer to escape betrayal seemed almost more than she could bear at the moment.

But she was no coward, and it did not occur to her not to keep the appointment. Only in that way would she be able to judge the reality of the threat contained in that letter, or—if by some miracle—it might only be someone's idea of a very poor jest.

She was at least grateful not to be afforded much opportunity for reflection. No sooner had she reached Berkeley Square when visitors were announced, and she had time only to run upstairs and put off her habit before receiving Lady Cowper and Lady Jersey, two formidable patronesses of Almack's and old friends of Vidal's whom it was impossible to offend. By the time they had taken their leave luncheon had been announced, and it was nearly quarter to two before she was able to escape to her bedchamber. By then there was scarcely time to dress quickly in a plain dark gown and cloak and send for her carriage if she were not to be late. After the briefest of hesitations, she took all the money she had at the time, and left a message for Maby that she had some shopping to do. Then resolutely she went down stairs and sent for her carriage.

Once in Bond Street, however, she dismissed her coachman, and waited until he had turned the corner before hailing a hackney carriage to take her to the City. She was not very familiar with London, and had not felt able to inquire of anyone the location of Maiden Lane; but the driver's reaction to her request was not encouraging. His brows drew together in astonishment, then he looked her up and down in a slightly familiar manner before shrugging his shoulders and whistling up his team.

She sank back into the dirty squabs, feeling more than a little soiled, and tried to prevent her thoughts from dwelling on the contemptible thing she was doing.

Her first glimpse of Maiden Lane was less intimidating than she had been led to expect, however. It was neither particularly clean nor prosperous looking, but nor was it the back-slum she had been dreading, and her spirits picked up a little. The neighborhood seemed primarily given over to commerce, with a number of small shops jiggling against one another along the narrow street, and a great many people seemed to have business there at this hour.

She had the jarvey set her down at the corner, and toyed briefly with the idea of requesting him to wait for her. But since she had formed a rather unreasonable dislike for this particular driver, and had, moreover, no idea how long her business might take her, in the end she dismissed him. By the time he had bit the coin she gave him, and grinned unpleasantly at her, she was more than glad to see the last of him.

No. 10, when she found it, proved to be a perfectly respectable if somewhat shabby draper's shop on the opposite side of the road. She stood observing it for a moment, trying to discover why it had been chosen for such a rendezvous, then at last shrugged her shoulders and stepped into the street.

She was halfway across when there was a loud scream behind her. Her nerves already stretched, she started violently and turned to see what had caused it. Then suddenly she froze in the middle of the cobbled road, her legs no longer obeying the commands of her brain.

It was not a heavily traveled road, perhaps because of its narrowness and the number of pedestrians, and for that reason the speed of the heavy dray cart that had rounded the corner and seemed to be headed straight toward her was all the more shocking. Everyone else seemed to have scattered at the woman's scream, and she alone stood directly in the horses' path.

The woman behind her screamed again, then, and abruptly Dominique regained her wits. Desperately she picked up her skirts and with the speed born of terror, ran toward the side of the road. The sounds of the wagon seemed to echo deafeningly in her ears and the horses were almost upon her.

She tripped once, but managed to regain her footing, and had nearly gained the safety of the flag-way, when a loose pebble proved her undoing. Her foot twisted beneath her, and without warning she went sprawling headlong into the gutter.

The force of her fall thrust her among a little cluster of pedestrians who had stopped in horror to watch the tragedy being enacted before them. There were a number of shrill shrieks, and the group fled before the onslaught of the horses, which had almost seemed to swerve to follow her slight figure.

There was a moment of utter pandemonium, as the thundering hooves mingled with the shouts and screams of the passers-by. Then at the very last minute the driver of the cart sawed violently at his horses' heads and the heavy wheels passed within inches of her prone figure. In another second he had disappeared around the corner and was lost to view.

One or two women had given way to strong hysterics, and there was suddenly a great deal of noise in the small street. Dominique, stunned, could only lay there, the breath knocked out of her body, and reaction setting in. Her heart seemed to have lodged itself in her throat and was pounding there abnormally rapidly and painfully.

Then a stout man had reached her and was helping her up. He half-supported her, his arm under her elbow and his round face drained of all color. "Gawd!" he said baldly. "Are ye all right, miss? Damme—begging your pardon, miss—but I swear that's give me the fright of my life!"

She was dirty and bruised and her knees were painfully scraped, but she managed to smile a little shakily at him, not wholly trusting her voice yet. Another man said angrily behind her, "Somebody ought to report it, is what I say! If 'e weren't drunker'n a lord, I'll *eat* this 'ere package my missis sent me after!"

There were a number of endorsements. "I think it was done deliberate!" a woman said stridently. "You can't tell me 'e didn't 'ead as if it straight toward 'er, for I seen it with me own eyes, I did!"

This, however, was going a little far for most, who, now that it was over, could forget the terror they had felt. There was some uncomfortable mumbling, and Dominique, alarmed as well by the trend the conversation was taking, looked up and said hastily, "No, no! I assure you I don't think it was anything other than an accident! Indeed, I fear I have only myself to blame, for I stepped into the street without looking."

A number of those assembled, including the man who had helped her up, looked relieved, and the crowd began slowly to disperse. Dominique was about to thank her stout rescuer and escape, when a familiar voice said harshly behind her, "Let me through! I must get through, I say!"

She jerked around, appalled, and looked up into the face of Lord Carleton as he ruthlessly thrust his way through the crowd toward her. His hat was missing and his usually ordered hair was disarranged, and he was breathing hard as if he had been running.

He reached her, and they stared at each other almost in horror for a brief second. Then Dominique closed her eyes and said distinctly, "Oh, no! What the devil are you doing here?"

It was scarcely a felicitous remark, but Carleton seemed too distracted to notice. He was still very pale and he tugged abruptly at his neckcloth as if it were too tight, and said blankly, "My God, it *was* you—! I could scarcely trust my eyes when I saw—and then that wagon—! Are you all right?"

He became aware belatedly that they still had an audience then, and turned to glare at the interested onlookers, until they sheepishly recalled themselves to their original errands and took themselves off. He turned back to her then, his voice strained, and said urgently, "You haven't answered me! Are you hurt?"

It was all suddenly too much. She put her head down and weakly began to giggle.

Carleton, looking very much alarmed, put his arm abruptly around her shoulders and said almost desperately, "Dominique—! No, my dear, don't! I promise you I'll get you home as soon as possible."

He signaled urgently to the driver of a hackney who had been interestedly observing the whole, and then said roughly, "My God, when I realized it was you—!" he shuddered slightly and mopped his brow, then did not finish.

Her conscience stirred then, and she stilled the laughter still threatening to escape, and put up her hand to him. "No, no, I'm behaving very badly! I promise you I am not about to give way to hysterics. Only—only what are you doing here of all places?"

He answered her almost abstractedly, his thoughts clearly elsewhere. "I was looking for a particular kind of snuff I used to buy in Spain, and someone told me I might find it here—" He broke off when she went off helplessly into another peal of laughter, and looked sharply into her face before bundling her unceremoniously into the cab, evidently not trusting her assurance she was not hysterical.

It was only then that she remembered her original errand, still uncompleted. She stiffened, wondering frantically what she was to do now. Then after a quick look at Carleton's face, admitted defeat and subsided meekly beside him.

She was scarcely conscious of the first part of the journey. Her thoughts were centered almost entirely upon the possible outcome of her failure to keep that appointment, and only after some time had elapsed did she recall the awkwardness of her present situation. She glanced nervously at her companion, and was not reassured.

Carleton was not looking at her, but his face was grave, and it was easy to tell he had finally begun to put two and two together, and was far from happy with the total. She sighed and watched him, and after a moment said gently, "It is not what you think, John."

He looked at her a little grimly, but said quietly, "I hardly supposed it was, my dear."

She sighed again, and could not quite meet his eyes.

"I—I would appreciate it if you did not feel it necessary to—to mention today's accident to Vidal."

Carleton's eyes were on her averted face. "I won't, of course, if you tell me not to. I think you know you don't have to ask. But if you are in trouble, my dear, you would do very much better to trust Justin."

She made an involuntary gesture of denial, hardly knowing what she was doing.

His lips tightened, but he said only, "I see. I don't know—I won't ask— But it is obvious that things are not as they should be between you. It makes it necessary for me to say what I have no right—and indeed, never meant to bring up. If you won't trust Vidal, and you are ever in need of any help—for any reason—I can think of no greater honor than being allowed to serve you. I think you must know there is very little I would not do for you, Dominique."

She put up her hand to keep him from saying anything more, the tears very near. She had been so concerned with her own problems that it had never occurred to her that Carleton—but if so, she had been unconscionable not to have seen it.

He was still watching her, but he said quietly, "I'm sorry, my dear. I did not want you to know, and I will say no more. But I hope you will at least remember what I said."

She attempted a very wobbly smile, and when shortly afterward they pulled up in Berkeley Square, she gathered her things quickly and said a little incoherently, "Thank you—! You needn't get down!"

He ignored her, and helped her down, then stood holding her hand. After a moment she sighed and looked up, meeting his eyes frankly, her own expression affectionate and sad.

He smiled crookedly at that and said soothingly, "You needn't worry, my dear. I am perfectly aware of which way the wind lies." He looked at her hand a moment, then surprised her by raising it to his lips before turning away and climbing back into the hack.

She watched him go, then at last climbed the stairs and waited drearily for the door to be opened, not even concocting a story to explain her appearance if she encountered anyone.

But for once the luck seemed to be favoring her, for it

was not Lymings, but a very junior footman who opened the door to her. If he was shocked to see his mistress returning in such a bedraggled state, he was too well-trained to betray it, and she was able to escape to her bedchamber without meeting anyone else. There she removed her torn and dirty gown and shoved it to the back of her wardrobe, then at a glance at the clock, sighed and rang for her bath. She would have given a great deal for the luxury of an evening free for a change, but it was time to be changing for dinner, and she would have to make at least an appearance at Lady Fairley's card party if she were to avoid arousing Maby's suspicions.

She thought she had endured all she could take that day. She was mistaken. When she returned home at last sometime after midnight, Vidal was there before her. He looked up sharply as she came in, then said lightly, "Ah, my love, I'm glad you're home early. There was something I wished to speak to you about."

Her eyes guarded, she suppressed a yawn and said politely, "Certainly, sir. But could it not wait until morning? I'm afraid I'm a little stupid tonight and fit only for my bed."

He stood looking down at her for a long moment, and she could not read his expression in the dim hallway. All of the events of that dreadful day came pouring back then, and she had to exercise the greatest restraint to keep from bursting into tears and disgracing herself.

But she must have given away more than she realized, or else Vidal was adept at reading her moods, for his face softened a little. He put out his hand and said ruefully, "My dear! Can we not do better than this?"

Her throat ached with the effort to hold back her tears. She put out her own hand a little blindly, and when he took it in his warm clasp, came very near to blurting out the whole. Her lips were actually parted when, unbidden, came once more the picture of Vidal bending over Lady Caroline in the park that morning.

She closed her eyes, and was lost. The next instant Vidal's hand had come away, and he shrugged indifferently and turned toward his library.

He had almost reached it, when he stopped and said curtly over his shoulder, "The next time you give Carleton your hands to kiss so devotedly, I would suggest you choose a little more secluded place than my doorstep!"

It was so unexpected that she gasped, not quite crediting what he had said. In another instant he had closed the library door behind him and she was left alone in the hall. She sighed then, hardly knowing whether to laugh or to cry, and climbed the stairs wearily to her room.

At that moment in a very different part of London, a man sat staring into his gin, growing steadily drunker. He seemed to be oblivious to the noise around him, and only roused himself periodically to call for another drink before lapsing once again into his own thoughts.

That these were far from being pleasant, however, became apparent when someone entered the dark tavern some time later. He started, spilling some of his drink, and stared at the newcomer with dislike and something very like fear in his eyes, before downing the contents of his glass in one gulp.

The newcomer looked around briefly, his nose wrinkled fastidiously at the malodorous atmosphere, then crossed the room leisurely.

"Well?" he said without emotion.

The first roused himself suddenly. "It ain't my fault if some hag screams and nabs the rust, is it?" he muttered angrily. "I never bargained for running down a whole gaggle o' gawkers as well."

The other's expression did not change. "You force me to deal with the matter myself. Let us hope you have not spoiled the game with your clumsiness. I have no further use for you."

"That's as may be!" the first said belligerently. "But I'll see me money now, if it's all the same to you! No one cheats Ned Breamish out of what's due him!"

A spasm of distaste crossed the other's face and he almost wearily threw a handful of notes on the stained table. "You may get even more than you bargained for if I ever learn you have spoken out of turn. Do I make myself clear, my friend?"

His cynical eyes moved expressionlessly over the sprawled figure before him, then he turned and walked out.

Breamish watched him go, then shrugged and picked up the money. He counted it, then called loudly for another drink. He could afford it now, though he'd not re-

ceived as much as he'd been promised if this afternoon's
job had been successful.

When the drink was brought he downed the gin, then
rose abruptly and paid his shot, not at all certain he
wasn't glad to be shut of that business, all the same.

Chapter Fourteen

By morning Dominique had had time to recall every reason why she could not confide in Vidal. And any inclination she might still have had to unburden herself, whatever the consequences, died when Vidal informed her at breakfast that he was called unexpectedly out of town and would be away a week to ten days.

He did not explain or invite her to accompany him, and while he was perfectly civil, there was no softening in his manner from the previous night. Before she had managed to think of a suitable reply, he had excused himself and left the room.

She saw him again only briefly, when he kissed her cheek in front of Lymings and two footmen, and advised her coolly not to racket around too much while he was away.

She resisted the desire to watch his traveling chaise out of sight, and if she was conscious of dismay at the knowledge that his large figure no longer stood between her and the world, she resisted that as well. Her own folly had created the present situation, and it was up to her to extricate herself.

Indeed, while so much stood between them, it was better that Vidal was away. He had always possessed an uncanny ability to discover what he was least expected to know, despite his lazy demeanor, and she did not mean him to learn anything of yesterday's nightmare events.

But at the end of a week spent feverishly searching through each day's post, and starting every time a note was brought in to her, she had received no more communications addressed to her in that large black lettering. If the events of that day had not been so indelibly etched on her brain, she might almost have begun to believe she had imagined the whole.

The strain of the last few weeks soon began to tell upon her. She lost weight, and even Bates' considerable skill could not hide the fact that there were unaccustomed shadows under her eyes. She lived daily in the fear that the rumors would begin and she would be undone.

She knew she was being stupidly morbid, but the blackmailer's continued silence preyed on her nerves in a way that a renewal of his demands would never have done. That at least she would have been able to deal with, but helplessly waiting for the axe to fall was almost unbearable.

She knew that Sally was concerned, but Sally thought only that Vidal's absence was making her unhappy and took pains to see that she should not be left alone to fret. Carleton, too, looked sharply at her the next time they met, then purposely set himself to keep her amused. She had been feeling a slight restraint, but he did not refer to that dreadful day, and she soon was able to relax in his presence. His manner was that of a trusted friend, and not by word or look did he betray any feelings he might have for her.

Oddly enough, only Miss Mabington gave no sign of having noticed anything amiss, for which Dominique could only be profoundly grateful. Maby, once aroused, would be far more difficult to reassure, and she did not feel up to making the attempt. Luckily, however, a crisis in the household—in the form of Mrs. Bundy at last serving in her notice—had distracted Maby's usually sharp attention, and apart from saying a little caustically that Dominique was looking decidedly jaded, Maby did not tax her with uncomfortable questions.

But that Maby was very far from being ignorant of certain facts became soon apparent. Dominique, having no engagements, had spent a quiet evening at home for a change. They had a light dinner, since Miss Mabington was never a robust eater and Dominique had failed to do more than pick at whatever was set before her in days. Afterward they retired to the small sitting room: Miss Mabington to her basket of mending, and Dominique with a book Sally had lent her.

But despite everything, Dominique's mind refused to concentrate on the written page, and after she had read the same paragraph three times without being aware of a single word, she threw down the book and wandered restlessly about the room, her thoughts no longer to be denied.

She had halted in front of the window and had drawn back the curtain to stare out into the square below, when Maby said harshly behind her, "All right, Dominique! I'm perfectly aware you don't wish me to meddle, but I've stood by and watched you break your heart long enough. I thought you had grown to love Vidal."

Dominique turned blindly, hardly aware of the expression in her eyes. But Maby, at sight of her face, crumpled suddenly, and said in very real pain, "Oh, my dear—! Don't—! I didn't mean to make you unhappy!"

Dominique, her eyes bright with unshed tears, shook her head and said a little disjointedly, "No, it's all right, Maby. I have always known where I stand."

At that Maby sniffed and recovered her temper. "Do you?" she said fiercely. "Do you? Then you've got a remarkably odd way of showing it! From fighting with him every time you meet, you've gone to treating him with a politeness that even chills my blood. I tell you Vidal's not the man to put up with such starts! You'll lose him if you're not careful!"

Dominique, her smile infinitely sad, said gently, "You don't understand. I never had him, Maby."

The maid came in with the tea tray then, and they did not speak of it again. But some time during the long night that followed, Dominique gave in to what had always been inevitable, no matter how much her pride had struggled against it. Vidal must be told the truth as soon as he returned. Not because of the threat to expose her, not even because she loved him, but because whatever his feelings were toward her, she was his wife and she owed him that much. She had been dreadfully wrong to keep it from him all these months for no other reason than that her vanity had been wounded.

With that decision came a certain peace. The next day passed uneventfully enough, with a shopping expedition with Sally in the morning, and a visit to the Elgin marbles in the afternoon. She was engaged to be one of a party to Vauxhall Gardens that night, and wore a new gown of pomona-green crepe that had just been sent home from the dressmaker's.

For some reason or another she had not yet paid a visit to the famous gardens, and when Linville had learned of the oversight he had instantly proposed a select group to initiate her into the delights of one of the celebrated gala nights. Lady Sarah had grumbled that the place was growing common, but in the end good-naturedly agreed to make a member of Linville's party.

But when Dominique came down stairs that evening, it was to find Vidal in the hall, his baggage still being carried in. He looked tired, and her heart gave a little involuntary leap at sight of him.

The next minute she had recalled everything, and the brief light in her eyes died out. There had been no responsive light in Vidal's eyes, and he looked her over now, a sudden frown between his brows. Abruptly he strode across to her and forced her chin up.

He grimly took in her pale cheeks and shadowed eyes, and said curtly, "Well, ma'am. I see you have not taken my advice!"

She was startled, and very conscious of the presence of the servants. Her cheeks flamed, but she said evenly, "You are back early, sir. Did you enjoy a pleasant journey?"

He let her go then and answered carelessly, "Yes, I finished sooner than I had expected. You are going out, I see. Is it something I should have remembered?"

When she explained where she was going, he raised his brows but only shrugged. "You will not like it," he said coolly, "but I suppose you can come to no harm if Sally is with you."

She stiffened at this reflection on her own good sense, and said with great cordiality, "Then why do you not come to make certain of it, your grace? I have no doubt Linville would be delighted."

For answer he shrugged out of his travel-stained cloak and said indifferently, "No, I think not, my dear. It is not quite in my style. Perhaps I will have a look-in at Whites later."

She came periously close to flouncing out. It was clear that while he had seldom been out of her thoughts for the past week, Vidal had scarcely spared a thought to her. He had certainly spent little time in repining that last evening, as she had done almost continually since. She hurried out to Linville's carriage, and did not even blink at the subsequent intelligence that their previously respectable party had dwindled to only four: Lady Sarah, Linville, herself and Sir Gareth Kingsley.

Linville was a shocking flirt, but a harmless rattle who

might always be counted upon to toe the line. Sir Gareth was a different proposition entirely. He was in his early thirties, a little older than her usual beaux, and possessed such a bored, world-weary air that she disliked him and usually sought to avoid him.

But now she only smiled at Lady Sarah's helpless little shrug, and set herself to enjoy the evening at all costs. Since Linville obligingly entertained Lady Sarah, Dominique found herself abandoned to Sir Gareth's gentle eloquence, and they passed a not-unpleasant hour in strolling about the grounds.

Despite her determination not to be, Dominique found herself almost shocked by some of the antics going on around her. There was a great deal of coy, genteel giggling of young ladies in dominoes and masks, and much rapping of hands by outraged damsels, and once a young lady fled shrieking past them, hotly pursued by a fair young man somewhat the worse for drink. Dominique began to perceive some of the justice of Vidal's remarks.

But she steadfastly refused to agree with Sally that they should not have come after all, and professed herself delighted with the fairy lights and a concert that was all but drowned out by the loud talk around them.

She was in truth rather amused by the fireworks display afterward, and found herself hungry enough to do justice to the light supper Linville had bespoken. But when Sir Gareth suggested that they should go out upon the lake, she had had just enough champagne, on top of an unfortunate reference to Vidal, to ignore Lady Sarah's small shake of the head and defiantly agree.

It was a defiance she was to regret, however, since Sir Gareth had grown emboldened by a previously unsuspected excess of wine to forsake his usual weary air and protest his undying love for her. When she sought to change the subject he laughed at her and told her cynically that she would soon change her tune. No wife was expected to be anything but discreet, and if she were naïve enough to believe that Vidal, whatever his present show of devotion, had really changed his spots, then she was a great deal greener than he had given her credit for.

It was close enough to the truth to make her exceedingly angry, but she held her tongue and icily requested to be returned to shore. After a moment he apologized,

THE DUCHESS OF VIDAL 161

but then attempted to kiss her. In a fit of fury out of all proportion to the crime she ended by tumbling him into the lake and rowing herself back.

She was, therefore, in a far from amiable mood when she at last reached home, only to find Bates had once more waited up for her, contrary to all orders. Something would have to be done soon about Bates. But not tonight. She sighed wearily and put herself into her dresser's hands.

Bates was just finishing the last strokes with the hairbrush while Dominique struggled to keep her eyes open, when there was a light tap on the door and Vidal entered. She looked up and met his eyes in the mirror, trying desperately to keep the dismay she felt from showing in her face, while Bates began hurriedly braiding her mistress's hair.

"That will be all for tonight, Bates," Vidal said firmly. When the dresser hesitated, he added calmly, "Leave her hair the way it is. I like it that way."

Bates, after a hurried glance at Dominique, put down the hairbrush, curtsied and walked quickly toward the door, not quite managing to hide the smirk upon her lips.

Dominique had wanted only to put off the moment when they were alone as long as possible, but she said crossly, "You've embarrassed her."

"Nonsense, my love. Bates must be very used to seeing me here by now. Anyway, I'd wager she's seen a great many more shocking things than a husband entering his wife's bedchamber late at night."

She ignored his tone and turned wearily again to her mirror and picked up her hairbrush.

"And how did you find Vauxhall?" Vidal inquired politely.

"I enjoyed it very much," she said untruthfully.

He did not look as if he believed her, but he leaned his shoulder against the wall and inquired almost idly, "And did you miss me while I was away, my dear?"

She glanced up sharply, then dropped her eyes and said dully, "Certainly. I hope you had a pleasant journey." She had both longed for and dreaded his return, and she did not understand the strange mood that was upon him.

Something of what she was feeling must have showed in her face, for Vidal's black brows drew together and he said a little cruelly, "Ah, yes! Ever the dutiful wife!" He straightened and came across to her, taking the brush from her suddenly still hand.

He stroked it through her hair for a moment, then drew it down and gathered her hair into his hands. "Your hair is afire with the candlelight in it," he said in an odd voice, then bent his head and pressed his lips to her bared nape.

She started violently, but when he released her busied herself very much at random with the contents of her dressing table, her hands trembling.

"You are very beautiful, Dominique. But then you don't need me to tell you that, do you?" he said harshly.

Her voice trembled woefully. "Thank you, sir. It—it is always pleasant to be told that one is beautiful."

Something hardened in his eyes, and he went on as if driven, "Oh, yes, you are beautiful! I think I am envied by half the men in London."

She kept her eyes down and made no answer. After a moment he added deliberately, watching her, "And they cannot know even the half of it, of course! You are beautiful, accomplished, intelligent, calm, capable of managing my houses beautifully, asking no questions and making no demands. And, if you will permit, my love, delightful after dark." He laughed harshly. "In short, the perfect wife!"

She would not let him see how much his words had wounded her. She did not know why he was doing this, and she wished only to be left alone. She said, through lips that seemed frozen, "You flatter me, your grace."

He shrugged. "Not in the least, my dear. You are a paragon among women." His eyes and voice were cold.

She was very pale, but she looked up at that, something seeming to snap within her. "Was it not what you wanted, your grace?" she cried defiantly.

"Why certainly, my dear. It makes things so much tidier, don't you think?" he drawled.

"I am happy to think I conform to your expectations!" She hardly recognized her own voice.

He merely shrugged and sat on the corner of her dressing table, watching her.

She moved abruptly away from him, laughing a little wildly. "Indeed, I must be very honored, your grace! Everything you possess is of the best. Your estates, your stables, your wife! But then you can afford it, can't you?"

In one stride he was across the room and had gripped her shoulders cruelly. "You little fool!" he grated. "Did you think I wanted a mealy-mouthed, submissive non-entity of a wife? I could have had my pick of the cream from the last dozen Seasons if that was what I was looking for!"

"Why certainly! I have no doubt any one of them would have leaped at the chance to become the Duchess of Vidal!"

"I can afford the best!" he snapped.

She gasped, but the next moment had achieved the calm of utter despair. "Yes," she whispered. "Even me."

His fingers tightened on her arms. "Goddamn you!" he said slowly and distinctly. "Goddamn you to hell! I want a woman, not that cold and proper wife you've created for me out of your pride. I flattered myself you knew me better than that."

She had not meant to go so far, but her pride would not let her retreat now. "Yes, I know you!" she cried passionately. "You are above all a practical man, are you not? I think I must be exactly the wife you've always wanted. Available when you want me and without too many questions when you don't. Presentable, entertaining, complacent, well bred—and as you have said, delightful after dark!"

She faltered suddenly before the look in his eyes. For a moment she thought he would strike her.

Then he seemed to have gained control of himself again. "As usual, my dear," he drawled, "you are exactly right." He bowed and in a moment the door had closed behind him.

She closed her eyes, then moved blindly toward the bed.

Vidal, in the throes of such a black anger as he had not known for many years, stormed down stairs and ruthlessly roused Hollings to saddle the chestnut. He had not meant to quarrel with her. He had had something far different in mind since he had been totally unable to get her out of his mind for the last week. He had even gone so far as to make a fool of himself in front of his bailiff by postponing his business and haring back to London two days early like any love-sick youth.

He had been conscious of an overwhelming gladness to

see her, only to have her face close up at sight of him. He had struck out at her, hurt; but it had only been later, when she taunted him about affording the best, that he had at last lost his iron control.

He supposed it was true that when he bothered to think about it he had fully expected to choose a bride who would bear his children without upsetting his routine too much, while leaving him free to pursue his own entertainments. But she must have known that he had not thought of that mythical, bloodless creature in months. She had been wholly buried in the reality of a tempestuous, headstrong beauty who had tumbled his well-laid plans about his ears, defied his orders, given him no reason to suppose she was anything but indifferent to him—and had succeeded in delighting him in a way he had long ago given up as impossible.

He swore to himself, then cursed Hollings roundly for his tardiness in bringing the chestnut around, mounted and was gone into the black night.

Hollings, left standing in the scanty attire he had donned when roused so precipitately from his bed, shook his head and grinned to himself. He had seen his grace in the devil of a taking over the years, but he disremembered when it had ever been caused by a woman. Aye, he had it bad.

Dominique did not see Vidal the next day. She pleaded a headache and retired early to bed, and Maby, after one worried glance at her pale face and shadowed eyes, made no comment. But although she lay in bed, she did not sleep, her ears strained for the sound of Vidal's footsteps. Like the night before he did not return.

The next day her pride came to her rescue, and she resolutely went about the day's activities as if nothing had happened. She went with Lady Sarah to Almack's and gave no one any reason to suppose she was in anything but excellent spirits, and it was not until she had gained the solitude of her bedchamber in the early hours of the morning that she allowed the determined mask of gaity to drop away from her. Vidal had been angry with her before, but never the cold icy fury that had been in his face that night. She could not think. She only knew she had never been so miserable in her life before.

When the door opened behind her, she lifted her head slowly, her eyes huge in her face, as if she were ill.

"I did knock, my dear," Vidal said stiffly. "You must have been daydreaming." His voice was cold, but then he took another look at her face and his manner changed abruptly. "Dominique—my dear—what is it?"

She made a supreme effort to pull herself together. "I —I—forgive me!" she said a little stupidly. "I was wondering about a new gown I had just had made up. I had quite decided it would do nicely with that amber necklet, but now I am not so certain. Rubbishing stuff you will not be the slightest bit interested in! D-did you wish me, sir?"

His eyes still rested penetratingly on her face, but after a moment he accepted her lead. "Of course I am interested, my dear," he said quietly. "You must know I am generally considered quite a hand at advising women on their gowns. May I see it?"

She started, then blindly produced it. Vidal studied it, and immediately embarked upon a long discussion of its merits that gave her time to recover.

She heard very little of it, but when he paused expectantly, she was able to say with tolerable composure, "You are experienced, aren't you?"

"Certainly, my dear," he drawled. Then as her eyes widened he added righteously, "I am a married man, you know." When her mouth curved reluctantly, he reached out to smooth a curl away from her ear. "Ah, that is much better, my dear. You don't look quite so lost and forlorn. What is it, my dear?" he asked gently.

After the last few days, this unaccustomed gentleness was almost her undoing, but she managed to shake her head, not quite able to meet his eyes.

After a moment he gently lifted her chin. "I know that we have had our—our differences, my child. But I would be very unhappy if I thought you did not trust me enough to tell me if you were troubled or upset."

His words were like a knife twisted in her heart. She shook her head again, and desperately kept her eyes on the very elegant pin he wore in his neckcloth.

She thought he would leave her then, but instead he took her hands in his and said very qietly, "My dear, I hope you will accept my apologies. I can only excuse myself by saying that I was tired, and angry, and said a great many things I did not mean."

This was infinitely worse. For Vidal to apologize, when it had been she who should be begging for his forgiveness—! She dared not lift her head for fear she would betray herself for all time.

But Vidal misunderstood her silence. After a moment his hands came away, and he said in an oddly gentle voice, "I see. I will not trouble you any more, my dear."

Her eyes flew to his. At the darkness of their expression, she put up her hand and said incoherently, "No—please—!"

Vidal held himself rigidly. "Dominique?"

"Please don't go—!" she whispered brokenly.

Vidal's breath was expelled harshly as he pulled her violently against him. A long time later, she sighed his name and slept contentedly at last, everything else forgotten.

The next morning when she came down to breakfast he was waiting for her. She lifted her brows in surprise, for she was very late and he was usually gone before now. But he merely held a chair for her and poured a cup of coffee.

"You certainly slept well last night, my love," he said calmly, and despite herself her cheeks grew hot. His slow smile appeared. "You blush delightfully, you absurd child. Surely you are not still shy with me?"

"No, of course not! Now shhh!" She looked around quickly as the maid came in with fresh rolls and firmly changed the subject.

His eyes continued to tease her, but he obligingly discoursed at length on the very boring topic she had introduced, until she was forced to say crossly, "Oh, that's enough! I don't care in the least what Hollings is using on your bay's graze, which you know very well! And stop laughing at me!"

He did not do that, but he did change the subject once again. But then as she was rising, he said abruptly, "I think you could do with a rest, my dear. We will go to WainCourt for a few weeks. Would you like that?"

She smiled tremulously and knew she would like it above anything else.

Chapter Fifteen

Somehow Dominique felt a strange peace surround her from the first moment of entering WainCourt's sprawling bulk. She knew it to be one of England's principal country seats, and had unconsciously developed a picture of an imposing mansion that befitted a ducal residence, but the truth turned out to be very different. WainCourt was a charmingly haphazard building whose various wings and additions seemed to accurately mirror the changing fortunes of each succeeding generation. Almost from the first she found herself enchanted by it.

The interior of the house and the enormous grounds displayed all the quiet elegance she had grown accustomed to in Vidal's house in Berkeley Square, but the whole was overlaid by a relaxed atmosphere somehow at odds with so much wealth. There was an informality about the grounds that she never grew tired of, and any number of occupations to keep her busy from morning to night. Not even once did she regret the balls and entertainments they were missing. Indeed, those last weeks in London began to take on a nightmare quality, as if they no longer had any reality.

Maby, no doubt with her own thoughts about the projected trip, had announced that she preferred to remain in town, and Dominique had been unable to budge her from that stance. She had a great many things to do, and was by no means as fond of the country as Dominique. Besides, she rather thought she would pay a visit to her sister for a few days. She had been sadly neglecting her lately.

Dominique, by now ruefully familiar with this totally unexpected penchant of her old companion for matchmaking, allowed Maby to have her games.

And so the days drifted past, and the few weeks slipped into a month, almost without quite being aware of it. Vidal took her over his estates and introduced her to his tenants, and she experienced an absurd pride in their obvious affection for "Master Justin," as they still sometimes called him. She herself was accepted with a touching eagerness.

At her request they spent long hours exploring the house, and discussing the paintings and *objets d'art* collected over many succeeding generations. There, in Vidal's home, surrounded by the portraits of his ancestors and the simple pride of his retainers and tenants in being a part of such a great family, she began for the first time to understand that pride in ancient names and houses that she had denied for so long. It was not snobbery, only a quiet acceptance of what one was and what one owed to that inheritance.

On other days they explored the home woods, and Vidal kept her in whoops over tales of his youthful prowess and continual efforts to evade the stern eyes of his governess and tutor. And one day he even taught her to fish the stream he had fished as a boy, expressing shock that in her checkered career she had never learned such a useful art. It was discovered that the rod he had used as a boy was the exact length for her.

And on the inevitable days that Vidal was busy with his bailiff she was content to explore on her own. She took Serena on long rambles, and indulged herself in the mad gallops she had so much missed in the very proper environs of Hyde Park.

In the evenings they played piquet for fabulous imaginary sums, or backgammon, or just talked quietly. She found Vidal very far from the man his reputation proclaimed him, and thought his friends in London might scarcely recognize him. She had long known of his shrewd intelligence, but she found herself again and again quietly impressed by the amount of his knowledge. She, who considered herself particularly well-read, was often pressed to keep up with him, and she learned in surprise that he had traveled as extensively as she herself had done, and they knew many of the same places. They talked easily and endlessly, and if she was sometimes aware that she was revealing more of herself than she had ever intended, it too was somehow unimportant.

Only one thing disturbed her growing contentment. Despite her decision, the time to tell Vidal the truth at last seemed never to occur. She despised herself for her cowardice, but could not bring herself to destroy these few magical weeks—whatever price she might be called upon to pay for them later. She clung desperately to each golden day and blindly refused to think about the future.

And it sometimes seemed to her almost as if Vidal, too, was taking care that nothing should mar their growing understanding. She might be aware sometimes that his eyes rested on her in an expression she could not define, but nothing disturbed the succession of long lazy days; and little by little she allowed herself to fall into a peace that was as comforting as it was false. They did not speak again of that last dreadful quarrel.

She realized soon in amusement that Vidal's staff frankly beamed upon them, and she was greeted with delight and a touch of relief. It was time and past that "Master Justin—er—I should say his grace, of course—" stopped playing and settled down. There was general expectation that they might see more of his grace now, for they missed him sorely, racketing around as he always was in that great house in London. Not that he neglected things, mind you. Only a house needed a master and a mistress, and perhaps before long there would be a need for the nurseries again, and old Nurse would come into her own.

Vidal, who had come in in time to hear the last of this discussion, quizzed Dominique with his eyes, and though the color stole to her cheeks, she did not look away. She had never thought of Vidal as a father, before, but it occurred to her then that he would be a good one. "Do you want a son?" she asked seriously.

He smiled slowly, a hint of lazy intimacy in his eyes, and said softly, "All in good time, my love. But I think first, a hoyden of a little girl who will have her mama's hair and eyes and never give us a moment's peace."

She blushed scarlet, and he added caressingly, "Unless, of course, you would prefer to begin with a son. There has never yet been a Waincourt with red hair, but if you would like to scandalize the world with the heir to the dukedom looking nothing like his father, I am perfectly willing!"

When she only laughed, he straightened and after a moment added easily, "I thought we might have a picnic today, if you'd care for it. You've been wanting to go again to the lake, I believe."

She agreed readily to it, and went away to change. They were halfway to the lake when Vidal asked idly, "Do you resemble your father's family at all?"

She started, suddenly on edge. "I—I don't know—perhaps a little. W-why do you ask?"

He shrugged. "You never mention them, and I wondered if you took all your looks from your mother's side of the family. She was Scots, I believe you said?"

She answered somewhat disjointedly, hardly knowing what she said. Her pleasure in the day was destroyed. She felt weighted down by guilt and all the old doubts, and she could only wonder why Vidal had chosen such a topic on this day of all days. He had shown an amazing lack of curiosity about her past, but until she chose to confess the truth to him, even such a mild question had the power to cut up her peace of mind. She rode blindly to the lake, her lighthearted mood gone, and dismally aware that the past had intruded at last to spoil the idyll.

But when they reached the spot where Hollings was waiting with a trap loaded with hampers and supplies, Vidal spoke easily to his groom and directed the arrangement of the picnic without betraying any awareness of her sudden withdrawal. She attempted to take her cue from him, and teased Hollings as he unpacked several hampers filled to overflowing with the chef's idea of the sustenance required to sustain two people between breakfast and dinner.

Since this included several roasted fowl, a large array of cold meats and hams, platters of fruits and creams and jellies, a number of bottles of wine, and even a dozen bottles of iced ale, her amusement rapidly came to the fore.

And when Hollings next unloaded a hamper filled with plates and silver and crystal goblets, she could not prevent herself from laughing. "Good God! There is enough food here to feed an army." Her eyes twinkled. "In fact, I've seen armies make do with considerably less and think themselves lucky."

Hollings grinned cheekily and Vidal smiled and said, "You must know what snobs servants are, my dear. I would never dare to suggest that a packet of sandwiches and a few apples were all we required. It doesn't suit with their notions of my consequence."

"Certainly," she agreed promptly. "I know in what dread you stand of your servants' displeasure! The first time we met I remember you were in the greatest terror of what Clay would have to say about your spoiling your boots."

Vidal sighed in resignation, and Hollings' grin grew broader. "Oh, aye, Clay's a nasty customer when he gets his dander up, there's no denying!" he agreed in appreciation.

Dominique watched in fascination as Hollings finished unpacking the last hamper. "But where's the ducal plate?" she demanded when that task was completed. "I must tell you that I firmly expect no less than the ducal place." As Vidal's lips quivered, she added suddenly, "*Is* there a ducal plate?"

"Oh, certainly! We'll have 'em out for dinner tonight if you wish."

She declined the promised treat, then seated herself on a convenient rock as Hollings gathered up the hampers and departed. She watched as Vidal seated himself on a rug nearby, and said suddenly, "You are a very good master, you know."

At his grin she colored, but insisted, "No, I'm serious. Sometimes it seems you are as trapped by your wealth as others ever are by their poverty." She shook her head and grinned self-consciously. "It is certainly strange. Perhaps it is no wonder that sometimes you feel you must do shocking things." She sighed and added honestly, "I do them myself."

His grin grew more satanic. "Certainly, my love. But, I think mine are perhaps a trifle more shocking than yours. Do you think me a sheep merely disguised in wolf's clothing?"

Her smile flickered. "Well, not that. But I have known for a very long time that you are not very black, despite your reputation. Why do you enjoy perpetuating the myth?"

"Boredom, mostly," he replied promptly.

When she laughed he flicked her cheek with a careless finger and gave his attention to filling a plate with delicacies for her.

She accepted the plate he handed her and picked lightly at its contents. "You *are* a good master," she said quietly. "I know you must often wish them all at the devil."

He shrugged. "Oh, very frequently. But it would be both unkind and stupid to offend their sensibilities, my dear."

She set aside her barely touched plate and came to join him on the rug. After a moment she wrapped her arms around her knees and said almost dreamily, "You love WainCourt, don't you?"

"Yes, my dear, I do."

Her cheek rested on her knees and her eyes were wide

and unseeing. "How much?" she asked quietly. "Enough to lie for it—to cheat for it? Would you do almost anything to keep it?"

There was a frown between his eyes, but he answered her seriously, "I don't know, Dominique. I hope I would place my—honor—above it, but I don't honestly know."

She shivered slightly, but went on doggedly in that same, flat voice. "And if you lost it? Would everything else cease to matter? And everyone?"

He put his hand on her bent head. "You are thinking of your father?" he asked gently.

She looked up and nodded, not even wondering how he had known.

"You said once that there was only one thing he cared about. It was his home, wasn't it?" Somehow it was not a question, and she nodded again.

"Seeing you here, being here," she said slowly, "I begin to understand a little of what he must have felt." She looked up and added gruffly, "I have never had a home, you see. So I cannot know."

His hand moved gently in her hair. "You have now, Dominique," he said quietly.

She lifted her head and her eyes were very grave as they met his.

"Dominique . . ." he said slowly. As she frowned he hesitated, started to say something more, then shook his head almost sadly. "No, never mind. I think it is not yet time, my love." He straightened and said lightly, "Right now you had best make a better effort on your plate, or I can guarantee you will have the ire of the chef to deal with when we get back." He refilled her wine glass.

Her eyes were puzzled, but after a moment she dutifully picked up her plate again and they talked lightly of other things.

When they had finished eating, while she set aside the uneaten food Vidal stretched hugely and lay back in the shade of the trees, his eyes closed. In a short while his breathing grew deep and even.

She studied him for a long time, oddly content to have him relaxed and asleep beside her. Then she reached out a hand and gently smoothed back a lock of his dark hair that had fallen forward.

Immediately his hand came up to capture hers and bring

it to his lips. He opened his eyes slowly. "Why do you only do things like that when you think I am asleep?"

She blushed painfully and tried to withdraw her hand. He held it firmly. "You are my wife, Dominique," he said quietly. After a moment she nodded. His hand tightened on her fingers. "Say it!"

"I am your wife," she repeated slowly, almost dully.

He sighed. "You could make it sound less a dirge, my love." Then he shook his head, released her hand and took out his snuff box and carelessly flicked it open. "Will you ever learn to trust me, I wonder?" he remarked conversationally.

She started and color swept her face. "I don't know what you mean," she whispered.

His mouth tightened. "Yes, you do, my love," he said. "Oh, yes, you do."

She looked quickly away, more upset than she cared to admit, and said with quiet intensity, "I do trust you, Justin."

For answer he only shrugged and raised his brows in his old mocking way. She sighed, then leaned forward and gently touched his cheek with her lips, in an oddly touching little gesture that she had never dared do before.

He cursed suddenly and spilled the contents of his snuff box. "Never, *never* do that when I have my hands full, you abominable child!" He pulled her roughly against him.

When he lifted his head her eyes were wide and slightly dazed. He smiled ruefully and kissed her again before lightly putting her away from him. "And not, I think, when we are in quite such a public place, hmm, my love?"

After a moment she sighed and lay back to rest her head upon a cushion. There was a little silence, then Vidal leaned over her and said quietly, "Will you tell me now what has made you so unhappy these past weeks, my child?"

She sighed again, her eyes wide and defenseless, but did not look away. But when she still made no answer, he prompted gently, "I am not an ogre you know, my love, and I am long past the age of being shocked at anything. Surely nothing can be as bad as that?"

She was very pale, and she said pitifully, "It may be worse."

He smiled and reached out to smooth away the frown between her brows, his eyes loving. "No, little one, I give you my word it is not."

She had no defenses against Vidal in such a mood, and she accepted that the moment <u>had</u> come at last. "No," she said bravely. But before she could say anything more, Vidal's head lifted suddenly, his black brows registering disgust, and he said wrathfully, "Hell and the devil confound it! It's Hollings!"

It was so unexpected that she laughed nervously, and once more the moment had been lost. There was nothing to do but rise to greet a very red-faced Hollings, painfully aware he had come for the baskets at a most awkward time, and say soothingly, "No, no, Hollings, it is all right. We were quite through."

Hollings took in Vidal's black visage, and hurriedly set about gathering together the remains of the picnic.

On the way home she turned to Vidal, unaccountably light-hearted, and said mischievously, "I think the last time we raced you had an unfair advantage, your grace. You wouldn't care to try me again?"

After a moment he smiled in mocking challenge. "To the oak tree?"

For answer she laughed and dug her heels into Serena's ribs. She was soon several lengths ahead, and began to suspect he meant to let her win. She turned in the saddle to glare at him, only to see him let his big chestnut out. Swiftly she turned, determined he would not beat her again.

But despite Serena's valiant efforts, he gained slowly on her, until they were neck and neck. She leaned lower and urged Serena forward, murmuring to her all the while.

As they reached the agreed marker Serena came slightly out in front. Dominique laughed in delight and pulled Serena up, then held out her hand to Vidal. "That was marvelous!" She hesitated, then added very softly, "And—thank you."

When they reached the house a figure was just alighting from a traveling chaise. She frowned and said in surprise, "Why, it's Charles Hastings. Did you know he was coming?"

Vidal only shook his head slightly and dismounted to meet his secretary.

They chatted easily for a few minutes, and then Dominique, becoming conscious of some undertone she did not understand, excused herself to go away to change. Charles looked up at that, and said quickly, "I brought your post, ma'am. I thought you might be interested in seeing it."

She smiled and accepted the pile of letters he handed her, for once lulled into forgetting her new fear. She stood in the hall, idly looking through them, while Vidal and Hastings discussed some paperwork Hastings had brought for his perusal.

Then at the sight of that dreaded black scrawl, she turned abruptly and climbed to her room, her heart leaden within her.

The two men glanced up at her going, then Vidal led the way to his library. "What is it, Charles?" he asked quietly.

Hastings, without another word, produced a large envelope from the case he carried, and handed it to Vidal. "This is the investigator's report, sir. I—I thought you had best see it right away."

Vidal pulled out the pages and began reading. As his eyes moved quickly down the pages his mouth grew grim, and at one point he swore softly before going on. At last he raised his eyes.

"You will say nothing of this, of course," he said automatically.

Hastings remained silent.

Vidal put the report carefully away. "I think we had best go back to London tomorrow."

That night when he entered Dominique's room, the dresser was still brushing her hair. Dominique looked up at his entrance, then said calmly, "That will be all for the night, Bates, thank you."

It struck him that she was looking a little as she had looked those last weeks in London, her eyes bruised and her face pale, but she said huskily, "Is anything wrong, sir?"

He frowned, then forced himself to smile lightly. "Not wrong, precisely, my dear. It is just that we must go back to London tomorrow, I'm afraid."

He had expected her to protest, for she had settled in here in a way she had never done in London. But she looked up, her eyes pained, and said dully, "Yes, it is time we returned. The magic has gone."

His eyes narrowed, but in the end he did not question her.

Chapter Sixteen

Dominique had recovered herself by the next morning, and if she looked a little subdued over the breakfast table, managed to chat lightly with Hastings and then supervise the hasty preparations for departure.

Vidal, watching her, was not fooled. He wondered what could have been in her post to make this change in her. The confiding creature from the past weeks was gone, and in her place had been set the charming, reserved woman he had become familiar with over the last months.

He had hardly failed to be aware for many weeks that something was troubling her. But while he might suspect she had at long last begun to chafe at the deceit between them, he could not be certain that that was all it was. She still did not confide in him, and a number of things had conspired to raise doubts in his mind. He did not know whether she was unhappy because she had lied to him, or whether something else had put that haunted look back in her eyes. He had never quiet managed to rid himself of the picture of her looking up so desperately into Carleton's face while he raised her hands to his lips.

He swore suddenly under his breath, and had an impulse to put off the business at hand. He did not like to leave her now, and while he preferred to have her in London, under Maby's eyes, he wished that this—what had she called it? magical?—yes, magical time together could have stretched out a little longer.

In the end, of course, he was forced to remember that he dare not ignore what he had just learned. He had long been ruefully aware that her fierce pride continued to stand between them, and if he were ever to lay that particular ghost, he must pursue this new lead.

Therefore, when they returned to Berkeley Square, he stayed only to have his bags repacked before setting out once more, this time for Paris. He had hoped to be gone less than a fortnight, but inevitably the business stretched out interminably, and he was forced to remain in Paris for five days, chafing at the delay, while the lawyers sifted through the evidence and debated points of law.

He had been virtually certain, by now, but when the proof was at last in his hands, he stood staring at it a long while, wondering if it would be the end of all his hopes after all. Then abruptly he straightened and ordered his bags packed.

He pushed himself on the journey home, inexplicably anxious to be back and impatient of delays. He arrived in Berkeley Square at dinnertime on the eighth day and strode in, travel-stained and weary, just as they were going in to dinner. He sighed and was aware of his tiredness dropping away from him at the stab of pure joy he saw in Dominique's eyes as she saw him standing there.

To be sure, she had recovered herself almost immediately, but that brief moment had told him all he needed to know. Unmindful of the presence of Maby, the butler and two housemaids, he crossed swiftly to her and took her into his arms.

She returned his embrace a little convulsively, and he was aware that something was wrong. But the next instant she had recalled their audience, and pulled herself out of his arms reluctantly, her eyes clinging to his face.

He smiled tenderly down at her, but did not release her. "Forgive me, my dear. I'm very dirty."

She made a little negative shake of her head and said only, "Yes, and tired, too. Will you have dinner set back, or would you prefer to have a tray in your room a little later?"

"No, if you will give me fifteen minutes, I'll come down." Out of the corner of his eye he saw Lymings, an oddly benevolent look in his eyes, slip out to warn the cook; and the others, too, with a start seemed to recall suddenly pressing business elsewhere.

When they were alone he looked her over, his eyes hungry, then shook his head and said ruefully, "I must go. Are you promised somewhere tonight, or dare I hope we can have the evening together?"

He was unprepared for the swift change his words wrought. She stiffened abruptly, an oddly stricken look in her eyes, and said quickly, stumbling a little over the words, "I did not expect you back so soon—I'm afraid I did promise—! That is, you must know that tonight is

Lady Fitzhugh's drum, and I have already said I would attend—!"

He frowned, suspecting she cared not a whit for Lady Fitzhugh's drum. He wondered whether it was only an excuse to avoid being left alone with him, or if she had an assignation.

But she looked so guilty and upset, that his eyes softened and he said gently, "By all means go to your party, my love. I would come too, only Lady Fitzhugh will not be expecting me."

She started violently at the suggestion, then made a valiant effort to cover up her slip by saying disjointedly, "That would not matter—I am sure she would be delighted—only I have promised Sally that I would pick her up on the way."

After a moment he forebore to point out to her that there was room for three in their carriage. It had been a moment of weakness only that had made him suggest it, for he had meant to go out again after dinner himself. The sooner this damnable business was over the better. But then he had every intention of settling matters between them and he would not be put off.

He took very little more than the allotted fifteen minutes to change, and though Lymings explained somewhat apologetically that Alphonse declared the scallops of veal had been sadly compromised and the asparagus souffle destroyed, none of the three who sat down to dinner that evening complained of anything amiss. Dominique, as if dreading silence, chatted gaily of the latest gossip and told Vidal of the dedication of the new Waterloo Bridge they had attended that day. She painted an amusing portrait of the poor stout Regent, sheltering beneath the mantle of Wellington's popularity, and bowing with great benignity to all his subjects, just as though their cheers had been intended for him. Then she told him of how Lady Sarah was complaining that now that Prinny had removed to Brighton for the summer, London was positively empty.

He laughed, and dinner passed in easy conversation. Only when the footman came in with the intelligence that Dominique's coach was at the door did she pale and break off what she had been saying for a brief telltale moment, before rising quickly and excusing herself.

He almost prevented her from going. He had only to stretch out his hand and tell her he wished her to remain home that evening, and she would have been left with very little choice. Then he had recalled his own urgent business again, and did not make the gesture. Tomorrow would be soon enough.

Dominique went quickly out to her carriage, and purposely did not look back. She had an assignation, but it was hardly what Vidal thought, and she would have given anything to stay home with him and ignore the outside world for a little while.

But the outside world would not be ignored. The letter Hastings had brought her at WainCourt had said very little, only that the writer was disappointed she had failed to keep their last appointment, but he would give her one last chance. He would send word to her later as to where and when, and he hoped she was not going to be so foolish as to force him to do what they must both regret.

The terms of the letter had been less cordial that time, and the third missive that had arrived only that morning had been quite abrupt. She was to attend Lady Fitzhugh's drum that night, and leave promptly at midnight. She would be met.

It was foolish, of course, to be afraid in such a familiar and crowded meeting place. And she had, moreover, developed a strong desire to meet her mysterious correspondent and tell him exactly what she thought of him. She was going for only one reason: to inform him that he might do as he pleased with her blessing, his threats no longer had the power to harm her. She herself intended at the first opportunity to inform the world of her identity and background.

He was not to know, of course, that the only world she had ever cared about was Vidal. And she had long ago made up her mind that as soon as Vidal returned from this trip she would confess the whole to him. She had come to know him a little better in those weeks at WainCourt, and she thought now that he would in the end come to understand and forgive, but it made no difference if he did not. She knew a profound sense of relief at the thought that she would soon be free at last, no matter what the consequences.

Vidal's sudden appearance had come close to ruining everything, of course, but she could not be sorry to see him. The thought of him, waiting patiently at home for her to return, sustained her through the short carriage ride and the much longer hours of the party.

Lady Fitzhugh's party seemed more insipid than usual, but she had no doubt her own impatience to be home was to blame. She laughed and danced, all the while wondering what Vidal was doing, and what it was that had taken him away so unexpectedly. She had even wondered during the past week whether this sudden activity might mean that he had suffered monetary reverses. She herself cared little for such things, and had never concerned herself with his wealth, but she did not like to think what such a thing would do to his pride. She wished he might confide in her, then remembered with a pang how very little reason she had given him to do so.

The hours seemed to drag, the night unexpectedly sultry, and a hint of thunder in the air. She wandered restlessly through the too-hot rooms, longing for midnight, and seeing no one she particularly cared to talk with. Despite what she had told Vidal, Lady Sarah had stayed at home with a child who had thrown out a rash the day before, and she had not seen Carleton since she had returned to London. Perhaps he was away.

At last, shortly before midnight, she took the opportunity of supper being announced to slip away. She was just congratulating herself upon successfully eluding a young man emboldened to extreme romantic fervor by an unusual quantity of liquor and wishing she might never attend another drum again, when she stepped into the hall to find it occupied by Lady Caroline and several of her particular court.

Dominique spoke civilly, but Lady Caroline turned her head away and drawled something to her companions, before sweeping out. There were several gasps and a few titters, before the rest of her party hurried after her.

Dominique straightened abruptly, an angry sparkle in her eyes. She had for the most part mastered her jealousy of the woman, and had even felt a certain pity for her. It could not have been easy for her after Vidal's marriage. Lady Caroline had made no secret of her position or her ambitions.

But it was clear that Lady Caroline's malice had become bitter hatred. Dominique would not have minded the direct cut, although it made them both appear foolish, but the cold malevolence in the glance Lady Caroline had given her as she swept out made Dominique shiver a little and hasten outside.

It was an odd relief to discover that the heavy atmosphere and oppressive heat had given way to the rain at last. She stood on the steps, with her taffeta cloak clutched tightly around her, and stared out into the darkness, wondering how long she might be required to wait.

The rain had extinguished the two flambeaux on either side of the door, and the street was unexpectedly dark. There seemed to be very few people about at this time of night. The two linkboys huddled just around the corner, attempting to keep their torches alight, unaware of her presence.

Then a dark, bulky figure detached itself suddenly from one of the waiting carriages. He held an unbrella over his head, so that in the dim light his face was in shadow, but he came quickly toward her. "Your grace? You will come with me, please?"

There was an urgency in his tone, and he spoke with a slight accent. She wondered why it had never occurred to her that her correspondent might be French. But she certainly had no intention of going anywhere with him. She pulled away and said coldly, "No, indeed! We will discuss it here, if you don't mind!"

He looked around, then shrugged, and appeared to accept it. He urged her a little away from the door, holding the umbrella solicitously over her head to ward off the rain. "As you wish, madame."

Then abruptly his fingers closed tightly on her arm, and he was hurrying her forward, his grip bruising and his actions concealed by the sheltering umbrella. She attempted to jerk away from him, bitterly aware of how foolish she had been to come alone to such a meeting, and looked frantically around for someone to help her. There was no one but the linkboys, still huddling miserably against the rain, but she opened her mouth to scream to them when his blow caught her on the side of the head.

She crumpled without a sound, and to any onlookers it must have seemed that milady had fainted and was being helped solicitously into her carriage.

When she opened her eyes a long while later, she was being rocked at great speed in a badly sprung carriage. She closed her eyes faintly again, her head aching abominably and the motion of the vehicle making her slightly ill.

Then as her memory returned, she sat up abruptly, instinctively clutching her bruised head, and tried to make her dizzy brain concentrate. She looked a little blankly around the carriage, not recognizing it as one of Vidal's, then leaned forward to stare out the window. It was still raining, the night very dark, and she could see little. But there was no lights, and it was clear she was no longer in London.

With the intention perhaps of seeking some cool air to clear her head, she tried to let down the window. But it, and all the others she tried, were stuck. Some of the reality of the situation at last penetrated her consciousness, and without being quite aware of what she was doing, she reached desperately for the door. Her hand scrabbled uselessly against the cracked leather. The inside handles had been removed.

She bit back a sob then, and forced herself to lean against the dusty cushions, until the throb in her head had receded a little, and her heart had ceased to pound so desperately. Hysteria would do no good at all at the moment, and she needed all of her wits about her.

She thought suddenly of Vidal, sitting home waiting for her, perhaps before the fire in his library with a book, then forceably pulled her thoughts away. That particular direction could only undermine what courage she had left, and she was very much on her own for the moment.

But oddly enough, the thought of Vidal did calm her. She leaned her head back against the squabs, her eyes staring blindly into the dark interior of the coach, her mind working suddenly with painful clarity.

She had been a fool—worse than a fool!—she had been unforgivably stupid not to see what was now so dreadfully obvious. Everything that had happened in the past month had been part of a horrible pattern, and only the fact that her thoughts had been taken up with other, more pressing problems, had prevented her from realizing it long before now. Those odd blackmail threats: the first letter that had taken her so conveniently to a strange district in the city where she had almost been run down, and only a woman's screams had saved her from serious accident or death. The next, that had set her up for this even more desperate attempt. She wondered a little blankly why whoever it was had bided his time so long between attempts. Then she thought she knew the answer. Vidal, of course. His presence and the long stay at WainCourt had stilled his hand. She thought suddenly he must not be aware that Vidal had returned tonight so unexpectedly.

At least there was hope in that thought, for Vidal would discover her absence very soon, if he had not already done so. Vidal would be far more of a threat to her abductor than Maby alone would have been while Vidal was far away.

She wondered suddenly what time it was, and if Vidal would even now have begun to worry at her delay in returning home. The thought strengthened her, and although she was cold and a little sick, she managed to keep up her spirits and refused to give in to the terrible fear that threatened to overwhelm her if she once weakened.

So many things were clear now—but not the reason. Why—*why*—would someone go to such elaborate lengths to frighten her and then kidnap her? The thought of ransom was oddly appealing, for there was hope in that. But she was past the point where she could lull her fears with comfortable falsehoods. Someone had attempted to run her down, and when that had failed they had had her abducted. But what could anyone possibly gain from having her harmed? She had nothing, and while Vidal was a very wealthy man, her death would hardly benefit anyone.

Suddenly, unbidden, came the thought that she might have deceived herself about that, too, all these months . . .

After that she lost all track of time. She dozed a little, only to start awake at the slightest jolt or change in direction, her heart beating suffocatingly when she remembered where she was. But even that was a relief, almost, since her dreams proved worse than the waking. She became cramped, and she was now very cold, her taffeta cloak damp and no protection against the night chill invading the carriage. The rain continued steadily outside the carriage windows.

She had no idea how long they had been traveling when the carriage made a ponderous turn and at last drew to a halt. Her heart leaped against her ribs, and she was instantly awake. Had they reached their destination, or were they forced to change horses? She leaned to stare out the streaming window, and nearly tumbled down when the door was jerked open abruptly.

She drew a deep breath and forced herself to step stiffly down from the carriage, looking around her quickly as she did so. But there was little enough to see. There were no lights anywhere except in the small two-story house they were standing in front of. She pulled abruptly away from the bulky figure when he would have taken her arm, and walked firmly toward the cottage's open door. Even before she had reached it the carriage had pulled away again.

At the door she lifted her head and walked through, a strangely bedraggled figure in her jewels and evening silks. For a moment the light dazzled her eyes and she was conscious of the pain in her head, but then she walked calmly forward, contemptuously surveying the man who leaned so negligently against the mantel.

After a moment, when he made no sound, she lifted her brows and said drily, *"Bonjour, mon oncle."*

Chapter Seventeen

The man flushed darkly, then moved to politely set a chair for her.

She would like to have retained the advantage of standing, but feared her knees might betray her, so she accepted the seat. She made a show of arranging her cloak around her, well aware that the gesture was more to keep up her own spirits than impress her uncle. Then she lifted her clear eyes to his face.

His smile, incredibly, was almost kind. "Why, how are you, my dear niece?" he said easily. "It is so nice that we meet again at last, don't you think? I regretted very much that you could not accept my previous invitations."

"They at least were worded a little more politely!"

"Ah, you must forgive the rough treatment, my dear. Naturally I regret it very much, but what can one do?" He spread his hands in an eloquent gesture.

Her lips curled derisively, but she remained silent.

He stroked the side of his face for a moment. "I am very flattered, of course, to think that you remember me all these years, my dear. Flattered, and I must admit, rather surprised." He looked at her beneath his hooded eyes, and she thought there was something oddly guarded in his expression. "Or can it be that you have expected me?"

She shrugged. "You have somewhat the look of my father."

His expression relaxed suddenly. "Ah, no doubt that is it. While you, on the other hand, have a great deal the look of your mother. She was very beautiful, and so, my dear, are you."

She bowed mockingly. "You are very kind, Uncle."

His eyes narrowed and he studied her elegant gown, the jewels at her throat and her taffeta wrap. "Yes, you are beautiful," he murmured absently. Then he roused himself and snapped his fingers. "But I am forgetting my manners! You must be quite exhausted from your journey, my dear. Allow me to give you a glass of wine."

He raised his voice. "Georges, the wine and two glasses! My poor niece looks as if she could do with a drink."

The stocky figure from earlier that evening appeared from the other room, bearing a tray with a bottle and two glasses. She looked curiously at his face and wondered how many more men there might be, or if she had only the two of them to contend with.

Her uncle poured out two glasses and handed one to her. "You met Georges earlier my dear, I believe. Georges is very devoted to me, are you not, Georges?"

The man's expression did not change. She was suddenly conscious of the unreality of the scene: those two strange men, this place, the normal act of offering wine in such a nightmare. She drew her head up abruptly, weary of the game. "I am naturally enjoying this little tête-à-tête, Uncle, but perhaps you will be so kind as to tell me exactly what you mean by this—this invitation, and then I can go home again. My husband is waiting for me."

His eyebrows rose. "Ah, yes, the so estimable English *Duc.* You have done very well for yourself, my dear. Very well! And they say he is mad for you. But he is unfortunately away at the moment, and I fear you will be required to enjoy my hospitality for a little longer.

"Ah, but you are not drinking your wine," he said gently. When she only continued to stare steadily at him he laughed suddenly. "But of course! How stupid of me! But I can assure you, my dear, that it is perfectly safe." He took a sip from his own glass then proffered it to her. "You see? Quite safe."

After a moment she ignored his glass and drank from her own. Then her brows rose a little mockingly. It was an excellent wine.

"But, of course, I brought it with me, my dear child," he said in amusement. "One can never trust the barbarous taste of the English, or have you not found that to be true? Your father, I know, was a great lover of the English. And then, I suppose you must be half-English yourself." He studied the color of the wine in his glass. "Yes, you have done very well for yourself," he repeated. Almost idly he raised his eyes. "So well that I know you will not grudge your uncle a very little."

When she remained silent he added gently, "I am certain there will be no need for any harshness, my dear. I can see that you are a very sensible girl. You have only to sign a piece of paper renouncing any claim you may have to your grandfather's estate, and we shall all be happy. I will restore you to your husband upon the instant."

Her lips curled. "Why, yes, I imagine you would be very happy! I see that my grandfather changed his will in my father's favor? What a blow that must have been after all the effort you had been to to have my father disinherited in the first place! So, naturally you thought it would be easy to frighten a woman into doing whatever you wished."

Her voice was full of contempt, and for a very brief moment her uncle's rigid control slipped. But almost instantly he had resumed his suave mask. "Come, come, my dear," he chided gently. "There is no need for this unpleasantness. You have no use for more money and will gladly sign my document. Your Miss Mabington must be growing concerned at your absence. It is possible that if you are gone for too long she may come to believe that you have . . . er . . . eloped with one of your so-eager admirers."

She managed a creditable smile, although he had shaken her. "Obviously, it would suit your purposes to have her think so. So admirably, I feel certain you have overcome the difficulty of duplicating my handwriting in the note you have no doubt sent her informing her of that fact."

He smiled. "You are very quick, my dear. It was but a piece of luck that Lady Caroline happened to discover a note you had written to your dear sister-in-law and was able to quietly pocket it. After that, with a little diligence, the thing was easily done. I assure you neither your husband nor your beloved Maby will look too closely at the handwriting."

She was scarcely listening any longer. "Lady Caroline—?" she repeated frowningly, more to herself than to him.

For a moment he appeared to regret that brief slip of the tongue, but then he shrugged. "But of course," he said simply. "Lady Caroline was kind enough to offer me some slight assistance. I am certain you are aware she has little reason to feel a fondness for you."

Her pride had managed to sustain her thus far, but now fear suddenly constricted her chest, making it difficult to breathe. If she had ever deluded herself into thinking he was playing anything but a deadly game, the mention of Lady Caroline had disillusioned her.

But then as abruptly she was consumed by a colder rage than she had ever known. She would be *damned* if she would allow herself to be defeated now by them!

Nor would she let him see her thoughts. She lifted her head and remarked almost conversationally, "I see it all now, of course. I must confess I have been very stupid. But then, one does not normally expect that one's relations are trying to kill one, do they?"

"Come, come, my dear," he said chidingly. "There is no need for such talk. I mean you no harm. You have only to sign my paper and you can return to your home. I think I can safely promise that you will never see me again."

She drew herself up to her full height, a slight smile in her eyes. "You can go to the devil!"

If she had meant to anger him into losing his control again she was doomed to disappointment. He only laughed. "You are a young woman of spirit, my dear. I must confess I admire that! But I am sure that given a little time to think it over you will conclude that what I ask is after all very little in return for your freedom. Georges, show *Madame la Duchesse* to her room. I regret, my dear, that the comforts are somewhat lacking, but I am confident you will not require us to remain here long."

Georges came forward and took her arm, not cruelly, but as if he were only politely escorting her up the stairs. She eyed him for a moment, then obediently moved with him toward the narrow staircase.

"Oh, and my dear," her uncle's voice halted them at the first stair. "It will do you no good to scream, of course. I am sure you have noticed there is no one within miles. I will give you one hour."

At the top of the stairs Georges opened a door and stood back to allow her to enter a small room. She shrugged and did so. Almost immediately the door closed behind her and she heard the key turn in the lock.

She looked around the room slowly, determinedly keeping her thoughts at bay. There was a narrow bed against one wall, a chest of drawers and one chair. They were plain, sturdy pieces of furniture, scarred from years of use. A shabby quilt was thrown across the bed and the walls were covered in an ancient paper that was cracked and peeling and showed dark stains spreading from the ceiling. But someone, sometime, in a touching desire for something pretty, had hung ruffled curtains at the room's only tiny window. They hung listlessly on either side of the dirty panes, time slowly removing their incongruity in the drab, ugly room.

She crossed to the window. It was an old-fashioned casement type, opening outward from the center. The opening was scarcely large enough to permit even a small woman to pass through, but they were nevertheless taking no chances. A lock had been installed, the pile of shavings under the window attesting to the newness of the alteration.

Her spirits sank, but she forced herself to search methodically through the rest of the room. She looked through all the drawers, behind the chest, under the bed, searching for something—she hardly knew what: a loose board, a weapon, anything she might use. The room had been prepared well. There was nothing.

For a long time she stood in the center of the room, the single candle they had left her flickering over her and throwing shadows on the wall. She was dry-eyed, strangely calm.

She had no illusions. She knew that once she had signed her uncle's paper he would have no choice but to kill her. He dared not allow her to leave.

Or rather, he would have her killed. She doubted if he would soil his hands with the actual deed. He would leave that to the so-devoted Georges. If she had doubted it before, her uncle's mention of Lady Caroline had confirmed it. Lady Caroline would not take the risk of assisting him unless she were very sure her part would never be discovered—and unless she had a very great deal to gain. In short, a second chance to become the Duchess of Vidal.

Her only hope lay in the fact that her uncle seemed to need her signature. Something had occurred between the accident and now to make him believe that he no longer dared do anything until he had it, for she felt certain he had meant to kill her then. She could not think what it could be—unless he had learned of the Settlements she had signed. She almost laughed at the thought. She had never thought to be grateful for those hated Settlements, but they might be the only thing that was keeping her alive for the moment.

But time, her only ally, seemed to stretch endlessly now, tightening her nerves unbearably and undermining the little courage she had left. No doubt her uncle had depended upon that. An hour in which to think, he had said. She dared not allow herself to think, or the fear inside her could no longer be controlled.

Gervaise, her uncle, had written to her shortly after her father's death. She had no idea how he had known, but his letter had been kind, even affectionate. He had said it was past time that old feuds be forgotten, and invited her to come and live with them.

But somehow she could not forgive what had been done to her father so many years ago. He had rarely talked of his youth or the rift with his family, and it had not been until he was dying that she had learned exactly how much the loss of his heritage had meant to him. He had always been gay, uncaring, never content to remain in any one place for very long. Her childhood had been one of constant movement, almost as if her father could not bear to be still for too long.

But only when it was too late had she realized that his determined gaiety and constant movement had masked a man haunted by his past. Because she had never had a home it had not occurred to her that her father had only ever really cared about one thing in his life. If he could not have it, he would have nothing else.

He had fallen ill, with a slight fever, but she had not worried too much. He was seldom ill, and invariably a bad patient, running both her and Maby ragged. But Maby had gone to her sister, and she had had to bear the brunt of his constant errands herself.

It was then the letter had come. He had read it, then laughed and laughed until the tears rolled down his face. At last he had gotten up and ridden away. He was away all night, and when he returned the next morning his fever was much worse.

Then he had been delirious, and had babbled endlessly of his home and his boyhood and the father he both loved and hated, as if the floodgate that had held him silent all those years had at last been opened. She had been terrified and searched frantically for the letter that had caused all this. She could not find it and he would not explain.

And he had talked of other things, things she only half understood. Of Annemarie, her mother, and the old Marquis, and the hate and anger unleashed by a thoughtless marriage born in a moment of youthful defiance. There had always been jealousy, for he was his father's favorite, and in the end his brothers had triumphed and he had been disinherited, sent away from the home he loved above all else.

She had sat with him and soothed him in his fever, and had known a strange pity for his wasted life and for her poor dead mother who had precipitated it all, and yet had meant so little.

Only after her father's death did she find the letter. It was from a firm of lawyers in Paris. Robert, the eldest son, was dead and the old Marquis was very ill. He wished the return of his long-lost son and heir.

With a feeling of revulsion she herself had scarcely understood, she had determined that she would never become dependent upon the charity of her grandfather. It was almost amusing, really. Her uncle might have spared himself this effort. She had not known about the will, or even the death of her grandfather, but it was an inheritance she would never claim. He had always been welcome to it for all of her.

Suddenly her head drooped and she did not know whether she longed to laugh or cry. She was so tired . . . so very tired . . .

Abruptly her head jerked up as her eyes narrowed on the pile of sawdust and shavings she had been staring at unseeingly for so long. Hardly aware of what she did, she flew to the window again, her fingers feverishly searching out the hinges buried deep in the ancient wood on either side of the window. It might work. It just might work.

Then she stiffened as steps sounded on the stairs. Her heart thudded sickeningly, but she made herself move away from the window and stand calmly in the center of the room. Time. She must have time.

She drew a deep breath as the key scraped in the lock. Her uncle came through the door, followed closely by Georges. "Well, my dear, have you decided to be sensible?" His voice was soft and affectionate.

For a moment she was tempted to appear to waver and allow her uncle to think that he had succeeded in frightening her. Then she bit back an hysterical giggle. Think! She had never been so terrified in her life.

But Gervaise was no fool, and he would by now have taken her measure quite accurately. And she was, after all, a de St. Forêt.

She met his eyes steadily. "I'm afraid you will have to kill me, Uncle. I shall not sign your paper."

His eyes narrowed angrily. "You are a fool if you think I will not! I have gone too far to draw back now!"

She smiled quite creditably. "And you are a fool if you think killing me will serve your purpose. Upon my death my husband inherits everything. I have signed a will in his favor. You will never see a penny of that money!"

His face was dark, but he smiled too. "Yes, my dear, you are like your mother. I see you are a very intelligent girl."

"Why, thank you, Uncle. If you accept that we shall deal together a great deal better. I have an alternative offer to propose to you. Restore me to my husband, and I will give you my word he will not kill you for this."

His laugh was quite genuine. "Yes, you have courage, my dear! And you are correct in one matter. It will avail me little to kill you. But even death can sometimes become —desirable."

But she was not to be frightened by such vague threats like any schoolroom miss! "Why, Uncle, I am surprised at you! Do you think me such a poor creature that I can be frightened into submission by idle threats and boasts? If you do not intend to kill me, and I think we have agreed that you do not, then we are both of us wasting our time here. I will not sign your paper, so let us call it a draw and part company like sensible human beings."

But the humor had disappeared from his face, leaving him suddenly older, and he did not rise to her taunt. "It is a great pity, my dear," he said quietly. "I hope you will not force me into something I will regret. I really do dislike hurting beautiful things."

The odd thing was, she thought he meant it. She paled a little, but lifted her head. "Why, come, Uncle! I had not expected such squeamishness. I have heard a great deal of my illustrious family, very little of it good. I cannot suppose you will balk at torture and murder to obtain what you want!"

Something flashed for such a brief instant through his eyes that she thought she must have imagined it. She would almost have said it was pain, if that had been possible. For some reason she could not explain an icy shiver ran through her.

But the look, if it had been there at all, was quickly gone. Her uncle said softly, no longer making any pretense of gentleness, "I think you are perhaps a very fool-

ish girl after all. Perhaps you desire a little more time. I
will give you until the morning."

He paused and added quite tonelessly, "I would advise
you to think it over very carefully, my dear. Your husband may not want you when I am through with you . . .
Georges?" He went down the stairs without a backward
glance.

As the man Georges came slowly toward her, Dominique involuntarily backed before him, the blood draining
from her face and her eyes huge. His mouth was still
curved in that eternal half-smile and his eyes held no
expression at all. His blow caught her full on the face and
sent her crashing into the wall.

He eyed her dispassionately for a moment, then locked
the door behind him as he left.

Angrily she shook the tears from her eyes and ignored
the taste of blood in her mouth. So she had her time.

Chapter Eighteen

She picked herself up wearily, unmindful of any pain, and moved swiftly to the window again. Her fingers sought instinctively to confirm what had caught her attention earlier. No, she had not been mistaken! The wood surrounding the window was rotting away, its unpainted surface swollen and rough to her fingertips.

Hastily she brought the candle over to look more closely at the hinges that held the casements in place. They were deeply imbedded, but she must just hope that the screws had no real anchor in the soft wood.

It was a desperate chance, she knew, but then, she *was* desperate. The casements fitted badly, and years of weather had taken their toll of the unprotected wood. It was rotten, the grain swollen and separated, so that it appeared as if she could almost peel away splinters of the wood with her fingernails.

But when she tried it, she only succeeded in breaking her nails and bruising her fingers. It would take something sharper. But what?

She looked around the small room a little desperately, conscious of how much time she was taking, searching for anything that might serve as a pick or gouge. But she had already searched the room too well. She knew there was nothing.

Her glance went down a little blankly, and fastened abruptly on the diamond brooch she wore on the front of her gown. She frowned quickly and unfastened it with trembling fingers. It was very old, part of the Waincourt jewels, and she knew the diamonds were good. But what mattered to her now was that, like many such old pieces, the pin that fastened it to her gown was both large and quite stiff. Bates had often complained about its difficult clasp. It seemed pitifully small, but it was all she had and it would just have to do.

It would take time, though; precious time to undermine the wood around the hinges sufficiently to release the casements from the window frame. Always supposing, of course, the thing could be done at all. She wished she had any way of knowing what time it was now. She tried feverishly to calculate. If she had left the ball at midnight —how many years ago that seemed—and the journey had taken, say, two hours, at the most, with another hour and a half here, to be on the safe side—why that would make it nearly four o'clock in the morning!

But it did no good to think of that. If she allowed herself to give way to panic she would be lost. Determinedly she went to work on the first hinge, doggedly chipping away at the soft wood surrounding it.

The wood resisted her, every tiny chip she managed to dislodge taking precious minutes of her time, but she refused to acknowledge how little progress she was making with her ridiculous brooch. She knew it was hopeless, senseless. But at least it was a chance, and she must do something.

Before long her fingers ached and her eyes were strained with the effort to see in the dim light, but still she chipped stubbornly away at the hinge, the pile of splinters at her feet pitifully small. She did not allow herself to think of the time she was taking. But she could not prevent her eyes from going now and then to the sky to reassure herself that it had not yet begun to grow light.

When the first hinge came loose, the screws pulling free of the soft wood, she could only stare stupidly for a long moment, scarcely believing it. She had actually done it! Hope flared within her then so sharply it was almost a pain.

She leaned her head against the cool panes of the window briefly, then attacked the top hinge with renewed energy, the tiredness falling away from her. If she could just manage to release it, she would be free. She thought she would be able to pull the window open without having to loosen the other side as well. Just one more hinge.

In the end, it was almost ridiculously easy. With the first hinge freed, the increased pressure worked to her advantage, weakening the hold of the screws still further, so that it took much less time to gouge out enough wood to release the top hinge as well. When it came free she was hardly expecting it, and only caught the casement just in time as it sagged within its frame.

She had planned to fold it back against the wall on the

inside, but she discovered it was not necessary. The wood was so rotten that the screws on the other side of the window could not withstand the weight of both casements. The hinges ripped from the wall and she was barely able to prevent the whole window from tumbling to the ground outside, and undoing all her work.

She supported the casements, still bound together by the now useless lock, and carefully lifted them down, standing them against the wall. Then she leaned recklessly out the window, drinking in great draughts of the cool air, full of quiet elation.

But her relief was short-lived. In truth she was hardly any better off than before. She had succeeded in opening the window, but she was still on the second floor, many feet from the ground and freedom. Even if she thought she might be able to climb down, the sides of the house were perfectly smooth, with no vines or creepers or even jutting stones to give her support. Nor dared she jump. A broken leg would hardly improve her circumstances and would ruin any chance she might have of escape.

The window was to the front of the house, and she could see a lighted window immediately below her own, so that any escape at all would be doubly difficult. But she could only deal with one problem at a time. Right now she must find a way to reach the ground. She was so buoyed up by her recent triumph that it did not even occur to her to admit defeat now.

She looked around the room again, then grinned to herself wearily. Of course. What else but the time-honored resort of all desperate heroines? She might be no heroine, but she was certainly desperate enough. She went to strip the sheets from the bed and knot them together.

That done, she eyed them a little dubiously. Even tied together they made a dreadfully short length, and did not look particularly strong either. She wondered a little hysterically whether romantic heroines traditionally escaped from much lower windows, or if indeed anyone actually ever had climbed down knotted sheets. Then she shrugged. Well, she would soon find out.

She returned to the window and carefully let down her makeshift rope. As she had feared, it did not extend very far, but since she could hardly dangle her sheets in front of the window below her, she supposed it did not matter so very much. Now, of course, she needed something to anchor it to.

The bed was the most likely possibility, for it was quite heavy. But it was also at present against the far wall. It took another endless time to inch it across the wooden floor, terrified that at any moment someone must hear the noise she was making and come to investigate. But either the house was better insulated than she had supposed, or they were asleep below, for no one came, and at last she had succeeded in positioning the bed beneath the window. For a long moment she leaned panting against it, before she at last straightened herself and tied the sheet-rope to the head of the bed and carefully lowered it out the window again.

To her anxious gaze it seemed that the darkness was softening already, the sky growing lighter. She knew it got light very early in the summer, but surely she could not have taken so much time! She must be far away before the sun rose. On foot she would be no match for her uncle, unless she had gained enough of a lead that he could not tell in which direction she had gone.

There was no time to even consider now whether her rope would actually bear her weight. She hitched up her skirts tightly, wishing momentarily for her breeches, and wriggled through the window, using the sheet to balance herself. It seemed secure so far, so she held her breath and allowed it to take her weight.

The bed creaked protestingly and for a dreadful moment she felt herself slipping. Then the bed had come up against the wall and she was caught and held firmly, her heart in her mouth and her hands trembling. She closed her eyes and grimly began to lower herself down the side of the house.

Her soft slippers made no sound against the wall, but it was very slow going. She was not used to climbing, and her arms ached unbearably before she had negotiated half the rope's length. But at least her rope held, and there was still no cry from either window to tell her that she had been discovered.

When she at last reached the end of the rope she was just above the lighted window. A good twelve feet still lay between her and the ground. She took a deep breath and determinedly kicked herself away from the wall, throwing her weight as far to the left as she could to land away from the lighted window.

She landed badly, the breath knocked from her body, and vaguely conscious of bruises she would notice later. But at least she was out of the light. She lay there, her heart pounding, for what seemed an eternity, waiting to be found out.

From where she lay just below the window she could hear the occasional low rumble of voices, so that they were still awake. But there was no other sound in the still night. It seemed, incredibly, that she was free.

She picked herself up very quietly and crept around the side of the house, away from the lighted window. Then she gathered her skirts and ran as fast as her legs would carry her across the open field.

She did not stop or look back until she had reached the belt of trees beyond the field. Then she stood leaning against a tree, her lungs straining for air, and her ears cocked for the sound of pursuit. There was none, and she could see the house standing as she had left it, the light shining peacefully from the window.

She grinned, then, foolishly in the dark, and set out in what she fervently hoped was the direction of London.

She did not make the mistake of believing she was out of danger. She had managed, against all odds, to escape—but she had very little time before the sun rose. She had not been mistaken earlier. The dark trees around her had already become more discernible, and the birds twittered noisily above her head. It would be fully light in less than an hour.

She tried to calculate how much time she could reasonably expect before the alarm was sounded. She was not optimistic. She had taken far too long to release the window, and it could not be many hours before they came upstairs for her and discovered her escape. She could only hope she had at least that much time. If for any reason one of them went outside earlier, they must surely discover her gaping window and the telltale sheet dangling from it.

She had a panicked, hunted feeling, as if at any moment she might turn her head and find her uncle just behind her. But she dared not run. She would only exhaust herself, and she had no idea how far she might have to go to find help. So she made herself walk steadily, keeping to a pace she could sustain. She determinedly ignored the sharp stitch in her side and her feet, already protesting in their thin slippers.

Far too soon for her peace of mind the sun rose behind her, steaming softly on the wet earth. She had felt safer in the dark, as if she were somehow invisible. But with the coming of the light walking became much easier, and it was warmer.

She had no idea where she might be, of course. But she thought they had come east from London, so she went west now, keeping the rising sun ever at her back. She knew it was hardly a rational plan, since they might have altered direction a dozen times during that nightmare journey. But still she clung stubbornly to that direction, thinking she must come to civilization soon.

When she emerged from the woods at last she cut across the fields, until she came within sight of a road. It did not look to be a major one, but she dared not use its smoother surface. She saw no one. She might have been the only person alive in all that silent, golden morning.

She was never afterward able to remember much of that strange journey. She walked hour after hour, attempting blindly to keep to the direction she had chosen, tripping wearily over obstacles in her path, falling headlong once or twice in the soft earth, then dragging herself up to go on. The sun rose higher in the sky, but she was no longer aware of it.

At first she had started at the slightest sound, her heart hammering and her mouth dry. But soon she grew too weary even for that. She plodded on, her feet blistered, her hair tumbling down her back, aware of nothing but the weary images dancing inside her head.

But those would not leave her alone. Her mind circled endlessly, haunting her. Her father, tormented by what he could not have; her uncle, so very much like him in many ways, cheated at the last minute of what he had given so much to gain. She wondered how a piece of ground could have the power to ruin so many lives.

And there were other things—not even thoughts so much as images she did not recognize and did not want to. There had been a lake. She did not know where. A lake, yes, serene and blue in the sun; and a woman and a child. It was strangely peaceful there, the woman and the

child and flowers to be gathered on the hillside. Strange
flowers she did not know, of red and gold.

But suddenly there was a man, intruding on that peaceful scene. A man with anger in his eyes and a loud voice.
Then the man and the woman had struggled briefly together on the edge of the blue, blue lake, and the sun
streamed down while the child screamed in terror. And
then there was nothing but red and gold blossoms, spilling
out on the lake . . .

At last even the images were gone and there was nothing but the necessity of putting one foot in front of the
other, and not letting herself fall to the soft grass because
she might never get up again.

Sometime in that morning she heard the sound of a
vehicle approaching on the road beside her. She had no
idea how long or how far she had come, but in sudden,
mindless panic she threw herself in the ditch beside the
road. She lay there, her eyes closed tightly and her body
tensed with terror.

From seemingly far away came a querulous voice.
"Ma'am?" it said uncertainly. "Ma'am? Are ye hurt,
ma'am?"

Slowly she sat up. A very old man stood at the edge of
the ditch, his watered blue eyes staring down at her in
concern and something very like wonderment. She became aware then of what she must look like, in her torn
and muddy gauze and jewels. She put her head down and
laughed weakly, helplessly, knowing she was safe at last.

But at the old man's start of fright she controlled herself with an effort. "No, please!" She rose painfully and
limped toward him. "I'm not mad! Really I'm not."

He did not look to be convinced, but he held his
ground. She sighed then and said simply, "Please, sir, I
need your help. Will you take me to London?"

The old man eyed her obliquely for a long moment,
then nodded slowly. Without a word he helped her into
the back of his cart. She had fallen asleep even before the
cart moved forward, the sweet smell of hay in her nostrils.

Chapter Nineteen

Maby, dwelling on the scene she had witnessed earlier, retired early to her room to indulge in one of her chief vices—a novel from the lending library. She would read just until she had heard Dominique return, then go to sleep.

But as it grew later and later her eyes drooped and then finally closed, her book sliding unnoticed to the floor. Sometime later her candle guttered and went out.

Bates, forbidden to wait up for her mistress any longer, looked into her room at half-past twelve, and seeing her still not returned, sniffed and went to bed.

When Vidal returned after one, he paused to tap on Dominique's door. Receiving no answer, he almost turned the handle and went in. Then he shook his head a little ruefully and crossed to his own room.

He was seated at the breakfast table the next morning, the paper propped before him, when Maby burst in upon him, a sobbing Bates at her heels.

"Your grace! Dominique did not return home last night!" Maby wrung her hands. "She's nowhere in the house and Bates says her bed's not been slept in!"

He listened to her story in frowning silence, barking an occasional question and at one point ruthlessly dispatching a nearly hysterical Bates to her room.

"Oh, your grace!" Maby finished. "I meant to stay up until she was in bed last night, but I fell asleep like the foolish old woman I am! I—" Her kind, plain face was suddenly old and haggard.

He put out his hand to grip her shoulder just as there was a discreet cough at the door of the breakfast room, left ajar by her hurried entrance. Vidal's head jerked around, frowning at this unprecedented breach of protocol by the usually impeccable Lymings. "Yes, what is it, Lymings?" he snapped.

The butler cleared his throat hesitantly, then advanced into the room. "I hope you will excuse this untimely interruption, your grace," he said apologetically. "I would naturally not have presumed to enter unannounced, but the door was ajar and I could not help overhearing . . ."

"Good God! Get to the point, man!"

Lymings allowed himself one more slight cough. "Certainly, sir. A lad has just this instant brought around this note. You will forgive me, but I thought under the circumstances you would wish to see it right away."

Vidal nearly snatched the proffered envelope from his butler's hand. The fact that Lymings had committed the further solecism of presenting it by hand rather than resting chastely on the silver salver reserved for such occasions told him how much his household already knew of the night's happenings.

He ripped open the seal and his eyes raced down the single page. "Who delivered this?" he demanded.

"A lad, sir. I took the liberty of trying to detain him, but I fear he slipped away." Lymings' usually impassive face was concerned and he shook his head regretfully. "I am not as young as I used to be, your grace," he said simply.

Vidal looked up at him for a moment, then nodded. "Yes, Lymings. That will be all. And—thank you."

He watched the butler withdraw and close the door carefully behind him. Then he wordlessly handed the brief note to Maby.

She searched his face for a moment, seeking some clue to its contents, before adjusting her spectacles and reading it. It was very brief and to the point.

My dear Justin:

By now you will have learned that I have gone away for a while. Please do not worry, or try to find me. And you must reassure Maby that I am safe and quite content.

I would give much not to have to tell you this, but I think you have known for some time that there is someone else. Please do not blame him, or judge either of us too badly. I give you my word I have not gone away with him. I must have time in which to consider everything carefully. If I give you pain, I hope you will in time be able to forgive me and see that I am trying to do what is best for both of us.

I have taken nothing with me. If in the end I find

I cannot return to you, I will send back the jewels I am wearing.

I can only again beg that you accept this, and allow me the time I need.

My love to Maby.

Dominique

When Maby looked up at last she was very pale. "I—your grace," she faltered. "I cannot believe she would do this. I—I have known that she—" she clamped her lips shut, unwilling to reveal too much. "I just cannot believe it . . ."

Vidal's voice was strangely gentle. "Is it her handwriting, Maby?"

She frowned and bent her head again to the letter. "It looks like it," she said unhappily. "I am no expert, of course, but it's very like. Do you think—?"

"I don't believe it either, Maby," he said quietly. "If it is not an outright forgery, which I rather suspect, then she was . . . constrained to write it."

The word rested between them for a long moment. At last she drew a deep breath and said slowly, "What do you suspect, your grace?"

"Her uncle, ma'am!" he replied baldly.

She gave a little moan and swayed on her feet. "It is my fault!" she whispered through colorless lips. "I have feared something like this . . . I should have—"

"Nonsense, Maby." Vidal's voice was very even. "If it is anyone's fault it is mine. Will you please send Lymings to fetch Hollings, and ask Charles to come to me? Then see what you can discover from the maids."

For a moment he feared she would not be able to respond. Then slowly she raised her head, stiffened her shoulders, and went without a word to do his bidding.

As soon as the door closed behind her he returned his attention to the brief note, as if by the very intensity of his gaze he could learn something more than the words conveyed. At last he savagely screwed up the sheet and thrust it away from him, his mouth very grim.

Then he lifted his head sharply as his secretary came quickly into the room. "Charles! You know? Good. I want you to check all of the hotels for anyone fitting the description of the Marquis de St. Forêt. Take as many of the stable lads as you need and do it as quickly as possible."

Vidal's expression was forbidding, and after his initial start Hastings made no comment, but turned on his heel, his questions remaining unspoken. As he reached the door he encountered Hollings. They exchanged quick worried glances and passed each other without a word.

Hollings' usually gruff face was full of concern. "We'll find her, sir," he said awkwardly. "Never you fear."

Vidal gripped the older man's shoulder for a brief moment. "Yes, Jeremy, we will. Send the coachman to me, and saddle the black, then go to Lady Fitzhugh's and see if you can discover exactly what time her grace left last night and anyone who may have seen her go."

Hollings was almost to the door when Vidal's voice stopped him. "And Jeremy," he said quietly. "I don't need to tell you to keep this as quiet as possible."

In a very few minutes the coachman came in, his hat in his hands and his eyes miserable. "Sir, 'er grace sent a message to say she was to come with Lady Sarah and not to wait for 'er. Believe me, sir, I wouldn't 'ave 'ad nothing 'appen to 'er for the world. I swear it to yer!"

Vidal eyed him for a long moment. "All right, Sturm. I believe you. What time was this?"

"Why, about eleven, sir. I remember because I 'ad the 'orses seen to and was in my bed before I 'eard the stable clock striking midnight. I never thought—"

Vidal was frowning heavily. "Did she often send you home?"

"Why, not often, sir. But now and again."

"Who brought the message?"

Sturm fingered his cap. "I don't know, sir," he said unhappily. "A footman, I thought . . ." He swallowed convulsively. "Sir, I—"

He was so obviously concerned that after a moment Vidal dismissed him. "Don't worry, Sturm. It's not your fault. See if you can find any of the others that might know anything more."

It was a refrain he was to repeat often. In the next half hour every member of his household who might have been held even remotely responsible for the safe return of her grace found business in the library where Vidal had repaired. And it said much for the esteem in which Dominique was held that instead of seeking to excuse themselves from blame, each one held himself personally responsible for not seeing that her grace was safely home.

While Vidal endured a tearful and almost wholly unintelligible apology from the upstairs maid, who somehow seemed to feel that she alone should have made certain her grace was safe in bed, there was a sudden commotion in the hall. In a minute Hollings entered, dragging a young boy by the collar.

"Young Jemmy has something to say to you, sir," Hollings said grimly.

Jemmy knuckled his eyes and squirmed, but finally blurted out that a foreign gentleman had been asking about the mistress. Wasn't he proud to work for such a beautiful and kind lady? Did she go riding every morning?

Hollings frowned. "I'm sorry, sir. I never dreamed anything like that was happening. It's my fault. I should have warned the lads to keep quiet. I don't think Jemmy meant any harm."

Jemmy, in the meantime, had burst into noisy sobs. "I *loves* 'er grace, sir! I didn't mean no 'arm, 'onest I didn't! I just told them how kind and pretty she is, sir!"

There was an expression no one could ever remember seeing in Vidal's eyes before, but he merely smiled and said wearily, "No, of course you didn't, Jemmy. Is my horse ready, Hollings? Good. I'm going to Lady Sarah's. I should be back in half an hour."

But Lady Sarah knew nothing. She had not gone to the ball because young Jonathon had thrown out a rash.

"Justin—?" She faltered before his look.

"Don't worry, Sally. I'll find her."

He next went to Lord Carleton's lodgings in Clarges Street. Carleton was still at his breakfast, but he waved his hand and cheerfully greeted his old friend. Only at a closer look at his face did he frown suddenly and rise to meet him.

Vidal, without emotion, passed Carleton the note to read.

Carleton swiftly read it, then looked up and said abruptly, "Justin, you don't think—?" He stared intently into Vidal's eyes, and must have found something to reassure him there, for he relaxed a little. "Justin, I won't deny how I feel," he said quietly. "But I give you

my word there has never been anything like that between us. Surely you know she's too deeply in love with
you to even know anyone else exists?"

Vidal nodded, and gripped his old friend's hand. "I
had counted on that, of course. But I saw you together
once, standing together with her hands in yours."

"Oh, my God!" Carleton said, suddenly pale.

Vidal frowned abruptly. "I trusted both of you better
than that, John!"

But Carleton brushed that aside. "No, no! That day—!
The cart that almost ran her down—! It never occurred
to me that it might be more than an accident, and she
made me promise not to—" He broke off at the grim look
in Vidal's eyes, and told him then what had happened.

Vidal swore long and dreadfully beneath his breath,
his face gray. Then without a word he strode out. Carleton, after a moment's hesitation, picked up his hat and
followed him.

When they reached Berkeley Square, Charles was just
entering the house, a heavy frown between his eyes.
Vidal shook his head slightly and ushered him into the
library, once more in control of himself. "Now, Charles,"
he said quietly.

Charles glanced hesitantly at Carleton, then said
simply, "The Marquis de St. Forêt has been putting up
at one of the better hotels in the City for more than a
month. He left only two days ago."

Vidal's face was grim. "He used his own name? He
does not lack for effrontery, damn him!"

Charles shook his head, a brooding expression in his
eyes. "Sir, I know there was the will in her favor, but
surely you don't think—I mean it's preposterous, sir! He
cannot hope to get away with it, and what does he think
to accomplish?" He looked up sharply. "A signed renun-
ciation—? Why, then sir, perhaps he will let her go when
she has signed it . . ." He faltered and said desperately,
"I mean, sir, he can gain nothing by her death . . ."

"He has gone too far. He cannot set her free now."
Vidal's voice was steady. "But he dare do nothing until
he obtains her signature. I am counting on Dominique to
stall him as long as possible."

Charles was very pale. "Sir—I—shouldn't we call in
the Bow Street runners? How can you hope to find her
yourself?"

"Not yet, Charles. Once we do, we cannot hope to keep it quiet. If there is a general hue and cry, de St. Forêt will not dare to keep her alive any longer." There was no trace of emotion in his voice.

Charles closed his eyes for a moment and lapsed into silence.

In a very few minutes Hollings returned. "Well, sir I told Lady Fitzhugh's butler that her grace was missing a diamond eardrop and thought she might have lost it there." He grinned briefly. "He immediately jumped up in the boughs, and a nastier, more stiff-rumped blighter I've seldom seen, but the long and the short of it is that he saw the Duchess of Vidal out shortly before midnight. He called for her carriage, but did not see her into it because her ladyship desired his assistance just then. Her grace was alone."

Hollings hesitated, and dropped his eyes. "There was only one other thing he recalled, sir. The Lady Caroline Graham was in the hall when her grace left."

The paper knife Vidal had been lightly holding snapped with a loud sound. After a moment Vidal said quietly, "Thank you, Jeremy." He strode out without another word. Charles and Hollings exchanged worried glances and hastily departed.

Vidal had for so long had the entree at Lady Caroline's house that her butler made no attempt to stop him. He merely smiled politely and informed his grace that the Lady Caroline was in the upstairs drawing room.

When Vidal strolled in a few minutes later Lady Caroline glanced up sharply, and a flicker of something showed briefly in her eyes, before she lowered her lashes. "Why, Vidal, my dear!" she drawled. "Don't tell me your wife's charms have palled so quickly."

Instantly she regretted the words. But although Vidal's mouth thinned, he only stood before her, lightly drawing his riding crop through his hands.

Lady Caroline was no fool, but neither was she a coward. She decided to brazen it through. "Ah, but then you do not like me to speak of your wife! How is the dear creature, by the way? I vow she was looking quite ravishing at Lady Fitzhugh's ball last evening. At least your friend Lord Carleton seemed to think so." She smiled archly.

Vidal's expression did not change. If anything his eyes

lightened. "Yes, my dear Caroline. Why don't you tell me about last night. But then I understood you to leave early, so perhaps you missed the exciting part."

Despite herself she felt her cheeks grow a little pale. She tossed her head. "Why, what is this? Some scandal brewing? But tell me!" she commanded lightly and patted the sofa beside her.

Vidal smiled. "I shall almost miss you, my dear," he said softly. "I must admit I had underestimated you." His smile thinned. "In fact, that seems to be a mistake I have made rather often of late."

She managed to laugh almost successfully. "But you are talking nonsense, my dear Vidal! I am going nowhere!" Then at his look she faltered.

In an instant Vidal had crossed the room and grasped her wrist cruelly, dragging her ruthlessly to her feet. "I have never used violence toward a woman, but I must confess you tempt me strongly!" he grated. "You had better tell me exactly what you know, before I forget myself."

To her credit, once she understood the game was up she did not pretend to misunderstand him. She drew herself up proudly and told him coldly and succinctly what she knew. It was not much. She had merely provided information to the man claiming to be the Marquis de St. Forêt. And on the night of Lady Fitzhugh's ball she had undertaken to send a footman to Vidal's coachman with the message that her grace would not require his further services that night. She had not thought he meant to harm Dominique. He only wanted her signature on a certain document.

Vidal did not release her wrist. "I see," he said contemptuously. "And what were you to gain from this very obliging assistance?"

At that her careful control deserted her. "I would have done anything to be rid of her!" she spat. "You loved *me* until she came along with her high airs and wheedling manners! Currying favor everywhere and setting everyone to laugh at me. I saw through her immediately, and you would have too, in time! You will still! She was nothing but a fortune hunter, and I'm glad she's dead! Glad! Do you hear me?"

Only then did she become aware of exactly what she had said. Still she would not give in before him. "Well,

Vidal! What do you intend to do with me?" she asked drily.

His eyes were very cold. "Do you know where he meant to take her?"

"I—" She shrugged. "No. I did not particularly care."

After a moment he released her wrist, as if he were scarcely aware of her. "I think perhaps a trip abroad is necessary for your health," he said curtly. "I have been noticing you have looked rather pale lately. I do not think we shall meet again." He bowed and walked out.

She stared for a long while at the door he had closed quietly behind him. Then at last she shrugged. Well, at least he was allowing her that. She rang for her maid.

Vidal spent the remainder of the day in the saddle, seeking leads or information. Ambersley came to help, and so too did Lord Carleton. But no one could turn up any sign of her. It was as if she had vanished into thin air.

At a little after eight that night Vidal returned to Berkeley Square, to find them all gathered in the hall. None of them could quite meet his eyes.

"Good God! She can't have just disappeared!"

"Justin, we are as worried as you. But you can't hope to find anything more tonight!" Ambersley urged. "We will all start at first light tomorrow."

Vidal merely turned on his heel and called for a fresh horse. They watched in silence as he swallowed a glass of brandy and set off once more.

They were seated in the drawing room, a strangely silent and subdued group, when he returned again shortly after eleven. One look at his face and all questions died upon their lips.

He strode to the fire and stood staring bleakly down into its depths.

"Justin, she'll be all right!" Lady Sarah laid a pleading hand on his arm. "Let me get you something to eat."

He stared down at her absently, as if he hardly knew her, then shook his head. There were tears in her eyes as she turned away.

Time dragged slowly. Each seemed loath to leave, yet each knew there was nothing more that could be done that night. Maby sat in blind misery, and after a moment Lady Sarah went to comfort her. But there was, after all, little she could say. She contented herself with squeezing her hand and sitting beside her.

Lord Ambersley had just stood up at last, when Vidal's ears seemed to pick up something no one else had heard. In one stride he was across the room and had flung open the drawing room doors. For a long moment he stood staring at the bedraggled, muddy figure that stood before him. Then she was in his arms and his face was buried in her hair.

"Oh, Justin, Justin!" she half laughed and cried, flinging her arms tightly around his neck. Only when he had at last released her did she seem to become aware of the beaming, tearful faces surrounding them.

"Oh, my goodness! I didn't mean to give you all such a fright. I am perfectly fine, I promise you!" She moved suddenly to hug Maby, then Sally, and even Ambersley and Carleton, and smiled gaily at them. "What, you too, Hollings!" she cried lightly. "And Charles! You should have known I could take care of myself."

She looked around again and added irrepressibly, "I have no idea what I look like, but it must be terrible! You all look as if you had just seen a ghost!"

Then her laughter died as she again met Vidal's eyes. "Really, I am not hurt!"

Wordlessly he lifted her in his arms and carried her up the stairs. Those left in the room below smiled a little foolishly at each other and quietly withdrew.

In her bedchamber Vidal set her down slowly, and keeping her within the circle of his arms, gently traced a finger over her cut lip and bruised cheek. His eyes were like death.

She smiled a little uncertainly. "Oh. I'd forgotten that! Is that what everyone was staring at?" Then quickly, "Justin! Don't look like that! It is nothing!"

At that moment there was a tap on the door, and a tearful Bates entered with a can of water, then quickly left. Dominique's eyes met his teasingly. "Well, I am certainly having the oddest effect on people tonight!" she murmured.

He ignored her, and with unbelievable gentleness washed the blood and dirt from her face. Her color rose and she said quickly, "I must look like a pig sty! Justin, this is not necessary."

For the first time he spoke. "Hush, my darling," he

said quietly, and unfastened her cloak and let it fall. Her once elegant gown was in tatters, and there were long scratches on her white skin.

"Justin," she said guiltily, "I'm afraid I lost that diamond brooch. I—I hope it was not too valuable."

"Shhh," he said again, and without another word unfastened her gown and pulled it off.

She blushed hotly and protested, "Justin! Really, I—" Then at the look in his eyes she broke off and stood mutely while he undressed her before the fire as if she had been a child. He gently sponged her bruised body, and slipped her soft silk nightdress over her head. Then he lifted her and held her in his arms as she sank into a low chair before the fire. Her color was high, but she allowed her hand to steal out and cradle his cheek.

At last some of the darkness left his face. She smiled tremulously up at him, and after a moment his lips curved in response. "Are you ministering to me, my love?" he asked gently, with a spark of his old humor.

She sighed, content to lay in his arms and be safe.

After what seemed a very long time, though, he said quietly, "Don't you think it's time you told me the truth, my love?"

She roused at that and met his eyes, her own very grave. And because in the end there was no other way, she said almost baldly, "My name is not Forrester."

"No, my love, I know it is not," he said calmly. When she started, he added gently, "It is Waincourt. Surely you had not forgotten?"

She shook her head insistently, not believing he could be teasing at such a moment. "No, you don't understand!" she said harshly. "I lied to you from the very beginning!"

"I see," he said in an expressionless voice. "Why did you not tell me this before?"

Her eyes were very dark and she said dully, "In the beginning because it would not have changed anything. And then, later, I was too proud. It would have been as if I were making excuses for myself, trying to prove that although I was poor and a governess, I was of good family, so that our marriage was not such a—a *mésalliance*, as you so clearly thought it."

When he said nothing, she added almost to herself, "Later, of course, I began to regret it—but by then it seemed too late. I could not bear for you to despise me as you must have done when you found out how I had deceived you."

Something reached his eyes, and he touched her cheek and said very quietly, "You might have spared us both a great deal of unhappiness, my love. I have known from the very first."

She gasped, and then grew very pale. "No—! Maby promised she would not—!"

"Maby kept your secret, much as she disapproved. You yourself told me. You signed your real name to the marriage certificate."

She stared disbelievingly at him, then laughed with a touch of hysteria. "Good God, what a fool I am! All that time—and you knew—!" Suddenly she was violently angry. "And you let me go on making a fool of myself, when you had known from the very beginning!"

"I could not help hoping you would learn to trust me enough to tell me yourself," he said very quietly.

Suddenly she dropped her head, her eyes full of shame.

"Did you never mean to tell me?" he asked.

Her eyes were deeply showed. "I don't know," she said in despair. "Perhaps if we had—" Then she shook her head and would not continue.

He did not press her, and after a moment she asked, because she had to, "If you know that much, how much more do you know?"

"Practically everything," he admitted quietly. "It was your uncle, wasn't it?"

"Yes," she said dully. She knew she ought to feel anger to learn he had had her thoroughly investigated. But she was suddenly too weary to care.

"Last year my father received a letter. He would not let me see it, but it—killed him. He had been ill, but after that he was like a wild man. Sometimes I would come upon him and he would be laughing in a horrible, mocking way, as if the world were nothing but a huge jest. He died a few weeks later.

"It was not until after his death that I found the letter. It was from a firm of lawyers telling him that his elder brother had died, and he was now the heir to the title. The old Marquis, his father, was ill and wished to see him."

She closed her eyes briefly. "I can only guess what had

been between them and what those years had cost my father. And then the old man thought he could erase those years and all that bitterness as if they had never been."

With an effort she steadied her voice. "Shortly afterward I received a letter from my uncle, inviting me to come and live with them. He was sorry to learn of my father's death and hoped we could forget all the anger of the past.

"I am afraid I was still very bitter, and wrote coldly that I did not consider I had any relations. He wrote again, more insistently, pleading that my grandfather deeply regretted his actions and wanted me near him."

She drew a deep breath. "I have no way of knowing how much of that was true. I think now my grandfather was probably already dead. Even then I began to suspect that there might be more to it than that. No one had betrayed the least interest in my father or myself for all those years, so I hardly believed they were suddenly so concerned about me.

"Old Jacques, my father's groom, became worried and insisted I should go immediately to Maby. He would not tell me exactly what he feared, but I guess his suspicions were more just than I gave him credit for. But then, he had known my—family."

After a moment she went on in the same toneless voice. "Because of . . . other . . . things, I had not thought of it in a great while, and even when I received the letter I confess I did not—" She stopped abruptly as Vidal swore violently beneath his breath.

In a moment he had gained control of himself. "What letter?" he inquired in a flat, blank voice.

She sighed. It was all so much worse than she had expected. "I received a letter several weeks ago threatening to—to betray me. I tried to keep the appointment, but—but was nearly run over by a cart. Even then I thought it was only an accident, and only last night did I realize what a fool I had been."

"And you did not think it worth while to apprise me of any of these things?" he demanded harshly.

"I—I can't excuse myself," she said miserably. "I was stubborn and proud, and even the few times I almost broke down and confessed everything, something always happened to prevent me. And then, we have not been on the—best of terms—always."

His eyes were bleak, but after a moment he said only, "Go on."

She sighed, wishing to have it over. "Naturally when I—became aware of what had happened, I saw how stupid I had been. The old Marquis was dead, and had changed his will in my father's favor. Perhaps he really did regret what he had done all those years ago." She looked up suddenly. "Did you know that, too?"

At his nod, she lowered her head for a moment before going on woodenly, "My uncle wished to force me to sign a document renouncing all claim to my share of the estate. He said he would keep me until I agreed." She remembered something then, and asked abruptly, "Did he send you a note saying that I had eloped with another man?"

Some of the grimness left Vidal's eyes. "Not that, exactly, but close enough."

She nodded. "I see. Did—did you believe it? I know I have given you very little reason to trust me."

His mouth softened. "No, Dominique. I did not believe it. I know you too well for that—even though you and Carleton between you have done your best to teach me an emotion I thought I was above."

She sighed and said after a minute, "I am at least glad of that. There is very little more to tell. He locked me in an upstairs room to think it over. I knew whatever he said he dared not let me go free. He said as much as told me so when he mentioned that L—" Furiously she broke off and tried to retrieve her slip. "That is—that—"

"You do not need to protect me," Vidal said curtly. "I am already aware of her part in this affair."

"Y-you are?" she asked foolishly.

"I am. You need not worry about Lady Caroline. She will not bother you again."

"Oh. Well—well, after that I managed to escape from the window and came home, with the help of a kindly old man."

"And how came you by that?" His finger touched her bruised cheek.

She shrugged. "His man hit me. I think it was to make me more afraid."

Her matter-of-fact voice brought a twisted smile to his lips, but his eyes were frightening.

She said quickly, "Why, it was all very stupid, as I told him. If he had killed me, you would have inherited everything, not him." She smiled suddenly. "I never thought to be grateful for those Marriage Settlements you thrust upon me. My uncle naturally became very enraged and threatened to—and threatened all sorts of dire consequences if I did not sign," she amended hastily. Then she sighed and allowed her head to sink to his shoulder.

For a long while there was no sound then but the crackle of the fire in the grate and the clear beat of his heart under her ear. She had begun to drowse, his hand softly caressing her hair, when some half-forgotten images returned to her. "Justin," she said suddenly, "I think my uncle killed my mother . . ."

Then, when his hand did not still in her hair she sighed and allowed her lashes to droop again. In another second she was asleep.

Vidal lifted her gently and laid her in the wide bed, tucking the bedclothes tightly about her. For a long moment he stood looking down at her, then he strode from the room.

He made only two stops. One was to tap softly on Maby's door. She answered immediately. "Is she all right?" she asked anxiously.

"Yes, Maby," he said gently. "Will you stay with her tonight?"

She searched his face, then nodded grimly.

The second was the library, where he took a pistol from its case and calmly loaded it before pocketing it and moving toward the door.

Chapter Twenty

Some hours later he walked into the cottage in the clearing. The room was in darkness, save for the soft glow of the fire, and a man sat sprawled before the table. At Vidal's entrance he looked up sharply.

"Ah, come in, *Monsieur le Duc*. I have been expecting you." He lifted his glass in greeting, then laughed. "Do not worry! I am not too badly dipped to give you satisfaction. But come! You must join me. I think we have a great deal to discuss first, eh?"

It was nearly noon when Dominique woke the next morning and no sooner had she opened her eyes than she was conscious of a cowardly urge to close them again and prolong her moments of peace. The room was carefully darkened, as for an invalid, and Maby was firmly ensconced in a chair beside the bed, an implacable expression on her face.

Dominique sighed, then leaned over to kiss Maby's soft cheek and announced her intention of getting up.

Almost immediately the door opened a crack and Lady Sarah stuck her head in, then whisked through the door. "Oh, you're up, my love! Ambersley said I should leave you in peace, but of course I must come to see how you went on. That was certainly quite an entrance you made last night!"

Dominique never liked being fussed over, so she gently shooed Maby and Lady Sarah out while she bathed and dressed. But after enduring a full half-hour of Bates's tearful ministrations and tragic countenance she was glad to escape down stairs. It was clear it was going to be a very trying day.

She was right. Bates took advantage of every opportunity that presented itself to publicly castigate herself, and insisted upon providing warm shawls, screens and smelling salts to fortfy her mistress. Dominique expected at any minute to have a hot brick placed at her feet.

In addition, it soon became apparent that virtually the entire household found excuse to linger near the small front parlor where Dominique sat with her friends, in order to assure themselves of her well-being, and blame themselves for their negligence. And since Alphonse spent the day in whipping up delicacies designed to tempt the appetite of a confirmed invalid, in the form of wholly improbable creams, jellies and soups, it was not to be wondered at if Dominique's temper grew a little short.

When Lady Sarah and even Maby, too, began to berate themselves for their part in the affair, she thought it was time to call a halt. "Good God! If you two begin I shall lock myself in my room, I promise you!" she shouted roundly. "I think the whole household is gone mad! Every time I look up Bates is weeping like a watering pot at my elbow, Hollings is stationed in the hall like a watchdog guarding a bone, and if Alphonse sends up another *consommé gelée*, I shall probably throw it at him!"

She then changed the subject, ignoring the grins on her friends' faces. Fortunately for her peace of mind, Lord Carleton was at that moment announced, and though he brought her a huge bouquet of spring flowers—for all the world, she chided him, as if she were at death's door—she could forgive him that lapse, since his calm good sense served to lessen the highly charged emotional atmosphere.

Soon afterward Lord Ambersley arrived as well, and immediately took command, dispatching the tearful Bates and any other of the more importunate household, and the afternoon passed pleasantly enough.

Conversation was kept intentionally light, and no one mentioned Vidal, a kindness that placed considerable constraint upon the conversation. The events of yesterday were equally studiously avoided by all, so that Lady Sarah was put to considerable effort to keep the discussion running smoothly. Dominique could only be grateful to them all, and if she herself could not help straining her ears at the sound of a carriage, only to relax again with a sigh when it passed on, she was careful to maintain her part in the light chatter.

The party easily persuaded to remain to dinner, each no doubt hesitant to leave her alone, and she was again touched by their kindness. But by the time the gentlemen had rejoined the ladies in the drawing room after dinner, and the tea tray was brought in, even Lady Sarah's considerable conversational abilities had been depleted.

So Dominique took pity upon them and gave them a highly abbreviated version of her "adventure" as she insisted upon calling it. She was aware that she glossed over her part in it, and was even less expansive in her explanations of her family, or her uncle's role, and no doubt her listeners found her version more than a little unsatisfactory, but they did not press her. She hardly knew whether to be grateful to them for their forbearance or exasperated at being treated as if she were wrapped in cotton. She thought she must possess an unusually wretched temper, for why else would she wish so desperately that her good friends would leave her alone to wait for the one person on her mind?

Shortly afterward Lord Ambersley announced firmly that they must leave, and Lord Carleton, too, stayed only to lightly kiss Dominique's cheek before departing. Even though she had longed for that moment, Dominique found herself reluctant to be left alone with Maby, for she had a pretty good idea what that lady's opinion of her escapade must be. But Maby, too, beyond saying rather grimly that she deserved to be horsewhipped, and if Vidal had any sense he would do so, abandoned the subject.

There was another awkward moment when Maby announced her intention of remaining on guard again that night. But that was something Dominique would not allow, and Maby at last was persuaded to seek her own room. Indeed, Maby's face was unusually lined and haggard, and Dominique realized guiltily that she should have insisted that her old friend retire hours ago. She could not have had much rest last night, and the strain of the last forty-eight hours had left its mark.

Surprisingly, despite a certain stiffness, and a rainbow-hued bruise on one cheek, she herself had suffered very little ill effects. She knew she would not sleep.

It was very late, and she was huddled listlessly in a chair before the dying fire, before she at last heard that familiar tread, and Vidal stood in the doorway.

She rose and searched his tired face. "He is dead, then," she said quietly.

He came to take her hands. "He is dead."

"You are not hurt?" she asked quickly.

He allowed his mouth to soften slightly. "No, my love."

"You fought him." It was not a question.

"He fired into the air," Vidal said gently. "I think he was almost glad it was over. He sent you his apologies and his compliments."

"His apologies——!" Her mouth curved slightly. "Yes, he was enough like my father to have done that. Did he need the money so badly?"

"I think he did, Dominique. He had done too much to gain his heritage, only to have the money to sustain it taken away from him by a last cruel twist of fate." He hesitated. "Let it wait until later, child."

"No, no, I want to know."

"Are you certain?" When she nodded he went on slowly, "Very well. I think you suspected that your uncle had a great deal to do with the break between your father and the old Marquis. It is true. Gervaise played successfully upon the old man's ambitions and temper until he could no longer forgive his favorite son for defying his wishes and disinherited him. I think it was an act your grandfather spent many years regretting, but his pride would not let him recant, and when he finally did, it was too late."

He watched her face for a moment, then went on evenly, "Robert, the eldest son, seems to have been a weakling and easily manipulated by Gervaise."

"But why? What did he hope to gain? My father was but the middle son, after all."

"Well, there doesn't seem to have been any love lost between any of the family, Dominique. But it was well known that the old Marquis was contemptuous of his oldest son and meant to leave as much of the estate as was unentailed to your father, with the proviso that although Robert must inherit the title and the chateau itself, your father would have the money needed to run it and must be given a free hand. So with your father out of the way Gervaise stood a gain to a very great deal. Robert had a passion for drink and gambling, and it was highly probable that he would not outlive the old Marquis, and while your father was in disgrace, Gervaise had little to fear from him. At any rate, it was well known that your father grew very reckless after the quarrel and your mother's death, and might be killed at any time."

She nodded and did not lift her eyes.

"I think you realized some time ago that what hounded them all was the chateau. It was a love your grandfather devoted his life to. He was even one of the first of the nobility to vow allegiance to the hated Napoleon in order to reclaim it. Only Robert seems to have escaped."

"Yes," she whispered. "I think it was a sort of madness with them. Even my father."

There was a little silence, then Vidal went on steadily, "After your father left, things went smoothly for a number of years. Robert had no interest in the estate, except what he could get out of it, and the old Marquis was so obsessed with restoring the chateau to what it had been before the revolution that he was more than content to leave the management itself in Gervaise's hands. And to his credit, I don't think it can have been an easy task. Robert seems to have been intent upon gambling away as much of his inheritance as he could lay his hands on, while the old man was equally determined that every available cent must be plowed into the chateau itself. And of course the war taxes at that time were crippling.

"When, a little more than a year ago, Gervaise came upon Robert in a field, badly injured from a jump he would not have attempted sober, it seems to have been relatively easy for Gervaise to convince himself that the estate would be infinitely better off without Robert, and that he, alone, deserved to inherit everything. So he left him to die."

She said nothing, merely clasping her hands more tightly together, and after a moment he continued. "Certainly, he knew that if your father were still alive he would inherit the title. So he set discreet inquiries afoot. It must have seemed an extreme stroke of fortune that your father died within a few weeks. The old Marquis himself died shortly thereafter, and he thought his dreams were at last to be realized."

"And then I got in the way," she said dully.

"And then you got in the way. He had gone so far, only to have it snatched out of his hands at the last minute. It must have been a considerable blow to discover that the old man had changed his will after Robert's death, leaving the bulk of the estate to your father, as heir to the title, with no provisions for it to revert to the head of the family upon his death. So legally you inherit everything not presently entailed. It must have seemed the last cruel irony that Gervaise now had the title and the chateau, but not the money to sustain it.

"He had gone too far to see it snatched away from him now. He wrote to you, thinking you would be a frightened girl and would be glad of his protection and his aid in your legal affairs. I don't honestly know if he meant for an accident to befall you even then, leaving your grieving uncle as your only known relative. But he had reckoned without your pride, of course." He smiled a trifle grimly. "I think throughout he made the great mistake of underestimating you, my love, to his sorrow.

"And then he lost track of you, until I blundered in and led him directly to you."

She shivered a little at the tone in his voice, and said the first thing that came into his head. "What happens now?"

"It is over. He is being taken back to France tonight and will be buried at home. He will have died in an accident, and no one will ever know differently. There is a distant cousin to inherit the title."

She smiled sadly. "So it has come to that, and it was all for nothing. Somehow I can only feel sadness for them all. They were all bound inevitably by the same compulsive love." She hesitated, then asked quietly, "And my mother?"

"It was an accident," he said very gently. "He loved her, you see. He encouraged your father to return to France shortly after you were born, with the false hope of reconciliation, in order to see her. But she scorned his advances and they struggled—and she was drowned. You were there, weren't you?"

She closed her eyes and nodded. "Did he know?"

"He suspected, but you were very small and nothing was said, so he decided you had been too young to understand. Your father took you away shortly afterward, and he felt safe. But I think when you recognized him so quickly at the cottage he realized that it was only a matter of time before you remembered."

After a long moment she shook her head and said with an effort to speak normally, "But I don't understand how you found my uncle. I did not tell you where—"

"Lymings knew I would wish to thank your kind rescuer, and very properly asked him to wait. From that lead it was not very difficult to find the cottage."

"I see. Lymings is always the perfect butler." She turned

almost blindly to the fire. "I am tired. Perhaps you will excuse me."

His hands were gentle on her shoulders as he turned her to face him. "It will have to be dealt with sooner or later, my love. I am perfectly aware you have spent the day convincing yourself I betrayed you by having your family discovered."

"And didn't you?" she asked dully.

His lips tightened. "No, I did not! When you signed a different name on the marriage certificate I naturally became curious. That you were not the simple governess you claimed had been apparent to me from the first, and I can hardly be blamed for seeking to discover exactly what you were up to.

"Nor do I regret it in the least. It explained a great deal about you that had puzzled me. Your pride, for instance, and your spirit and independence."

"And did you satisfy yourself that I was worthy to marry into the great Waincourt family?"

His fingers tightened on her arms and he almost shook her. "Be quiet! You have known from the first, with those witch's eyes of yours, that I loved you!"

But that was too much. Her lips curled and her eyes sparkled with scorn. "You must forgive me if I mistook the signs, your grace, since we seldom met without quarreling!"

He smiled ruefully. "I know, my love, but you put me in the devil of a temper. I did not wish to fall in love with you."

"I was aware of that, sir!" she snapped.

This time he did shake her. "If you utter another word to me in that tone I promise you I shall—"

"What? Beat me?" she taunted furiously.

In reply he pulled her roughly into his arms.

When he at last lifted his head she was very pale. He looked at her for a long moment, then said softly, "My love, I have been arrogant, overbearing and careless of your feelings, all the things you have delighted in taunting me with. But I think I have been more than repaid by your damnable pride and your stubborn refusal to trust me, no matter how hard I tried to convince you that you might. Indeed, we have wasted a great deal of precious time by not trusting one another.

"No, let me finish! I know you have heard a great

deal of nonsense from everyone today, claiming responsibility for what you have been through, but I alone am responsible. I knew that there was some question about your mother's death, and even the rumors about Robert's timely accident, and I even knew about the will in your favor, but I was too arrogant to believe that your uncle would dare to touch you here. For *that* I will never forgive myself."

Despite herself she reached up and gently touched his cheek. He gave a twisted smile then. "While as for you, if I beat you, as Maby recommends, it will be no more than you deserve!" His arms tightened about her.

After a moment he said into her curls, "You are now a very rich woman, Dominique. What do you intend to do with it?"

She drew a little away so that she could see his eyes. "Will you take it?" she asked hesitantly.

At his thunderstruck expression she added unwillingly, "I have thought perhaps you might be having some difficulties—I have cost you a great deal I know—and I . . ."

"May I ask what put that into your head?" he asked quietly.

She colored a little. "I was not prying. Only you have been away a great deal on business, and have seemed preoccupied, and I began to suspect—"

"Good God! Let that be a lesson to both of us!" When she frowned he shook his head and said lightly, a strange expression in his eyes, "So you wish me to take your fortune, to make up for the one you think I have lost?"

"I—yes," she said simply.

He smiled at her very gently. "I do not require your money, my love. If I have been somewhat preoccupied the last few weeks, I apologize, but I have been involved in rather lengthy negotiations in order to obtain your inheritance for you."

He put her away from him very quietly. "You can now be independent of me, Dominique. Is that not what you wanted?"

Her eyes were very wide. "You mean you would finally let me go if I wished?"

He tucked his hands in his pockets and nodded curtly.

At that a gentle smile curved her lips. "And you would not bully me and coerce me shamelessly if I decided to go?"

His brows drew together and he warned softly, "Do not try me too far, Dominique!"

She laughed and threaded her arms around his neck. "Then I think it would be a shame to deprive my unknown cousin of the means to support his new inheritance, don't you?" she inquired demurely.

For answer he snatched her so roughly to him that the breath was knocked from her body. She ignored this minor discomfort and raised her lips to his, perfectly content.

After a long while she turned her face into his coat and murmured tremulously, "Oh, Justin . . ."

He tipped her face up to his and his expression held such tenderness she scarcely recognized him. "I love you, Dominique. I won't pretend that my disposition will improve, or promise not to bully you or rake you over the coals when you're up to one of your ridiculous starts, because I'm sure I couldn't keep it. I have a devilish temper," he admitted ruefully.

"Yes, your grace," she agreed obediently.

His eyes began to dance. "As for you, my love, you are spoiled, willful, and thoroughly unbroken to bridle. But I don't doubt that a stern husband and a passel of brats will soon change that."

She stiffened instantly, a martial light in her eyes. "You think to change me, your grace?" she challenged softly.

Vidal, a superb fencer, slipped under her guard. "No, my love," he said instantly. "I place my faith in the fact that you love me."

But she was not to be won over yet. "I have never said I loved you!"

"No," he agreed promptly. "Why don't you?"

Her lips twitched, but she said sternly, "Why are you so very certain that I do?"

"Because, my naïve little darling, no matter how coldly formal your manners to me were during the daytime, you still lay with such delightful abandon in my arms at night."

"Justin!" Her green eyes glittered wrathfully, but at his deep laugh she abandoned all attempts to reform him and allowed herself to be swept up into his arms.

And when he laid her among the pillows she was so far lost to all propriety that she held up her arms to him and whispered deliciously, "Justin . . ." before his body descended to hers.